The Dark Eyes of London

The Dark Eyes of London

by Edgar Wallace

Contents

The Dark Eyes of London

Larry Holt in Paris

LARRY HOLT sat before the Café de la Paix, watching the stream of life flow east and west along the Boulevard des Italiens. The breath of spring was in the air; the trees were bursting into buds of vivid green; the cloud-flecked skies were blue; and a flood of golden sunshine brought out the colours of the kiosks, and gave an artistic value even to the flaring advertisements. Crowded motor-buses rumbled by, little taxis dashed wildly in and out of the traffic, to the mortal peril of unsuspecting pedestrians.

A gendarme, with cloak over his shoulder, stood in a conventional attitude on the kerb, his hand behind him, staring at nothing, and along the sidewalk there were hurrying bareheaded girls, slow-moving old men, and marching poilus. Itinerant vendors of wares loafed past the tables of the café, dusky-faced Arabs with their carpets on their arms, seedy-looking men who hawked bundles of picture post cards and would produce, at the slightest encouragement, cards which were not for the public gaze. All these things and people were a delight to Larry Holt, who had just returned from Berlin after four years' strenuous work in France and Germany, and felt in that holiday spirit to which even the mind of a detective will ascend.

The position occupied by Larry Holt was something of a mystery to the officials of Scotland Yard. His rank was Inspector, his work was the administrative work of a Commissioner; and it was generally understood that he was in the line for the first vacant assistant commissionership that came along. The question of his rank, of his prospects, did not trouble Larry at that particular moment. He sat there, absorbing the sweetness of spring with every breath he drew. His good-looking face was lit up with the sheer joy of living, and there was in his heart a relief, a sense of rest, which he had not experienced for many a long day.

He revealed himself a fairly tall man when he rose, after paying the waiter, and strolled round the corner to his hotel. It was a slow progress he made, his hands in his pockets, his soft felt hat at the back of his head, a half-smile on his parted lips as he gripped a long black cigarette holder between his white teeth.

The Dark Eyes of London

He came into the busy vestibule of the hotel, the one spot in Paris where people hustle and rush, where bell-boys really run, and even the phlegmatic Briton seems in a frantic hurry, and he was walking towards the elevator, when, through the glass door leading to the palm court, he saw a man in an attitude of elegant repose, leaning back in a big chair and puffing at a cigar.

Larry grinned and hesitated. He knew this lean-faced man, so radiantly attired, his fingers and cravat flashing with diamonds, and in a spirit of mischief he passed through the swing doors and came up to the lounger.

"If it isn't my dear old friend Fred!" he said softly.

Flash Fred, Continental crook and gambler, leapt to his feet with a look of alarm at the sight of this unexpected visitation.

"Hullo, Mr. Holt!" he stammered. "You're the last person in the world I expected to see——"

"Or wanted to see," said Larry, shaking his head reproachfully. "What prosperity! Why, Fred, you're all dressed up like a Christmas tree."

Flash Fred grinned uncomfortably, but made a brave show of indifference.

"I'm going straight now, Mr. Holt," he said.

"Liar you are, and liar you will always be," said Larry without heat.

"I swear to you on the Book——" began Fred vigorously.

"If," said Larry without resentment, "you stood between your dead aunt and your failing uncle, and took an oath on Foxe's Book of Martyrs, I wouldn't believe you."

He gazed admiringly at Fred's many adornments, at the big pin in his tie, at the triple chain of gold across his neatly tailored waistcoat, at his white spats and patent shoes, and then brought his eyes back to the perfectly brushed hair.

"You look sweet," he said. "What is the game? Not," he added, "that I expect you to tell me, but it must be a pretty prosperous game, Fred."

The man licked his dry lips.

"I'm in business," he said.

"Whose business are you in now?" asked Larry, interested. "And how did you get in? With a jemmy or a stick of dynamite? That's a new line for you,

Fred. As a rule, you confine yourself strictly to picking crumbs of gold off the unwary youth of the land—and," he added significantly, "in picking the pockets of the recently deceased."

The man's face went red.

"You don't think I had anything to do with that murder in Montpellier?" he protested heatedly.

"I don't think you shot the unfortunate young man," admitted Larry, "but you were certainly seen bending over his body and searching his clothes."

"For identification," said Fred virtuously. "I wanted to find out who did it."

"You were also seen talking to the man who did it," said Larry remorsefully. "An old lady, a Madame Prideaux, looking out of her bedroom window, saw you holding him and then saw you let him go. I presume he 'dropped.'?"

Fred said nothing at first. He hated a pretended gentleman who descended to the vulgarity of employing the word "drop" for "bribe."

"That's two years ago, Mr. Holt," he said. "I don't see why you should rake that thing up against me. The examining magistrate gave me a clean bill."

Larry laughed and dropped his hand on the man's shoulder.

"Anyway, I'm off duty now, Fred. I'm going away to enjoy myself."

"You ain't coming to London, I suppose?" asked the man, looking at him quickly.

"No," said Larry, and thought he saw signs of relief.

"I'm going over to-day," said Fred, in a conversational tone. "I was hoping we'd be fellow-passengers."

"I'm grieved to shatter your hopes," said Larry, "but I'm going in the other direction. So long."

"Good luck!" said Fred, and looked after him with a face which did not indicate any desire for Larry Holt's fortune.

Larry went up to his room and found his man brushing his clothes and laying them out on his bed. Patrick Sunny, the valet he had endured for two years, was a serious young man with staring eyes and a round face, and he grew suddenly energetic on Larry's appearance. He brushed and he hissed, for he had been in a cavalry regiment.

The Dark Eyes of London

Larry strolled to the window and looked down on the Place de l'Opéra at the busy scene.

"Sunny," he said, "you needn't brush those dress things of mine. Pack 'em."

"Yes, sir," said Sunny.

"I'm going to Monte Carlo by the night train."

"Indeed, sir?" said Sunny, who would have said exactly the same if Larry had expressed his intention of going to the Sahara or the North Pole.

"To Monte Carlo, Sunny!" chortled Larry. "For six bright, happy, expensive weeks—start packing at once."

He picked up the telephone from the writing-table and called the Travel Bureau.

"I want a sleeper and a first-class reservation for Monte Carlo by to-night's train," he said. "Monte Carlo," he repeated louder. "No, not Calais. I have not the slightest intention of going to Calais—thanks." He hung up the receiver and stood looking at his servitor. "I hate talking to you, Sunny," he said, "but I must talk to somebody, and I hate your name. Who gave you that horrible name?"

"My forefathers," said Sunny primly, continuing his brushing without looking up.

"They rather missed the 'bus, didn't they?" asked Larry. "For if there is anything less like a bright spring day than you, I should like to avoid it. But we're southward bound, Sunny, to this Côte d'Azur, to the land of flowers and folly, to the orange-groves—do you like oranges, Sunny?"

"I prefer walnuts, sir," said Sunny, "but fruit of any kind means nothing to me."

Larry chuckled and sat on the edge of the bed.

"We're going to be criminals and take people's money from them," he said, "instead of nosing about the criminal practices of others. No more robberies, defalcations, forgeries and murders, Sunny. Six weeks of dolce far niente."

"I don't play that game myself, sir," said Sunny. "I prefer cribbage."

Larry picked up the afternoon paper and had turned its columns. There

10

were quite a few items of news to remind him of his profession and its calls. There was a big bank robbery at Lyons, a mail coach had been held up in Belgium by armed robbers; and then he came to a paragraph.

"The body of a man picked up on the steps leading down from the Thames Embankment has been identified as Mr. Gordon Stuart, a rich Canadian. It is believed to be a case of suicide. Mr. Stuart had been spending the evening with some friends at the theatre, and disappeared between the acts, and was not seen again until his body was discovered. A coroner's inquest will be held in due course."

He read the paragraph twice, and frowned.

"A man doesn't usually go out between the acts of a play and commit suicide—unless the play is very bad," he said, and the obedient Sunny said, "No, sir."

He threw the newspaper down.

"Sunny, I'm getting into bad habits. I'm taking an interest in lunacy, and for that same reason I notice that you've folded my trousers so that the crease comes down the side. Unfold 'em, you lazy devil!"

He spent the afternoon making preparations for his journey, and at half-past six, with his trunks in the hands of the porters and Sunny carrying his overcoat, he was settling his bill at the cashier's desk, had folded up the receipt and was putting it in his pocket when a bell-boy came to him.

"Monsieur Holt?" he asked.

"That's my name," said Larry, and looked suspiciously at the thing in the boy's hand. "A telegram?" he said. "I don't want to see it."

Nevertheless, he took it in his hand and opened the blue paper with a disapproving grimace and read:

"Very urgent, on special police service. Clear the line. Larry Holt, Grand Hotel, Paris.

"Very worried about Stuart drowning stop case presents unusual features stop would be personally grateful if you would come over at once and conduct investigation."

It was signed by the Chief Commissioner, who was not only his superior

11

but his personal friend, and Larry put the telegram in his pocket with a groan.

"What time do we arrive in Monte Carlo, sir?" asked Sunny when he joined him.

"About this day twelvemonth," said Larry.

"Indeed, sir?" said Sunny, politely interested. "It must be a very long way."

Sir John Hason

FLASH FRED, whose other name was Grogan, had a genuine grievance; for, after he had been solemnly assured by a reputable officer of the law that he intended going to Monte Carlo, he had found him on the Paris boat train, and though he carefully avoided him he knew that Larry was well aware that they were fellow-passengers.

At Victoria Fred made a rapid exit from the station, not being perfectly satisfied in his mind that Larry's business in London was altogether unconnected with Fred's own activities. Larry saw the disappearing back of the crook, and smiled for the first time since he had left Paris.

"Take my things to the flat," he said to Sunny. "I'm going to Scotland Yard. I may be home to-night, I may not be home until to-morrow night."

"Shall I put out your dress things?" said Sunny. All that concerned him was the gentlemanly appearance of his employer. To Sunny the day was divided into three parts—tweed, broadcloth and pyjamas.

"No—yes—anything you like," said his master.

"Yes, sir," responded the obliging Sunny.

Larry drove straight to the Yard, and had some difficulty in making an entry, because he was unknown to the local officials; but presently he was ushered into the big room where Sir John Hason rose from his desk and came across to meet him with outstretched hand.

"My dear Larry," he said, "it is awfully good of you to forgo your holiday. You are a brick! Of course I knew you would come, and I've given you room forty-seven and the smartest secretary I have seen in Scotland Yard for many a day."

Edgar Wallace

They were old friends and old school-mates, John Hason and Larry Holt, and between the two men there was an affection and a confidence which is rarely found between men in the same profession.

"I don't know forty-seven," said Larry, taking off his overcoat with a smile, "but I'll be happy to know the smartest secretary in Scotland Yard. What's his name?"

"It isn't a he, it's a she," smiled Hason. "Miss Diana Ward, who's been with me for about six months and is really the smartest and most reliable girl I've ever had working with me."

"Oh, a female secretary!" said Larry gloomily, then brightened. "What you say goes, John; and even this paragon of virtue doesn't worry me. I suppose she's got a voice like a file and chews gum?"

"She is rather unprepossessing, but looks aren't everything," said Sir John dryly. "Now sit down, old man; I want to talk to you. It is about this Stuart case," he began, offering his cigarette box to the other. "We only discovered yesterday that Stuart was a very rich man. He has been living in this country for nine months at a boarding-house in Nottingham Place, Marylebone. He was a mysterious individual, who went nowhere, had very few friends, and was extraordinarily reticent. It was known, of course, that he had money, and his bankers in London, who revealed his identity when they discovered he was dead, were in his secret; that is to say, his secret so far as his identity is concerned."

"When you say he went nowhere, what do you mean? Did he stay in the boarding-house all the time?"

"I'm coming to that," said Sir John. "He did go somewhere, but why, nobody knows. Every afternoon it was his practice to take a motor drive, and invariably he went to the same place—to a little village in Kent, about twenty-five miles out. He left the motor-car at one end of the village, walked through the place, and was gone for a couple of hours. We have made inquiries and we have discovered this, that he spent quite a lot of time in the church, an old Saxon edifice the foundations of which were laid a thousand years ago. Regularly as the clock he'd return after two hours' absence, get into

13

the car, which was hired, and be driven back to Nottingham Place."

"What was the name of the village?"

"Beverley Manor," said the Chief Commissioner. "Well, to resume. On Wednesday night, departing from his usual practice, he accepted the invitation of a Dr. Stephen Judd to go to the first night of a new show at the Macready Theatre. Dr. Stephen Judd is the managing director of the Greenwich Insurance Company, a small affair and quite a family concern, but having a pretty good name in the City. Mr. Judd is a genial person who dabbles in art and has a very beautiful house at Chelsea. Judd had a box for the first night of the show—which is a perfectly rotten one, judging by the newspaper notices—Box A. Stuart came, and, according to Judd, was very restless. In the interval between the second and third acts he slipped out of the theatre, unobserved, and did not come back, and was not seen again until we found his body on the Thames Embankment."

"What sort of a night was it?" asked Larry.

"Bright in the early part, but rather misty and inclined to be foggy later," said Sir John. "In fact, the constable who was patrolling that particular beat where the body was found reported that it was very thick between half-past three and half-past four."

Larry nodded. "Is there any possibility of his having mistaken his way in the fog and fallen into the water?" he asked.

"None whatever," replied Sir John emphatically. "Between the hour he disappeared and half-past two in the morning the Embankment was entirely clear of fog, and he was not seen. It was a very bright night until that hour."

"And here is another curious circumstance," the Commissioner went on. "When he was discovered, he was lying on the steps with his legs in the water, his body being clear—and," he added slowly, "the tide was still rising."

Larry looked at him in astonishment.

"Do you mean to say that he hadn't been deposited there by the falling tide?" he asked incredulously. "How could he be there, with his legs in the water, when the tide was low, as it must have been, when he came upon the steps?"

"That is my contention," nodded Sir John. "Unless he was drowned immediately he left the theatre when the tide was high and was falling, it seems almost impossible that he could have been left on the steps at daybreak, when the tide was rising."

Larry rubbed his chin.

"That's queer," he said. "There's no doubt about his being drowned?"

"None whatever," replied the Commissioner, and pulled open a drawer, lifting out a little tray on which were a number of articles. "These were the only things found in his pockets," he said. "A watch and chain, a cigar-case, and this roll of brown paper."

Larry took up the latter object. It was about an inch in length, and was still sodden with water.

"There is no writing on it," said Sir John. "I opened it when it first came in, but thought it better to roll it back and leave it as it was for another inspection when it dried."

Larry was looking at the watch, which was an ordinary gold half-hunter.

"Nothing there," he said, snapping back the case, "except that it stopped at twenty past twelve—presumably the hour of his death."

Sir John nodded.

"The chain is gold and platinum," mused Larry, "and at the end is a—what?"

There was a little cylinder of gold about an inch and a half long.

"A gold pencil fitted in here," said Larry. "Have they found the pencil?"

Sir John shook his head.

"No, that is all we discovered. Apparently Stuart was not in the habit of wearing rings. I'll have these sent to your office. Now will you take on the case?"

"But what is the case?" asked Larry slowly. "Do you suspect foul play?"

The Commissioner was silent.

"I do and I don't," he said. "I merely say that here are the elements of a terrible crime. But for the fact that he has been found on the steps with the tide still rising, and it was obviously low when he died, I should have thought it was an ordinary case of drowning, and I should not have opposed a verdict of accidental death if the jury reached that conclusion."

Larry looked at the watch again.

"It's strange," he said, speaking half to himself, and then: "I'll take these things into my room, if I may."

"I expected you would want them," said the Commissioner. "Now will you see the body?"

Larry hesitated.

"I'll see Doctor Judd first," he said. "Can you give me his address?"

Sir John looked up at the clock over his mantelpiece.

"He will be at his office. He's one of those indefatigable persons who work late. Number 17 Bloomsbury Pavement; you can't miss the building."

Larry gathered up the tray and moved to the door.

"Now for the unattractive secretary," he said, and Sir John smiled.

The Secretary

ROOM NO. 47 was on the floor above that where the Commissioner's office was situated. It lay at the end of a long corridor, facing the detective. He carried the tray in one hand and opened the door with the other, walking into a comfortable little bureau.

"Hallo!" he said in surprise. "Am I in the wrong office?"

The girl, who had risen from her desk, was young and extremely pretty. A mass of dull gold hair, dressed low over her broad forehead, gave an added emphasis to clear grey eyes that were regarding him with surprise. She was neat and slim of figure, and when she smiled Larry thought he had hardly ever seen so gracious and pleasant a lady.

"This is Inspector Holt's office," she said.

"Good Lord!" said Larry, coming slowly into the room and shutting the door behind him. He went to the other desk and put down the tray, and the girl looked puzzled.

"This is Inspector Holt's office," she repeated. "Are those things for him?"

Larry nodded, looking at the girl in wonder.

16

"What is that?" he asked suddenly, pointing to a glass and a jug on a side table which was covered with a small white cloth.

"Oh, that is for Inspector Holt," she said.

Larry looked into the jug.

"Milk?" he said in wonder.

"Yes," said the girl. "Inspector Holt is rather old, you know, and when I asked the Commissioner if he would like something after his journey, the Commissioner suggested invalid's food and milk; but I can't make invalid's food here, and—"

His shriek of merriment stopped her, and she stared at him.

"I am Inspector Holt," he said, drying his eyes.

"You?" she gasped.

"I'm the lad," said he complacently. "John, the Commissioner, has played a joke on you, miss—I don't know your name. Now, would you be good enough to ask the aged Miss Ward to step in?"

A smile twitched her lips.

"I am Miss Ward," she said, and it was Larry's turn to stare. Then he put out his hand with a smile.

"Miss Ward," he said, "we're companions in misfortune. Each has been equally a victim of a perfidious police commissioner. I'm extremely glad to meet you—and relieved."

"I'm a little relieved," laughed the girl as she went to her desk, and Larry, watching every movement, thought she floated rather than walked.

"Sir John said you were sixty and asthmatic, and told me to be careful that no draughts should come into the office. I've had a draught excluder specially fitted this afternoon."

Larry thought a moment.

"Perhaps it's as well I didn't go to Monte Carlo," he said, and sat down at his desk. "Now let us start, shall we?"

She opened her book and took up a pencil, whilst Larry examined the trinkets that lay on the tray.

"Take this down, please," he said. "Watch made Gildman of Toronto, half-hunter, jewel-balanced; No. A778432. No scratches on the inside." He opened the case and snapped it again, then tried the stem winder. "Wound less than six hours before death took place."

She looked up.

"Is this the Stuart case?" she asked.

"Yes," said Larry. "Do you know anything about it?"

"Only what the Commissioner's told me," she replied. "Poor man! But I'm getting so used to horrors now that I'm almost hardened. I suppose one feels that way if one's a medical student. I was a nurse for two years in a blind asylum," she added, "and that helps to toughen you, doesn't it?" She smiled.

"I suppose it does," said Larry thoughtfully, and wondered how young she had been when she started to work for her living. He put her at twenty-one and thought that was a fairly generous estimate of her age. "Do you like this work?" he asked.

She nodded.

"I love it," she said. "Sir John says that one of these days he's going to make me a——" She hesitated for a word.

"A sleuth? Don't say you're going to be a sleuth," begged Larry. "I thought we had this business to ourselves. Female competition to-day——"

She shook her head.

"You're neglecting your work, Mr. Holt," she said. "I've got as far as the watch."

He chuckled a little and resumed his inspection.

"Chain made of platinum and gold, length twelve inches, swivel at end, and container of a gold pencil—at least, I presume it was gold," he dictated. "The pencil wasn't found?"

"No," she said. "I particularly asked the sergeant who brought the goods whether the pencil had been found."

Larry looked at her in surprise.

"Did you notice that?"

"Oh yes, I noticed that too," said Marjorie calmly. "The knife has gone too."

18

He looked across at her in genuine amazement.

"What knife?" he asked.

"I guessed it was a knife," said she. "The swivel is too large to be attached to a pencil only. If you look you will see a little ring—it has probably got entangled with the ring holding the pencil. It was broken when it came in, but I pressed it together. It looked as if somebody had wrenched it off. I guessed the knife," she said, "because men so often carry a little gold penknife there."

"Or a cigar-cutter?" suggested Larry.

"I thought of that," she said, nodding, "but they'd hardly have taken the trouble to nip off a cigar-cutter."

"They?" he asked.

"Whoever killed Stuart," she said quietly, "would have removed all weapons from his possession."

He looked at the chain again and saw the other ring, and wondered why he had not noticed it before.

"I think you're right," he said after a further examination. "The ring is much larger—it had slid up the chain, by the way—and there are distinct scratches where the knife was wrenched off. Hm!" He put down the object on the table, and looked at his own watch. "Have you seen the rest of the things?" he asked.

She shook her head.

"I've only examined the watch."

He looked around for some receptacle, and saw a cupboard in the wall.

"Is this empty?" he asked, and she nodded. "Then we'll leave the examination of these until I come back. I have to see somebody."

He slipped the tray into the closet and locked the door, handing the key to the girl. He was half-way to the door when he remembered.

"You won't be here when I come back? I suppose you have some sort of office hours?"

"I make it a practice never to stay after two o'clock in the morning," she said gravely.

The Dark Eyes of London

She met the frank admiration in his eyes without embarrassment.

"I don't think I have ever met a girl like you," he said slowly, and as though he were speaking his thoughts aloud.

She flushed and dropped her gaze. Then she laughed and looked at him again, and he thought that her eyes were like stars.

"It may be that we have never met anybody like each other," she said.

And Larry Holt left Scotland Yard, conscious that a new and a very potent interest had come into his life.

Flash Fred Sees a Client

FLASH FRED had seen Larry Holt off the premises of the railway terminus; for, though he had left the station building first, he had waited until Larry's taxi had gone.

He had a particular desire that he should not be shadowed that evening, and to this was engrafted a wholesome respect for the perspicacity and genius of Larry Holt. On the Continent of Europe, whereever crook met crook, it was generally and unanimously agreed that the first person they wished to meet on the other side of the Styx was Larry Holt. Only they did not say "on the other side of the Styx"; they said, simply and crudely, "in hell." The ruthlessness of this man, once he got his nose on to the trail, was a tradition and a legend; and Fred, more than any other man, had reason to fear him.

He gave Holt ten minutes' start and then doubled back to the station, left his suit-case at the cloak room and came out at one of the side entrances where the cabs were ranked, and, choosing the first of these, he gave an address. Ten minutes later he was set down in a quiet Bloomsbury square, devoted in the main to lawyers' offices. There was an exception to these. The building at which he alighted was a narrow and tall erection of red brick, and though no light showed in the lower office, there was a subdued gleam in the windows of the upper floor. A commissionaire on duty in the hall looked at Fred askance.

"The office has been closed for hours, sir," he said, shaking his head. "We open at nine in the morning."

"Is Dr. Judd on the premises?" asked Flash Fred, shifting his cigar from one corner of his mouth to the other.

The commissionaire hesitated.

"Mr. Judd is still busy, sir, and I don't think he wants to see anybody."

"Oh, you don't, don't you?" sneered Fred. "Now, you go upstairs to the governor and tell him that Mr. Walter Smith wants to see him. Don't forget the name—it's an unusual one," he added humorously.

The commissionaire looked dubiously at the visitor.

"I shall only get into trouble," he grumbled, as he stepped into one of the two small elevators and, pressing the automatic knob, he went quickly up out of view.

Apparently Mr. Judd's office was situated on the top floor, for it was some time before the whine of the motor ceased. After a while it began again, and the commissionaire descended.

"He'll see you, sir," he said. "Will you step this way?"

"You ought to know me by now, sergeant," said Fred as he walked into the lift. "I've been here pretty regularly the past few years."

"Maybe I wasn't on duty," said the commissionaire as the lift slowly ascended. "There are two of us here, you know. Were you a friend of Mr. David's, sir?"

Fred did not chuckle, he did not even smile.

"No, no," he said airily, "I don't know Mr. David."

"Ah, very sad, very sad!" said the commissionaire. "He died suddenly four years ago, you know, sir."

Fred did know, but he did not confess the fact. The death of Mr. David had robbed him of a possible source of income by right, whereas now he only had that income by favour, and might at any time lose that and gain a term of imprisonment if the jovial Dr. Judd grew tired of paying blackmail.

The lift stopped and he stepped out and followed the commissionaire to a door, at which the uniformed man knocked. A loud voice bade them come in, and Flash Fred swaggered into the handsome apartment with a cool nod to its occupant.

The Dark Eyes of London

Dr. Judd had risen to meet him.

"All right, sergeant," he said to the commissionaire, and flicked a silver coin across the room, which the man caught deftly.

"Get me some cigarettes," he said. And when the door had closed: "Sit down, you rascal," said Dr. Judd good-humouredly. "I suppose you've come to get your pound of flesh."

He was a tall, stout man, florid of face and heavy of build. His forehead was bald, his eyes were deep-set and wide apart; he had about him an air of comfort and boisterous good humour. Fred, in no wise abashed, sat down on the edge of a chair.

"Well, doctor," he said, "I'm back."

Dr Judd shook his head and searched his pockets for a cigarette.

"What do you want—a cigarette?" said Fred, reaching for his case, but the doctor shook his head and his smile was broad, good-humoured but significant.

"No, thank you, Mr. Grogan," he said with a chuckle. "I don't smoke cigarettes that are presented to me by gentlemen of your profession."

"What is my profession?" growled Flash Fred. "You don't think I was trying to dope you, do you?"

"I was expecting you," said the other, without answering the question, and seated himself. "If I remember rightly, you have a strong objection to taking cheques."

Flash Fred grinned.

"Quite right, governor," he said. "That is still my weakness."

The doctor took a bunch of keys from his pocket, walked to the safe, snapped back the lock, and then, looking over his shoulder:

"You needn't watch this too closely, my friend; except when I have to pay blackmailers, I never keep money in this safe."

Fred made a little grimace.

"Hard words never killed anybody," he said sententiously.

The doctor took out a packet, slammed the door and turned the key, came slowly back to the desk and threw down a fat envelope. Then he consulted a little book which he took from a drawer.

"You're three days ahead of your time," he said, and Fred nodded admiringly.

"What a brain you've got for figures, doctor!" he said. "Yes, I'm three days ahead of my time, but it's because I've got to get out of England pretty quick to meet a friend of mine in Nice."

The doctor threw the packet across to him, and he caught it clumsily.

"There are twelve hundred pounds in that envelope. You needn't count them, because they're all there," said Dr. Judd, and leaning back in his chair, he took out a golden toothpick, eyeing the other straightly and thoughtfully. "Of course I am the biggest fool in the world," he said, "or I would never submit to this iniquitous blackmail. It is only because I want to keep the memory of my dead brother free from calumny that I do this."

"If your brother goes shooting up people in Montpellier and I happen to be on the spot," said Flash Fred unctuously, "and help him to escape—as I did, and I can prove it—I think I'm entitled to a little compensation."

"You're an unutterable scoundrel," said the other in his pleasant way, and smiled. "And you amuse me. Suppose, instead of being what I am, I were a bad-minded man? Suppose that I was desperate and couldn't find the money? Why, I might—do anything!"

He guffawed at the thought of doing anything very terrible.

"It wouldn't make any difference to me," said Fred. "But it wouldn't make any difference to you, either. I've got all the facts written down about that shooting—how I helped the man escape and recognized him in London as Mr. David Judd when I came back—and my mouthpiece has got it."

"Your lawyer?"

"Sure, my lawyer," said Fred, nodding. He leaned forward. "You know, I didn't believe your brother had died. I thought it was a fake to get me out of the way, and I shouldn't have believed it if I hadn't seen it in the papers and been to the funeral."

Dr. Judd rose and replaced his toothpick.

"That a man like you could besmirch a name like his!" he said. All the good humour had gone out of his voice, and he trembled with indignation and passion.

He had passed to the other side of the table and stood glowering down at Flash Fred, and Fred, who was used to such scenes—for this was not his first blackmailing case—merely smiled.

"He was the best man that ever lived, the cleverest, the most wonderful," said Dr. Judd, and his face was white. "The greatest man perhaps that this world has seen." His voice shook with the intensity of his emotion. "And for you——" He reached down, and before Fred knew what had happened, the big hand had gripped him by the collar and jerked him to his feet.

"Here, none of that!" cried Fred, and strove to break loose.

"The money I do not mind paying," Judd went on. "It is not that which maddens me. It is the knowledge that you have it in your power to throw mud at a man——" Here his voice broke, and the other hand came up.

With a cry like a wild beast, Fred flung himself back with all his might and broke the grip of his adversary. Suddenly, as if by magic, there appeared in his hand a revolver.

"Put 'em up and keep 'em up, damn you!"

And then a voice, the gentlest voice in the world, asked:

"Can I be of any assistance?"

Fred turned with a start. Larry Holt was standing in the doorway, an engaging smile upon his face.

The Will

FLASH FRED looked upon the intruder, a picture of comical amazement.

"You don't lose no time, do you?" The protest was forced from him, and Larry laughed softly.

"For carrying concealed weapons, you're pinched, Fred."

"It's no crime in this country," growled the other, putting up his gun.

By this time Dr. Judd had recovered himself.

"You know our friend, Mr. Grogan," he said easily. "He's a member of our amateur dramatic society, and we were practising a scene from the Corsican

Brothers. I suppose it looked rather alarming."

"Thought it was Julius Cæsar," said Larry dryly. "The scene between Cassius and Brutus, though I don't remember the gun play."

The doctor looked at Flash Fred and then at Larry.

"I'm afraid I don't know you," he said. He was still rather white, but his tone had recovered its good nature.

"I am Inspector Larry Holt from Scotland Yard," said Larry. "Now seriously, Dr. Judd, are you charging this man with anything?"

"No, no, no," said Judd with a laugh. "Honestly, we were only doing a little harmless fooling."

Larry looked from one to the other. The managing director of an insurance company, even a small company, does not fool with a known criminal.

"You know this man, I suppose?"

"I've met him several times," said Judd easily.

"You know also that he's a member of the criminal classes, and that he is in fact 'Flash Fred,' who has served penal servitude in this country and a term of imprisonment in France?"

The doctor said nothing for a while.

"I'm afraid I guessed that too," he said in a low voice, "and in consequence my association with the man must seem rather curious to you—but I cannot explain."

Larry nodded. The one perturbed person in the room was Flash Fred. He was in an agony of apprehension lest Dr. Judd told his secret and the reason for his visit. But Judd had no such intention.

"You can go now," he said curtly, and Fred, trying to summon up some of his old swagger, lit a cigar with a hand that trembled, and Larry watched the operation.

"You want 'Nervine for the Nerves,' Fred," he said. "I saw a chemist's shop open at the corner of the street when I came along."

Fred walked out with a pitiable attempt at indifference, and Larry watched him go. Then he turned to the doctor.

"I'm sorry I came in at such an inconvenient moment," he said, "though

I don't think you were in any danger. Fred gets all his fine dramatic effects by pulling, not by shooting."

"I don't think so either," said the doctor with a laugh. "Sit down, Mr. Holt. I certainly didn't expect to see you. I work rather late here at nights."

"There was nobody down below when I came," said Larry, "and that is my excuse for coming up unannounced."

The doctor nodded.

"I sent the commissionaire out to buy me some cigarettes, and here he is."

There was a tap at the door and the commissionaire came in and laid a packet on the table in confirmation.

"Now what can I do for you?" asked Judd, as he took a cigarette from the packet and lit it. "I suppose it is the Stuart case? I've seen one of your men to-day."

Larry nodded.

"It is the Stuart case," he said. "I wanted a few additional details. I've only just taken charge of the business, and interrupted my investigation of the—remains, in order to see you before you left the office."

"I know very little," said the doctor, smoking comfortably. "He came with me to the theatre the night before last. A queer, quiet, reticent man, I met him quite by accident. As a matter of fact, I was in a car that collided with his taxicab and I was slightly injured; he called upon me, and that is how the friendship began—if you can call it a friendship."

"Tell me about the night before last," asked Larry, and the doctor looked up at the ceiling.

"Now let me think. I can give you the exact time almost, for I am a somewhat methodical person. I met him at the entrance to the theatre at seven-forty-five, and we both went into Box A. That is the last box on the left, or O.P. side. The box is on a level with the street, the stalls and pit being below the level. We sat there through two acts, and then, just before the curtain came down on the second act, he made an excuse and went out of the box, and he was never seen again."

"None of the attendants saw him?"

"No," said the doctor, "but that, I think, is easily explained. It was a first night, and, as you know, the attendants are very interested in the action of a play, and fill the doorways and the entrances to gangways, looking at the stage, when of course they should be attending to their business."

"Did you know he was Stuart, a semi-millionaire?" asked Larry.

"I hadn't the slightest idea," said the doctor truthfully. "I knew nothing whatever about his past life except that he had come from Canada."

Larry was disappointed.

"I hoped I was going to get a lot of information from you," he said. "Nobody seems to have known Stuart, and naturally I thought that you would have been in his confidence."

"Neither I nor his bank manager was in his confidence," said the doctor. "It was only this morning that I heard from the manager of the London and Chatham that he was a client of theirs. We knew absolutely nothing of him except that he had plenty of money."

A few minutes later Larry was walking down Bloomsbury Pavement, and he was a very thoughtful man. What had Flash Fred been doing in that office? What was the significance of that flashing of the revolver and the white face of Dr. Judd? It was another little mystery, into which he had not time to investigate, and any way it was no concern of his. Ahead of him, his iron-shod stick tapping the pavement, was a man who walked slowly and deliberately. Larry passed him, and, waiting for a cab which he had signalled, saw him again.

"Blind," he noted casually, not interrupting his thought of Fred and the doctor.

But he had no time for side trails and side issues, and, entering the cab, he drove to Westminster.

He was not going back to the Yard immediately. First he had a gruesome little duty to perform. At the Westminster mortuary, whither the cab had taken him, he found two Scotland Yard officers awaiting him.

The examination of the body was a brief one. The only mark was an abrasion of the left ankle, and then Larry began an inspection of the clothing, which had been placed in an adjoining room.

"There is the shirt, sir," pointing to a garment which had been roughly folded. "I can't understand those blue marks on the breast."

Larry carried the garment under a light. It was a dress shirt, rough dried, and the purple specks on the breast were clearly visible.

"Made by an indelible pencil," said Larry, and in a flash remembered the missing pencil-case. But what meant those specks, which formed three rough lines of indecipherable pothooks and hangers?

And then the solution came to Larry, and quickly he turned the dress front inside out and uttered an exclamation. Written on the inside were three lines, and it was the indelible pencil markings which had soaked through that had caused the speckly appearance of the front of the shirt.

The water had made the purple pencil markings run, but the words were distinct.

"In the fear of death I, Gordon Stuart, of Merryhill Ranch, Calgary, leave all my possessions to my daughter, Clarissa, and I pray the courts to accept this as my last will and testament.—Gordon Stuart."

Underneath was written:

"It is now clear to me that I have been betrayed by——"

There followed a letter which looked like an "O," but at this point the writing abruptly terminated.

Larry raised his eyes and met those of his subordinate.

"Here is the strangest will that has ever been made," he said in a hushed voice.

He put down the shirt and walked back to the mortuary chamber, and again examined the body. One hand was clenched, and evidently this fact had been overlooked by the doctors. Using all his strength, he forced the fingers apart, and something fell with a tinkle to the stone floor. He stooped and picked it up. It was a broken sleeve-link of a peculiar pattern. The centre was of black enamel, the rim was of tiny diamonds. He made a further inspection, without discovering anything new.

Then he looked at his companion, and his forehead was wrinkled. What did this mean? What association had all these circumstances with each other? They could be connected, he felt sure of that—the strange encounter between Flash Fred and Dr. Judd, the will on the shirt, and now this new clue. An atmosphere of impenetrable mystery enveloped this case like a fog behind which strange and inhuman shapes were moving, dimly glimpsed and as dimly suspected.

Murder!

He knew it, he felt it—every shadowy shape he passed on his way to his office whispered the word "Murder!"

The Writing in Braille

THE GIRL was making tea on an electric stove when he came in.

"Hallo!" he said with a start. "I had forgotten you," and she smiled.

"Tell me," he asked quickly, "did Stuart have any cuff-links?"

She nodded and took a small packet from her table.

"The Commissioner forgot to send these on; they came in just after you left," she said.

He opened the paper. The links were of plain gold, without crest or monogram.

He took the enamel and diamond half-link from his pocket and inspected it.

"What is that?" she asked. "Did you find it in—" She hesitated.

He nodded.

"I found it in his hand," he said quietly.

"Then it is murder, you think?"

"I'm certain," said he. "It will be most difficult to prove, and unless a miracle happens, the villain who committed this crime will go free."

He opened the cupboard and took out the tray, adding to the collection the two gold links and the half-link he had found in the dead man's hand.

"Nothing at all," he said, shaking his head. Then he remembered he had not examined the little roll of brown paper. "I don't know what this is; it was found in his pocket."

The Dark Eyes of London

He flattened it out on the table, and the girl came to the opposite side and bent over, looking at the paper as he smoothed it out. It was a strip about four inches long and two wide.

"Nothing written here," he said, and turned it over. "Nor here. I'll have it photographed to-morrow."

"One moment," she said quickly, and took the paper from his hand, passing the tips of her delicate fingers over its surface.

He saw her face go white.

"I thought so," she whispered. "I was almost sure of that when I saw the embossing."

"What is it?" he asked quickly.

"There are some words here written in Braille—the language of the blind," she said, and again her fingers went over the surface, pausing now and again with a puzzled frown on her face.

"Braille?" he repeated in amazement, and she nodded.

"I used to read it when I was in the Institute," she said, "but some of these words have been damaged, probably by the water. Some are distinct. Will you write them down as I spell them?"

He snatched up a pen, pulled a piece of paper from the rack, and waited. Even in that moment he thought how curiously the positions had been reversed, and how he had become the secretary and she the detective.

"The first word is 'murdered,'?" she said. "And then there is a space, and then the word 'dear'; then there's another gap, and the word 'sea' occurs, and that is all."

With this weird message between them they stared at one another. What blind man, amidst those blind shades which had mouthed and gibbered to him in the fog, had sent this message?

What was there behind the ragged scroll of soaked paper? Whose link did the dead man hold in his stiffened hand? Why was he murdered? There had been money in his pocket, his possessions were untouched. It was not for robbery that he had been struck down. Not for vengeance, for he was a stranger.

One fact stood out, one tangible point from whence Larry knew his future movements would radiate.

"Murder!" he said softly, "and I'll find the man who did it, if he hides himself in hell!"

A Telegram from Calgary

DIANA WARD was looking at her chief with a new interest in her fine eyes.

"Braille," he said in a low voice. "That is the written language of the blind, isn't it?"

She nodded.

"Yes, there are books and newspapers printed in that type," she said. "It is a sort of embossed character made of a number of small dots, the relation of one with the other producing the letter."

She took up the paper again.

"When blind people write, they use a small instrument and a guide, but this has been written in a hurry by somebody who worked without any guide. I can feel how irregularly it is done, and the illegibility of the words which I cannot read is due almost as much to bad writing as to the action of the water."

He took this curious clue into his hands and examined it.

"Could Stuart have done it with his pencil?"

She shook her head, and then asked quickly:

"Have you found the pencil?"

"No," said Larry grimly, "but I've found what the pencil was used for."

He opened the parcel he had brought in and showed the shirt and its tragic message written inside the front.

"Why inside?" he said thoughtfully. "It's written on the left too."

Diana understood.

"It would necessarily be written on the left side if he used his right hand," she said.

"But why on the inside?"

She shook her head.

"I don't know. It would have been much simpler to——"

"I have it!" cried Larry triumphantly. "He wrote this will where it would not be seen by somebody or other. If it had been written outside, it would have been seen, and probably destroyed."

She shivered a little.

"I'm not quite hardened yet," she said with a smile. "There is something terrible about this, isn't there? I think you are right; and if we go on that assumption, that he wrote this will in such a manner in order to keep it from the eyes of a third person, we must suppose that that third person existed. In other words, there was somebody of whom he was afraid—or, if you like, at whose hands he feared death—and the murder was premeditated, for he must have been in the custody of that somebody for some time before he met his dreadful end."

She stopped suddenly, for Larry's eyes were fixed on her, and she dropped her own and flushed.

"You're rather wonderful," he said softly; "and if I'm not jolly careful I'm going to lose my job."

He saw a look of doubt in her eyes and laughed.

"Now, Miss Ward," he said banteringly, "we are going to start fair, and you must acquit me of any professional jealousy."

"Jealousy!" she scoffed. "That would be absurd."

"Not so absurd," said Larry. "I've known men to be jealous of women for less reason. And now"—he glanced at his watch—"I think you had better go home. I'll get a taxi. Have you far to go?"

"Only to the Charing Cross Road," she said.

"Then I'll take you home," said Larry. "It's nearly one o'clock."

She had already started putting on her coat and her hat.

"Thank you, I'll go alone," she said. "It isn't far. Really, Mr. Holt, I don't want you to get into the habit of taking me home every time I'm late. I'm quite used to being out by myself, and I won't have a taxi."

"We'll see about that," said Larry. He was writing rapidly on a cable form.

"If I can get this cable through in time, it ought to reach the Chief of Police in Calgary by tea-time yesterday!"

"Yesterday?" she said in surprise. "Oh, of course; they are nine hours late on Greenwich time," and Larry groaned.

"I'll have to try some new ones on you," he said.

They walked home together, but as it happened, the girl's tiny apartment lay in the direction that he had to take. Larry reached Regent's Park, where his own flat was situated, and found the patient Sunny laying out his pyjamas.

"Sunny," said Larry, as, clad in these garments and his flowered dressing-gown, he sipped a cup of chocolate, "somewhere in this city is a very unpleasant gentleman, name unknown."

"I expect there are many like that, sir," said Sunny.

"And somewhere in England is a man who is known as the Public Executioner, and it's my job in life to bring them together!"

He was at Scotland Yard at half-past eight the following morning, and to his surprise the girl was before him, and the departmental memoranda and the various documents which come to every head of Scotland Yard were neatly arranged on his blotting-pad.

"A cablegram has just come in," said the girl. "I didn't open it. You must tell me what you want done about cables and telegrams."

"Open 'em all," said Larry. "I have no private business—and the only scented notes which come to me can be read without bringing a blush to the youngest cheek."

She came across the room with the cablegram in her hand, and he took it.

"Calgary," he said, looking at the address. "That's pretty quick work." And then his mouth opened in amazement, for the telegram read:

"Stuart had no child. He was not married."

He looked at the girl.

"Check Number One," he said.

She took the telegram from him and examined the hour at which it was dispatched.

"This is a common-knowledge telegram," she said.

"What do you mean by common knowledge?" asked Larry good-humouredly.

"Well, it must have been answered just as soon as it arrived, and the man who sent this wrote from what is common knowledge. In other words, he didn't attempt to make any investigations, but took the fact for granted; probably he asked somebody in the office, 'Is Stuart married or a bachelor?' and when they said he was a bachelor, he dispatched the reply."

Larry folded the wire and put it away in his desk.

"If it is common knowledge that Stuart was not married, it merely complicates a situation which is not exactly clear. Here is a man who dies and is obviously murdered, and in a few moments preceding his death writes his will secretly on the inside of his shirt. It is possible, by the way, that he may have done this in the presence of his murderers without their being aware of the fact, and I should think that is most likely."

"I thought that," she agreed.

"He was murdered, and writes his will on the stiff breast of his shirt, leaving the whole of his property to his daughter. Now, a sane man—and there is no reason to suppose that he was anything but sane—does not invent a daughter on the spur of the moment; so it is obvious that the Chief of the Calgary Police is wrong."

"It is equally certain that if he was married it was not in Calgary or even in Canada, where the fact would be known," said the girl. "Secret marriages are possible in a great city, but in small places, amongst very prominent people—and apparently he lived not in a town but on a ranch—the fact that he was married could not escape knowledge."

On the way home the previous evening Larry had told the girl almost all that the Commissioner had told him. It was not usual for him to make confidantes so quickly, but there was something very appealing about Diana Ward, and his confidence, usually a matter of slow growth, had come to maturity in a flash.

The girl was looking thoughtfully down at her desk.

"If he was married secretly," she said slowly, "would it not be—in—"

"In London, of course," said Larry, nodding. "Send a cable to the Chief of the Calgary Police, asking him particulars about Stuart's known movements, when he was in London last before his present visit."

The Memorial Stone

SHE NODDED, took out a telegram form from her rack, and began writing. Larry glanced through the reports mechanically, initialed one, and put the others aside. Then he opened the cupboard and, taking out the tray, carried it to the table. He examined the watch again in the light of day, the swivel ring, the cigar-case, and lastly the roll of paper. By daylight the embossed characters were visible, and he put his finger-tips over them very gingerly. He was not, however, accustomed to reading Braille, and he realized that his hand was a heavy one compared with the delicate touch of his secretary. She had finished her writing, had rung a bell and handed the telegram to him to read.

"That's all right," said Larry, and, when the uniformed messenger had come and taken the telegram away: "Do you notice anything peculiar about this piece of paper?" he asked, pointing to the Braille message.

"Yes," she said. "I was looking at it before you came. You don't mind?" she asked quickly, and Larry laughed.

"You can examine anything except my conscience," he said. "Did you notice"—he turned his attention to the paper again—"that one end of this paper is less discoloured than the other?"

"I noticed that one end was drier than the other last night," she said, "and that of course is the reason. It was on the dry end that we got our best results. For instance, the word 'murderer' was almost untouched by the water; it was damp but not moist."

He nodded, and she opened a drawer of her desk and took out a sheet of brown paper.

"I brought this with me," she said. "It is a sheet from a Braille book, and I was trying experiments with strips I had torn from the book, soaking them

35

in my wash-basin. Here is the result." She took out a little roll of shapeless pulp, which skinned when she attempted to unwind it.

"Humph!" said Larry. They had both reached the same conclusion, but by different processes—she by actual experiment, he by deduction; and the conclusion they had come to was that the roll of paper had been placed in Gordon Stuart's pocket after the body had left the water.

"There would be enough moisture in the clothes to saturate it through," said Larry. "This paper is very absorbent, almost as much so as blotting paper. So we have come to this—that Gordon Stuart was drowned, and after he was drowned his body was handled by some person or persons, one of whom slipped this message into his pocket, and that person was either a blind man or one who believed——" He stared at her. "By Jove!" he said, as a thought struck him.

"What were you going to say?" she asked.

"Is it possible——" He frowned. It was an absurd idea. The man or woman who left this message on the body expected that Diana Ward would read it.

She held no official position, and the fact that she was Larry Holt's secretary was a purely fortuitous circumstance, which could not have been anticipated by any outside person. Yet a hasty telephone call to the Chief of Internal Intelligence revealed the fact that there was no Braille expert at Scotland Yard, the only man who knew the system being at that time on sick leave for six months.

"I think you can dismiss the idea that the message was intended for me," said the girl with a smile. "No, it was written by a blind man, or it would have been written better. A person with the use of his eyes, or——"

"Suppose he were writing in the dark?" asked Larry. He put the tray away and locked the cupboard.

The girl shook her head.

"If he were not blind, he would not be in possession of the instrument to make these markings," she said, and Larry felt that was true.

He spent two hours dictating letters to various authorities, and at eleven o'clock he rose and put on his coat and hat.

"We're going for a joy ride," he said.

"We?" she repeated in surprise.

"I want you to come along," said Larry, and this time his tone was authoritative, and the girl meekly obeyed.

There was a car waiting for them at the entrance to the Yard, and the driver evidently had already received his instructions.

"We're going to Beverley Manor, the village which Stuart was so fond of visiting," he said. "I particularly want to discover what attractions the old Saxon church had for this unhappy man. He doesn't seem to have been an archæologist, so the fact that the foundations were a thousand years old would not interest him."

It was a glorious spring day, with just a sufficient nip in the air to bring the colour to young and healthy cheeks. The hedgerows were bursting into vivid green, and the grassy banks were yellow with primroses. They sat silent, this man and woman whom fate had thrown together in such strange circumstances, enjoying the golden day and thankful of heart to be alive in that season of renewal. All the world was living. The air was lively with hurrying birds, going about their business of nest-making. They saw strange furtive shapes creeping across the road from burrow to burrow; and in one sheltered old-world garden which they passed white lilacs were blooming.

Beverley Manor was a straggling village at the foot of the Kentish Rag. Beyond its church it had few attractions for visitors, for it lay off the main Kentish road, a tiny backwater of rural England, where life ran a smooth unruffled course.

They pulled up at the inn, where Larry ordered lunch, and then they set forth on foot to the church, which lay a quarter of a mile away along a white and pleasant road. It was not a pretty church; its square tower was squat and unlovely, and successive generations, endeavouring to improve its once simple lines, had produced a medley of architecture in which Romanesque, Gothic and Norman struggled for recognition.

"It rather swears, doesn't it?" said Larry irreverently as they passed through the old lych-gate into the churchyard.

The Dark Eyes of London

The door of the church was open, and the edifice was empty. However disturbing its outside might be, there was serenity and peace and simplicity in the calm interior.

Larry had hoped to find memorial tablets placed in the wall of the church which would give him some clue to Stuart's movements. But beyond a brass testifying to the virtues of a former vicar, and the tomb of an ancient Bishop of Rochester, the church was innocent of memorials. Larry then began a systematic inspection of the graves. Most of them were very old, and their inscriptions indecipherable.

He came at last to the far end of the cemetery, where half a dozen workmen were carrying a new stone wrapped in canvas, and he and the girl stood side by side watching them in silence as they deposited their load by a well-kept grave.

"I'm afraid we've had our journey for nothing," said Larry. "We'll make a few inquiries in the village, and then we'll go back to London."

He was turning to go, when one of the men stripped the canvas covering from the headstone.

"We might as well know who this is," said Larry, and stepped forward to look.

The men stood on one side to give him a better view, and he read; and, reading, gasped.

To the Memory of
Margaret Stuart,
Wife of
Gordon Stuart
(of Calgary, Can.).
Died May 4th, 1899.
Also His Only Daughter
Jeane,
Born 10th June, 1898.
Died 1st May, 1899.

The girl had joined him now, and together they stood staring down at the headstone.

"His only daughter!" said Larry in a tone of bewilderment. "His only daughter! Then who is Clarissa?"

The Man Who Lost a Finger

AN EXAMINATION of local records produced no satisfactory result. Margaret Stuart had died at a farm three miles out of Beverley Manor, and the farm had changed hands twice since the date of her death.

"Twenty years ago?" said the farmer whom Larry interviewed. "Why, twenty years ago this place was a sort of nursing home. It was run by a woman who took in invalids."

Where the woman is, he could not say. She was not a local woman. He thought he had heard she was dead.

"I've been racking my brains to recall her name," said the farmer. "I told the gentleman yesterday that he'd best go to Somerset House——"

"A gentleman here yesterday?" said Larry quickly. "Was there somebody inquiring yesterday?"

"Yes, sir, a man from London," said the farmer. "He came down in a car and offered me fifty pounds if I could tell him the name of the woman who kept this place as a home, and a hundred pounds if I could give him any information about a lady that died here twenty-two years ago. A lady named Stuart."

"Oh, indeed?" said Larry, alert now. Nobody from Scotland Yard had made the inquiries he was well aware. "What was this gentleman like who called yesterday?" he asked.

"Rather a tall man," said the farmer. "I didn't see his face properly because he had his overcoat buttoned up to his chin. But I did notice that he'd lost the little finger on his left hand."

On their way back to London both Larry and Diana Ward were absorbed in their own thoughts. The car was threading through the traffic of Westminster Bridge Road before Larry made any reference to their visit.

"Who is in such a frantic hurry to discover all about the Stuarts," he asked, "and will give fifty pounds for information? And who is his daughter Clarissa, and how can he have a daughter Clarissa, when his only daughter lies at Beverley Manor?"

"You inquired at the stonemason's when we came through Beverley. Didn't they tell you anything?" asked the girl.

He nodded.

"The stone was put up by order of Mr. Stuart, who was in the habit of coming to the churchyard every day to sit beside the grave. The memorial was ordered two months ago, and the stone was seen and approved by Gordon Stuart only last week."

He bit his lip thoughtfully.

"Between last week and the night of his murder, Stuart must have discovered that he had another child." He shook his head. "That sort of thing doesn't happen," he said decisively, "not in real life anyway."

He spent ten minutes with the Commissioner, and afterwards went into the city, and the girl did not see him till seven o'clock that night. She had had instructions from him that she was not to wait, as it was a Saturday and her office hours ended at one. But she was sitting at her desk, reading, when he came in, and he was so elated that he did not reprove her.

"I've got it!" he said exultantly.

"The murderer?" she asked with a start.

"No, no, the story of Stuart. Has there been any reply to my cablegram?"

Diana shook her head.

"It doesn't matter very much," he said briskly as he paced the office. "I've secured the registration of the marriage. It occurred in the Diamond Jubilee year, in August, 1897, and was celebrated at a church in Highgate. Don't you see what happened?"

"I don't quite see," she said slowly.

"Well, I'll tell you. Gordon Stuart, a young man at the time, was on a visit to this country. I have found that he stayed at the Cecil Hotel from June to August, 1897. He married the girl, whose name was Margaret Wilson, and returned to the Cecil Hotel alone in March, '98. There is a record there that he left for Canada two days after he came back to the hotel. They keep a book in which they write down the addresses to which letters should be forwarded, and there was no difficulty whatever in tracing his movements so far. Then I went to see the vicar of the church where he was married; and here I had a great find."

He paused, rumpled his hair and frowned.

"I really should like to know who is that tall man who has lost the little finger of his left hand," he said irritably.

"Why?" she asked in surprise.

"He had been there a day before me," said Larry, and then, shaking off his annoyance: "Here is the story—the story told by Stuart to the vicar, whom he met in the Strand on the day before he sailed for Canada, never to return until he came back eight or nine months ago.

"The vicar married him, and remembered the circumstances very well. He said Stuart was a very nervous and somewhat conceited man, who lived in terror of his father, a rich landowner in Canada. Stuart confessed to him, over a cup of tea which they had together at the Cecil, that he was leaving his wife and going back to Canada to break the news of his marriage to his father. He was in considerable doubt as to what his father would say, or, to be more exact, he had no doubt whatever that the old man would kick up a shine. The impression left on the vicar's mind was that the old man would disinherit him. To cut a long story short, he said he was leaving London the next day, and at the first opportunity he should tell his father, and then he would return for his wife.

"There's no doubt in my mind," Larry went on, "that Stuart did not tell his father, that he kept the secret of his marriage carefully hidden, and in a panic at being found out, he broke off all communication with his wife."

The girl shook her head.

"One doesn't want to judge the dead too harshly," she said, "but it was not a manly thing to do."

"I agree," said Larry. "It wasn't sporting. He must have left his wife a considerable sum of money. At any rate, when the vicar saw her she was in comfortable circumstances and gave him that impression. Stuart left in March. In June, 1898, three months later, his child was born—the child he never saw, and about whom in all probability he never heard until years of remorse worked upon him and he came back to England to find his wife and establish her in the position to which she was entitled.

"He must have employed an inquiry agent. And the end of his quest was a discovery in the churchyard of Beverley Manor—the grave of his wife and his only child."

"What about Clarissa?" asked the girl, and Larry shrugged.

"That is Mystery No. 2 which has got to be cleared up."

She was silent, this thoughtful girl, and her pretty brows were wrinkled in perplexity. Presently she put down the pen she had been so assiduously biting, and looked across at him with a slow, triumphant smile, a smile which found a ready response in his face.

"You've solved it?" he asked eagerly, and she nodded. "You've solved the mystery of Clarissa?"

"I think it's one of the easiest of the problems to solve," she said calmly, "and I must have been silly not to have thought of it before. Have you the registration of birth?"

"I haven't got that; we're making a search for it to-morrow," said Larry.

"I can save you the trouble," replied Diana Ward. "Clarissa is the other twin daughter."

"Twins!" gasped Larry, and the girl nodded, her eyes dancing with merriment at his surprise.

"Obviously," she said. "Poor Mrs. Stuart had twin daughters. One of them died; the other is Clarissa, of whom Stuart learnt, perhaps, in the last few hours of his life."

Larry looked at her in awe.

"When you are Chief Commissioneress of the Metropolitan Police," he said, "I shall be very obliged to you if you make me your secretary. I feel I have a lot to learn."

Edgar Wallace

Mr. Strauss "Drops"

FLASH FRED had not left London: he had no intention of leaving London, if the truth be told. He had certain doubts in his mind which he had determined to set at rest, certain obscurities on his horizon which he desired should be dispersed. Flash Fred was a clever man. If he had not been clever, he would not have lived in the excellent style he adopted, nor possessed chambers in Jermyn Street and a motor-brougham to take him to the theatre at night. His working expenses were heavy, but his profits were vast. He had many irons in the fire and burnt himself with none of them—which is the art of success in all walks of life.

On the evening of the day that Larry had made his discovery Flash Fred, in the seclusion and solitude of his ornate sitting-room, had elaborated a theory which had followed very close upon a discovery he had made that morning. Men of his temperament and uncertain prospects suffer from a chronic dissatisfaction. This dissatisfaction is half the cause of their departure from the straight and narrow path, and is wholly responsible for their undoing. A hundred pounds a month, payable yearly, is a handsome income; but the underworld abhor anything that savours of steadiness, regularity and system—three qualities which are so associated with prison life that they carry with them a kind of taint particularly distressing to the lag-who-was.

Twelve hundred pounds a year for five years is six thousand pounds, or twenty-four thousand dollars at the present rate of exchange—a respectable sum; but five years represents a big slice taken out of the hectic life of men like Flash Fred. Twelve hundred pounds at best represents only two coups at trente et quarante, and can be lost in three minutes.

Dr. Judd was a collector. It had been reported to Fred that Dr. Judd's residence at Chelsea was a veritable treasure-house of paintings and antique jewellery. Fred had read a newspaper paragraph that Dr. Judd was the possessor of historical gems worth fifty thousand pounds. Though Fred had no passion for history, he had an eye to the value of precious stones. And the theory he had evolved was in the main arithmetical. If he could get away with ten thousand pounds' worth of property in twenty-four hours, he would not

The Dark Eyes of London

only have anticipated his income for eight or nine years, but he would be saved the fag of coming to London every twelve months to collect it. Much might happen in twelve months. It might not always be possible for him to make the journey, since prison authorities are notoriously difficult to persuade. Or he might be dead.

To get that movable property would be difficult, because the doctor was hardly the kind of man to leave his property unguarded. Indeed, the ordinary methods of effecting an entrance were repugnant to Fred's professional feelings. For he gained his livelihood by the cleverness of his tongue and the lightning adjustment of certain brain cells to meet emergencies, and to him a jemmy was an instrument of terror, since it implied work. But there was another method—and once he had made his get-away, would the doctor dare prosecute?

That afternoon, sauntering aimlessly through Piccadilly Circus at the midday hour, he had come face to face with a tall, stoutish man, who, after one glance at him, had attempted to avoid a meeting; but Fred had caught him by the arm and swung him round.

"Why," he said, "if it isn't old No. 278! How are you, Strauss?"

Mr. Strauss's face twitched nervously.

"I think you've made a mistake, sir," he said.

"Come off it," demanded Fred vulgarly, and, taking him by the arm, led him down Lower Regent Street.

"Excuse my not recognizing you," said Mr. Strauss nervously, "but I thought at first you were a bull—split we call them in this country."

"Well, I'm not," said Flash Fred. "And how has the old world been treating you, hey? Do you remember G Gallery at Portland, in B Block?"

The face of the stout man twitched again. He did not like being reminded of his prison experience, though in truth he had little against the prisoner who had occupied the adjoining cell.

"How are you getting on?" he asked. And it happened that that morning Flash Fred had gone out without any visible diamonds—he carried them in his hip pocket, for he trusted nobody.

"Bad," said Fred, which was a lie, but no good crook admits that he is prosperous. Then suddenly: "Why did you think I was a split, Strauss?"

Strauss looked uncomfortable.

"Oh, I just thought so," he said awkwardly.

"Are you at the old game?"

Fred looked at the other steadily and saw his eyes shift.

"No, I'm going straight now," he said.

"A liar you are, and a liar you will always be," said Fred, quoting Larry Holt. "I'll bet you're on the way to 'fence' something."

Again the man looked round as though seeking a way of escape; and Fred, who never despised an opportunity, however small, held out a suggestive palm and said laconically, "Drop!"

"Only a few things," said Mr. Strauss hurriedly. "Thing that were given to me or wouldn't be missed—just odds and ends like. A couple of salt-spoons . . ." He enumerated his loot.

"Drop!" said Fred again. "I'm hard up and want the money. I'll take a share and you shall have the money back—one of these days."

Mr. Strauss dropped, with a curse.

"Come and have a drink," said Fred briskly, when the transaction had been completed to his satisfaction.

"You've left me with about three pounds' worth," grumbled the man. "Really, Mr. Grogan, I don't think you're fair," and he looked at the other suspiciously. "And you don't look as if you're hard up either."

"Appearances are deceptive," said the cheerful Fred, and led the way into a private bar. "What are you now—valet or butler?"

"Butler," replied Strauss, tossing down a dram. "It's not a bad place, Mr. Grogan."

"Call me Fred," begged Flash Fred.

"It seems a liberty," said Strauss, and meant it. "I've got a butler's job with a very nice gentleman," he said.

"Rich?"

Mr. Strauss nodded.

"Yards of it," he said briefly. "But what's the good? He knows I'm a lag, and he's very decent to me."

Fred was eyeing him narrowly.

"You still dope, I see?" he said, and the man flushed.

"Yes," he said gruffly, "I take a little stimulant now and again."

"Well," said Fred, "who is your boss?"

"You wouldn't know him." Mr. Strauss shook his head. "He's a City gentleman, head of an insurance office."

"Dr.—Judd?" asked Flash Fred quickly.

"Why, yes," said the other in surprise. "How did you know?"

They parted soon after, and Flash Fred was a thoughtful man for the rest of the day, and his plans began to take shape towards the evening.

He dressed himself with care after dark, and strolled Strandwards, for he numbered amongst his other accomplishments that of an experienced squire of dames. He had a ready smile for the solitary girl hurrying homewards, and though the rebuffs were many, such conquests as he had to his credit added to the pleasures of memory. Between St. Martin's Church and the corner of the Strand he drew blank, for such girls as he saw were unattractive or were escorted. Opposite Morley's Hotel he saw a peach.

He caught one glimpse of her under a light-standard and was transfixed by the rare beauty of her face. She was alone, and Fred swung round and in two strides had overtaken her.

"Haven't we met before?" he asked, raising his hat, but asked no more. Somebody caught him by the collar and jerked him back.

"Fred, I shall really have to be severe with you," said the hated voice of Larry Holt, and Fred developed an instant grievance.

"Haven't you got a home to go to?" he wailed, and continued his journey to the Strand in a bitter mood, for the romance had been shaken out of him, and he could still feel the knuckles of the shaker at the back of his neck.

*

The girl passed on, unconscious of the fact that Larry Holt had been behind her. It was not an unusual experience to be spoken to in the street, and she had grown hardened to that also.

She lived above a tobacconist's shop in the Charing Cross Road, and Larry saw her open the side door and go into the dark passage; he waited for a few minutes, then continued his walk.

This girl had made an extraordinary impression upon him. He told himself that it was not her delicate beauty, or anything about her that was feminine, but that it was her genius, her extraordinary reasoning faculties which attracted him; and, to do him justice, he believed this. He was not a susceptible man. Beautiful women he had known, on both sides of the border line which separates the good from the bad, the honest from the criminal. He had had minor affairs in his youth, but had come through those fiery dreams unscorched and unmarked by his experiences.

So he told himself. It was extraordinary that it was necessary to tell himself anything; but there was the indisputable fact that he spent a great deal of his spare time in arguing out his attitude of mind toward Diana Ward. And he had known her something over twenty-four hours!

Diana Ward was not thinking of Larry as she went into her flat. Her mind was wholly occupied by the problems which the Stuart case presented. She felt that, if the missing Clarissa were found, they would be on the high road to discovering the cause of Stuart's death and the reason for this hideous crime.

She slammed the door and went up the dark and narrow stairs slowly. The upper part of the tobacconist's was let off in three flats, and she occupied the highest and the cheapest. The tenants of the other two were, she knew, spending the week-end in the country. The first floor was occupied by a bachelor Civil Servant, a hearty man whose parties occasionally kept her awake at night; the second floor by a newspaper artist and his wife; and she had no reason to complain of her neighbours.

She had reached the second landing, her foot was on the stairs of the final two flights, when she stopped. She thought she had heard a noise, the faint creak of a sound which she had felt rather than heard. She waited a second, and then smiled at her nervousness. She had heard these creaks and whispers before on the dark stairs, but had overcome her timidity to discover that they were purely imaginary. Nevertheless, she walked up a little more slowly and reached the landing from whence rose a short flight of stairs to her own apartments. The landing was a broad one, and as she turned, with one hand on the banisters, she put out the other in a spirit of bravado as though she groped for some hidden intruder.

And then her blood turned to water, for her hand had touched the coat of a man! She screamed, but instantly a hand, a big unwholesome hand, covered her face, and she was drawn slowly backward. She fought and struggled with all her might, but the man who held her had almost superhuman strength, and the arm about her was like a vice. Then, suddenly, she went limp, and momentarily the arm that held her relaxed.

"Fainted, have ye?" said a harsh voice, and as a hand came feeling down for her face, the other arm relaxed a little more.

With a sudden dart the girl broke free, ran up the remaining stairs and opened and slammed the door. There was a key on the inside and this she turned with a heart full of gratitude that she had never locked her bedroom door from the outside. She flew across the room, stopping only to switch on the lights, pulled out a drawer and took from its depths a small revolver. Diana Ward came from a stock which was not easily scared, and, though her heart was pounding painfully, she ran back at the door and flung it open.

She stood for the space of a few seconds. She heard a stealthy footstep on the stairs and fired. There was a roar of fear and a blunder of feet down the stairs. Only for a moment did she hesitate, and then raced down the stairway in pursuit. She heard the thump of feet on the landing lower down, heard the rattle of the door, and came down the last flight to find it open and nobody in sight.

Concealing the revolver in a fold of her dress, she stepped out into the Charing Cross Road. At this hour there were few pedestrians, and she looked round for some sign of her assailant. A light motor-van was driving away, and the only person she saw near at hand was an old blind man. The iron ferrule of his stick came "tap-tap-tap," as he stumbled painfully along.

Edgar Wallace

"Pity the blind," he wailed; "pity the poor blind!"

Burglars at the Yard

SUNNY," said Larry to his servitor, "London is a terrible city."

"Indeed it is, sir," said Mr. Patrick Sunny.

"But it has one bright, radiant feature which redeems it from utter desolation and abomination."

"I think you're right, sir," said Sunny. "I've often noticed that myself, sir. I'm very fond of the picture houses myself."

"I'm not talking about the picture houses," snapped Larry. "Nothing is further from my thoughts than the cinema houses. I am talking of something different, something spiritual."

"Would you like a whisky and soda, sir?" asked Sunny, at last securing a tangible line.

"Get out!" roared Larry, bubbling with laughter. "Get out, you horrible materialist! Go to the pictures."

"Yes, sir," said Sunny, "but it's rather late."

"Then go to bed," said Larry. "Stop a bit. Bring me my writing-case."

He was wearing his favourite indoor kit, a dressing-gown, a pair of old cricketing trousers and a soft shirt, and now he filled his polished brier with a sense of physical well-being.

"Believe me, Sunny," said Larry Holt impressively, "there are many worse places than London on a bright spring day, when your heart——"

There was a faint rat-tat-tat on the other door. "A visitor at this time of night!" said Larry in surprise. It could not be from Scotland Yard, because Scotland Yard use the telephone freely, a little too freely sometimes.

"I think there's somebody at the door, sir," said Sunny.

"That's a fine bit of reasoning on your part," said Larry. "Open it."

He waited and heard a brief exchange of questions. The visitor was a woman; and before he could guess who it was, the door opened and Diana Ward came in. He saw by her face that something had happened, and went to meet her.

49

"What is the matter?" he asked quickly. "That man didn't follow you?"

"What man?" she demanded in surprise.

"Flash Fred."

She shook her head.

"I don't know whether it was Flash Fred," she said grimly, "but if he is somebody particularly unpleasant, it was probably he."

"Sit down. Would you like some coffee? I'm just going to have a cup. Sunny, get two coffees."

"Yes, sir," said Sunny, and then, significantly, "Do you want me to go out to the pictures, sir?"

Larry blushed angrily.

"Get some coffee, you—you—you——" he spluttered. "Now, what is it?"

The girl told the story of her adventure without preliminary. Larry listened with a serious face.

"You say he was big? That rules out Flash Fred," he said. "Do you think it was a burglar—somebody who had broken in and whom your arrival interrupted?"

"I don't think so," she shook her head. "In fact, I know that it was a much more serious attack. When I got back to my flat, I went through all the rooms. In the dining-room, the room to which I would have gone first in ordinary circumstances, I found a long laundry basket."

"A laundry basket?" he repeated in surprise.

She nodded.

"It was lined with a sort of quilting, very thick, and the lid was padded in the same way. Inside of it was this."

She laid down the object she had been carrying. It looked like an airman's cap, except that there was no opening for the mouth.

He took it up and sniffed, though, there was no need for this, for he had noticed the sweet scent when she had come into the room.

"It is saturated in chloroform," he said. "Of course, this would not make you entirely insensible, but it would have quietened you."

He paced the room, his hands in his pockets, his chin on his chest.

"Did you find anything else?"

"When I got out into the street," she said, "a laundry van was just moving off. I noticed it particularly, because I thought at the time that the word 'laundry'—and that was all the inscription the van bore—had been written by an amateur, and very badly done."

"I can't understand it," said Larry, bewildered. "The brute couldn't have got you away. He must have had some assistants in the house."

"I don't agree with you," she said quietly. "This man was terribly strong. I felt like an infant in his arms, and it would have been a very simple matter for him to have slid the basket down the stairs and carried it out across the pavement with the help of the man who was driving the van."

"But why you?" he asked, bewildered. "Why should they bother about you?"

She did not reply immediately.

"I am wondering," she said at last, "whether I have by accident stumbled upon some clue which incriminates the Stuart murderers. Perhaps, without knowing that I have such a clue, I am in possession of information which they wish to suppress."

Larry was very thoughtful.

"Just wait here a little while and I'll change," he said, and disappeared from the room.

The girl looked round the cosy flat appreciatively and Sunny came in, bearing a tray, first stopping outside the door to cough loudly, to the intense annoyance of Larry, who heard him from the other room.

"Will you have sugar, miss?" asked Sunny solemnly, and when she nodded: "Some ladies don't like sugar. It makes them fat."

"I'm not very much afraid of getting fat," she smiled.

"No, ma'am, you wouldn't be," said Sunny agreeably.

On the way to the flat she asked Larry laughingly if Sunny agreed with everything he said.

"With everything I've ever said," said Larry. "He drives me to despair sometimes. I have yet to find the subject upon which Sunny has an independent, definite opinion."

Later he was to discover there was at least one matter in which Sunny had a mind of his own, but that time was distant.

They came to the apartment in Charing Cross Road, and Larry began his search. He had brought a flash lamp with him, and inspected every stair, without, however, coming upon a single clue that would identify the mysterious assailant.

"Now we'll have a look at your room."

He examined the laundry basket, which the girl had exactly described.

"Nothing new here," he said. "See if anything is missing."

She made an independent search and came back to him in the sitting-room with a puzzled face.

"My green coat, an overcoat I wear, and a hat have disappeared."

"A distinctive hat?" he asked quickly.

"What do you mean by a distinctive hat?" she asked in surprise.

"Is it rather striking?"

"It is rather," she smiled. "It is a golden yellow hat which I wear with my green coat."

He nodded.

"Have you worn it to the Yard?" he asked.

"Often," she replied in surprise.

"Then that's it," said he. "Come down with me. I don't want to leave you alone."

She followed him into the street, and he went into the nearest telephone booth and rang up Scotland Yard and got the officer on duty at the door.

"Has Miss Ward been in to-night? It is Inspector Holt speaking," he asked.

"Yes, sir," was the reply. "She's just gone out."

Larry groaned.

"But I haven't been to Scotland Yard," she said in surprise.

"Somebody has impersonated you!" he said shortly.

They were in the grim building on the Thames Embankment within a few minutes, and the door of 47 was apparently untampered with. He opened the door and switched on the lights.

"Oh, yes," he said softly, for the doors of the cupboard wherein he had kept the clues concerning the death of Stuart hung broken upon their hinges.

He pulled out the tray and gave a rapid glance at its contents.

The Braille writing had disappeared!

Fanny Weldon Tells the Truth

HE LIFTED the telephone, and presently:

"Send the first two officers in the building," he said, "and a messenger, quick!"

The girl was watching interestedly. Now she saw the real Larry Holt, the man of whom it is said by the Commissioner that "he slept trailing." At his request, she stood outside the open door whilst he conducted an investigation. The light jemmy which the intruder had used he had not troubled to take away. It lay on the floor, and he picked it up with a piece of paper and carried it to the light.

A short thread of cotton adhered to its rough end, which meant that its user had worn cotton gloves to avoid finger-prints. His only hope was the tray. It was a flat glass tray with wicker sides and handles, and he knew that if the gloves came off anywhere it would be here; for a person unaccustomed to working in gloves would remove them to examine the smaller objects. And his surmise was right. When he breathed on the polished back of the gold watch, a distinct thumb-print was visible.

By this time two officers had arrived.

"Is there a man on duty in the print department?" asked Larry.

"Yes, sir," replied the officer.

"Take this watch down. Hold it by the stem. If he cannot bring up the print by powder I want it photographed and verified within the next hour."

The burglar had made another faux pas. Larry had pulled out the waste-paper basket without disturbing its contents and had taken out three screwed-up pieces of paper, two of which proved to be nothing more important than memoranda in Diana's writing. The third, however, was a plan of the room, drawn in ink by a skilful hand, the cupboard being marked

53

and the positions of the desks shown.

"They thought there were three cupboards here," said Larry, pointing. "There is one supposed to be on the left of the fireplace," he looked up and raised his eyebrows. "By Jingo, they're right!" he said. "And another behind the door," he looked and nodded. "They know this room much better than I do, Miss Ward," he said, and looked at the paper again. "The man who drew this has a knowledge of architectural drawing," said he. "I think we'd better have a safe and a bodyguard," he added bitterly.

Somebody appeared in the doorway. It was Sir John Hason, who sometimes returned to his office at night to take advantage of the quiet and freedom from interruption which the evening hours afforded.

"What has happened, Larry?" he asked.

"Oh, nothing," said Larry airily, "only a burglar has broken into Scotland Yard! Don't you think we ought to send for the police?" he asked sardonically and Sir John grinned. But the smile came off his face instantly.

"They haven't taken the Stuart clues, have they?"

"The only clue that matters," replied Larry. "It would be a good idea if we brought some Boy Scouts into this building to look after our movable property!"

"I like you when you're funny," said the Commissioner, but he was serious. "We'll have the doorkeeper up."

The doorkeeper, when he came, could give no satisfactory explanation, except that he had thought it was Miss Ward who had passed. It was the practice to call the number of the room when its occupants came in for duty, and this was also the custom after office hours. The visitor had said "47," and had been allowed to pass unchallenged.

"There have been no strangers here, have there?" asked Larry.

"No," said the girl, and then: "There was a blind man here this afternoon: you remember, you wanted to see the instruments these poor people use, and I asked the little old man who sells matches on the Embankment to come up."

Larry remembered.

"At any rate, he couldn't have made a plan of the room," he said.

"The system seems to be a little bit groggy," said Sir John when the doorkeeper had gone. "We can't really blame this man. It is our own fault."

"There's hardly enough light in the main hall to read a newspaper placard," complained Larry. "Here is the finger-print gentleman."

The officer who came up had a broad smile: the smile of a man who had justified his hobby.

"Got it first time, sir," he said. "Fanny Weldon, 280 Coram Street. Here's her record." He handed the card to Larry.

"Twice gaoled for impersonation," he read. "That's the woman. But how did she come into this game?"

The officer who had taken the watch away, and who now restored it, supplied the information.

"Fanny's a queer woman, sir," he said. "She hasn't a spark of originality, and she's had all her trouble through helping other people in their schemes. Big Joe Jaket employed her to impersonate Miss Lottie Home, the actress, about two years ago; and then she was employed by somebody else to impersonate a barmaid whilst the landlord was away, when the Mannic gang cleared out three thousand from the Hotel Victor Hugo."

Larry was sitting at the table, his chin in his palm, thinking.

"That is what has happened," he said. "These people have got track of all the crooks in London, and it's just as likely they've employed Fanny. 280 Coram Street, I think you said? We'll see what Fanny has to say for herself."

He did not see Fanny until daylight. 280 Coram Street was a corner house, apparently rented out in rooms. Soon after daybreak a cab drew up to the kerb outside the door and a woman stepped out and paid the driver. As she walked to the door, Larry came behind her and took her arm. She turned round with an exclamation of fright. She was a pretty woman with a shrewish mouth.

"Here, what are you doing?" she asked in alarm.

"You're coming for a little walk with me," said Larry.

"Is it a cop?" she asked, going pale.

"A fair cop," said Larry, and, still holding her elbow, led her to the nearest police station, where Diana and his officers were waiting.

On the way to the station she bewailed her fate.

"This comes of being obliging," she said bitterly. "What's the charge?"

"Sacrilege," said Larry solemnly, and she was astonished.

"Sacrilege? What do you mean? Breaking into a church or something?"

"Breaking into Scotland Yard," said Larry.

She drew a long breath.

"Then it is a cop!" she said.

"You've said it," replied her captor.

They put her in the steel pen, but not before she had been searched by one of the woman attendants. The search produced £150 in bank-notes, which Fanny, who had now recovered her good spirits, insisted should be counted.

"I've lost things in police stations before," she said significantly.

She was not taken to the cells, but in a little waiting-room Larry and Diana interviewed her. And the presence of Diana was a source of great interest to the prisoner.

"You've brought your young lady along, I see?" she said flippantly. She was gamin right through, despite her smart clothes and her elaborate jewellery. "Is this the lady I 'took off'?"

"She's the identical lady," said Larry. "Now, Fanny, I'm going to talk to you like a father."

"Go ahead and don't mind me," said Fanny recklessly. "But I can tell you that I've been going straight for months," and Larry grinned.

"I should like to draw a line alongside that straight course of yours," he said. "It'd be a bit bumpy. Fanny, I'm going to give you a chance. And I shall be perfectly frank with you. Scotland Yard doesn't want the world to know that a female hook has broken in under its nose and pinched certain articles of value."

The woman laughed softly, and, catching Diana's eye, winked.

"It takes a woman to do that sort of thing, eh, dearie?" she asked. "Proceed with your story, Mr. Busy Fellow. But if you think I'm going to give anybody away, why, you're making a mistake."

"You will give away just what I want you to give away," said Larry sharply. "You are going to tell me who employed you to do this job."

She shook her head.

"You will also tell me who was the man to whom you handed the stuff, and where."

Again she shook her head, but she was in a good humour.

"There is no use in asking me questions," she said. "I'm not going to answer. You can put me into the cell just as soon as you like, and save yourself a lot of trouble."

"I'll put you into the cell after I've charged you," said Larry quietly, and the woman looked up sharply.

"You have charged me with breaking and entering," she said.

"That is not the crime which I shall bring against you," said Larry. "If I get no satisfaction from you now I shall take you back to the pen and charge you with being an accessory to the murder of Gordon Stuart on the night of the twenty-third of April."

She looked at him, speechless.

"Murder?" she repeated. "Good Gawd! You don't mean that I'm in——"

"You're in bad," said Larry. "You're assisting murderers to escape the processes of justice. You were employed to steal a very important clue which the police held, and which might have led to the conviction of the murderer—and that is sufficient offence to bring you under the gravest suspicion."

She was serious now.

"Do you mean that?" she asked.

"I do indeed," said Larry earnestly. "See here, Fanny, I don't want you to think I'm kidding you. I'm giving it you as straight as it's possible for one human being to give a thing to another. You went out to steal the clue which might have led to the arrest of the murderers."

"What is your name?" she asked.

"I am Inspector Larry Holt," and she gasped.

The Dark Eyes of London

"Suffering Moses! Then I am in bad!" she said. "I thought you were abroad. Now, Mr. Holt, I'll tell you. I've heard a lot about you, and I'm told that you always play straight with a hook. I knew nothing about this job until yesterday afternoon, and then I had a telephone call asking me to meet Big Jake, or Blind Jake as they call him."

"Blind Jake?" repeated Larry, to whom the name was new, and then he recalled the blind match-seller on the Embankment who had come to his office—but it could not be he. Diana had said he was a small man.

"Your men know all about him, Mr. Holt," Fanny hesitated. "He's a wicked man. Now, that sounds funny coming from me; but if you know what I mean, he's just wicked. I'm scared to death of Blind Jake, and there isn't a hook in London who isn't. He's been inside twice: once for unlawfully wounding and once for being in possession of property. There used to be three of 'em, all hooks together, and all blind! We used to call 'em the blind eyes of London, because they could get about quicker than you, and in a fog they'd beat the best detectives that ever lived, because fog never means anything to them. Blind Jake used to be the boss of the three, and then one of 'em disappeared and I heard he was dead. We never heard much about them for twelve months, and then Blind Jake turned up again with yards of money. I believe he is working for a big boss."

"Well, you met Blind Jake?"

"Yes," she nodded. "He gave me the plan——"

"Not his own—he couldn't draw," interrupted Larry.

"Not him," said the woman contemptuously. "No, he brought the plan with him. I've got it somewhere. Maybe it's in the bag you've taken."

"Don't worry about the plan," said Larry. "I found that in the office."

"Well, Blind Jake told me how to go about it, said he would give me a coat and a hat that this young lady always wore when she went to the Yard, and I got instructions that I was to say '47' when I went into the room, and run upstairs quick."

"What were you told to get?"

"A little roll of brown paper," said the woman. "They told me where it was and almost how it was placed in the tray." She shrugged her shoulders. "I can't guess how they knew."

"I can," said Larry and turned to the girl. "The little old match-seller recovered his sight! Where can I find Blind Jake?" he asked the woman.

"You won't find him," she said, shaking her head. "He never comes out by day—at least, very seldom."

"What is he like in appearance?"

"Very big and as strong as an ox."

Diana uttered an exclamation.

"Has he a beard?" she asked.

"Yes, miss," said the woman. "A little greyish kind of beard."

"It was the man on the stairs," said Diana, "I am certain of it."

Larry nodded.

"Well," he said, addressing the woman, "when did you hand over the stuff?"

"About two o'clock this morning. That was the time he said I was to meet him at the lower end of Arundel Street in the Strand, near the Embankment. And a pretty fine temper he was in, too."

"Do you know where he lives?" asked Larry.

She shook her head.

"Years ago they used to live in Todd's Home," she said. "That's an institute in Lissom Lane, Paddington, where they used to look after the blind hawkers. But I don't think he's there now."

Larry took the woman back to the charge room.

"You can release her on my recognisance," he said. "Fanny, you will report to me to-morrow morning at Scotland Yard at ten o'clock."

"Yes, sir," said Fanny. "What about my money?"

Larry thought a moment.

"You can take that," he said.

"If anybody tells me," said Fanny, as she collected and counted her notes with offensive care, "that the police are dishonest, I shall have something to say."

The Dark Eyes of London

Todd's Home

MY DEAR," said Larry gently, "you really must go home and go to bed."
Diana shook her head laughingly.

"I really am not tired, Mr. Holt," she said. "Won't you let me go along with you? You know, you promised to keep me in this case."

"I didn't promise to keep you up all night," he said good-humouredly, "and you're looking a wreck. I don't think I shall do anything much more this morning—except sleep," said he. "Now, off you go. There's a providential taxi crawling this way," he said, and whistled.

She was feeling desperately tired, and she knew his words were the words of wisdom. But she made one last ineffectual protest. Larry was adamant. The cab drew up and he opened the door for her.

"Sergeant Harvey will go home with you," he said, and drew Harvey aside. "Go upstairs to Miss Ward's room, search it thoroughly, and remain on duty on the lower landing until you're relieved."

He watched the cab out of sight, then turned to the second officer who had accompanied him.

"Now, sergeant," he said, "I think we will investigate Todd's Home."

It was some time before they found another taxi, and Larry had a constitutional objection to walking. Six o'clock was booming out from the church towers when the cab put them down before Todd's Home. It was a bleak, unlovely house, the windows covered with blue-wash. A long black board, covering the width of the house, was inscribed in faded gold letters: "Todd's Home for the Indigent Blind."

Larry expected he would have some difficulty in making the inmates hear, but he was mistaken; for, hardly had he knocked when the door was opened by a little man.

"That's not Toby and not Harry and not Old Joe," he said loudly. "Who is it?"

Larry saw that he was blind.

"I want to see the superintendent," he said.

"Yes, sir," said the man in a tone of respect. "Just wait here, will you?"

He went down a long passage full of turns and angles, so that he disappeared from sight, and presently they heard him shuffling back in his slippered feet, and behind him walked a tall man wearing a white clerical collar. His eyes were covered with dark blue glasses, and he too felt his way along the passage.

"Won't you please come in?" he said in an educated voice. He was a man of powerful build, and his clean-shaven face denoted a strength of character out of the ordinary. "I am John Dearborn—the Rev. John Dearborn," he explained as he led the way. "We have few visitors here, alas! I'm afraid Todd's Home is not very popular."

He did not speak resentfully but cheerfully, and as one who had a great spirit. Nor did he make allusion to the early hour they had chosen.

"It is a little farther along, gentlemen," he said. "I know there are two of you because I can hear your footsteps. Mind the step—this way."

He pushed open a door and they went in. The room was cosily furnished, and the first thing that Larry noticed was the bare condition of the walls; and then he remembered, with a little pang, that the blind have no need for pictures.

A curious little instrument stood by the side of the table, which was the principal article of furniture in the room, and a tiny wheel was spinning as they came in. The superintendent walked unerringly to the machine. There was the snap of a button and the wheel ceased to revolve.

"This is my dictating machine," he explained, turning to them with a smile. "I am engaged in literary work, and I can dictate to this cylinder, which is then transferred to an operator who types from my voice."

Larry expressed polite interest.

"Now, gentlemen," said the Rev. John Dearborn as he seated himself, "to what am I indebted for the honour of this visit?"

"I am an officer from Scotland Yard," said Larry, "and my name is Holt."

The other inclined his head.

"I hope none of my unfortunate men have been getting into trouble?" he asked.

The Dark Eyes of London

"I don't exactly know yet," said Larry. "At present I am searching for a man called Blind Jake."

"Blind Jake?" repeated the other slowly. "I don't think we have had such a name in the Home since I have been in charge. I've been here for four years," he explained. "It used to be run, and very badly run, by a man who got together quite the worst type of blind men in London. You know that the blind are wonderful and heroic, and the majority of them are positively an inspiration to those who have sight. But there are a class of men so afflicted who are the scum of the earth. You have probably heard of the Dark Eyes?"

"Not until this morning," said Larry, and the other nodded.

"We have got rid of those people, and we have now very respectable old hawkers who come here, where everything is done for them. You would like to see the home?"

"You don't know Blind Jake?"

"I have never heard of him," said the Rev. John Dearborn, "but if you will come with me, we will make inquiries."

The Home consisted of four dormitories and a common room; and in this latter, reeking with tobacco smoke, sat the inmates of the Home. Larry looked round and could scarcely repress a shiver.

"Just one moment," said Mr. Dearborn, when he had ushered the two men into the passage. He returned shortly, shaking his head.

"Nobody there knows Blind Jake, though one has heard of him."

They ascended to the first dormitory.

"I don't suppose you want to see any more," said Mr. Dearborn.

Larry raised his head.

"I thought I heard somebody groaning."

"Yes, yes, a sad case," said the superintendent. "There are cubicles upstairs for those men who can afford to pay a little more than their fellows. In one of them we have a man who, I fear, is going out of his mind. I have had to report the case to the local authorities."

"May we go upstairs?" asked Larry.

"With pleasure," said the Rev. Dearborn, after a moment's hesitation. "The only thing I am afraid of," he said as he led the way, "is that the language of this man will distress you."

In a little cubicle lay a wizened man of sixty, who tossed desperately to and fro in his bed, and all the time he was talking, talking to some invisible person. And Larry, watching him, wondered.

"Brute! Coward!" muttered the man on the bed. "You'll swing for it, mark my words! You'll swing for it!"

"It is very terrible," said the Rev. John Dearborn, turning away and shaking his head. "This way, gentlemen."

But Larry did not move.

"All right, Jake, you'll suffer too! Mark my words, you'll suffer! Let them do their dirty work! I didn't put the paper in his pocket, I tell you."

Larry took a step into the cubicle, and, bending over, shook the man.

"Let go my arm, you're hurting it," said the man on the bed, and Larry released his hold.

"Wake up," he said, "I want to speak to you."

But the man went talking on, and Larry shook him again.

"Leave me alone," growled the old man. "I don't want to have any more trouble."

"What is your name?" asked Larry.

"I don't want any more trouble," said the man.

"He's quite delirious," said John Dearborn. "He is under the impression that he's accused of a practical joke on one of his friends down stairs."

"But he said 'Jake,'?" said Larry.

"There is a Jake below—Jake Horley. Would you like to see him? He's a little fellow and rather amusing."

Disappointed, Larry walked down the stairs and took farewell of his conductor.

"I am very glad to have had a visit from the police," said John Dearborn. "I only wish that we could persuade other people to come to us. You have seem some of our work and some of the difficulties with which we are faced. Before you go," he added, "perhaps you will tell me why you are seeking

Blind Jake? The men will be consumed with curiosity to know the reason for this police visit."

"That is easy to satisfy," smiled Larry. "There is a charge against him made by a woman to the effect that she was employed by him to commit a felony."

The police officer who was with him gasped, for it is not the practice of the police to give away their informants.

Larry opened the door himself and paused with his hand upon the handle.

"Pardon my asking what may be a very painful question, Mr. Dearborn," he said gently. "Are you afflicted——?"

"Oh, yes," said the other cheerfully, "I am quite blind. I wear these glasses from sheer vanity. I think they improve my appearance." He laughed softly.

"Good-bye," said Larry, shaking his disengaged hand, and then he pulled the door open and came face to face with Flash Fred.

Flash Fred was dumbfounded, and he walked backwards down the few steps at some peril to himself. Larry surveyed him, his head on one side, like an inquisitive hen.

"Are you following me or am I following you?" he asked gently. "And why this early rising, Fred? Have you been out all night at your—business?"

For once Fred had no words. He had walked all the way from Jermyn Street to Paddington, and had been very careful to see that he had not been followed. At last he found his voice.

"So it was a trap, was it?" he said bitterly. "I might have guessed it. But you've got nothing on me, Mr. Holt."

"I have several things on you," said Larry pleasantly. He had unconsciously closed the door of the Home behind him. "I don't like your face, I don't like your jewels, I positively loathe your record. What is the idea, Fred? Have you called to deliver a contribution? Is your conscience pricking you?"

"Stow that stuff, Mr. Holt," growled Fred, and to Larry's surprise began walking away with him.

"Aren't you going to the Home?" he asked.

"No, I'm not," snapped Fred.

They walked on in silence, Fred between the two police officers, and his thoughts were very busy. They had reached the broad thoroughfare of Edgware Road before he had completed his mental exoneration.

"I don't know what you've got me for. You can't pinch me for ancient 'istory."

In moments of perturbation Fred suffered certain lapses of style.

"History," corrected Larry. "For the matter of that, I don't know why you're with us. But since you've forced yourself upon us, and since there's nobody to see the disgraceful company I keep, I will endure you."

Fred stopped short.

"Do you mean to tell me that I'm not pinched?" he asked incredulously.

"So far as I am concerned you are not," said Larry, "unless Sergeant Reed has a private engagement with you."

"Not me, sir," smiled Sergeant Reed. "Who told you you were pinched, Fred?"

"Well, that beats it," said Fred, aghast. "What was the game?"

"Don't you know somebody at the Home?"

"I don't know it from a cowshed," said Fred. "I had to inquire my way of a milkman."

"You should have asked a policeman," murmured Larry. "There are plenty about."

"There are too many about for me," replied Flash Fred vindictively. "Here, Mr. Holt," he said with sudden seriousness, "you're a gentleman, and I know you wouldn't put me wrong."

Larry passed the compliment without comment.

"Well?" he said, and Fred dived into his inner pocket and produced a letter.

"What do you make of this, sir?" he asked.

Larry opened the letter, which was addressed to Fred Grogan, and began:

"They are going to arrest you to-morrow. Larry Holt has the warrant for execution. Come to Todd's Home in Lissom Lane at half-past six in the morning and ask to see 'Lew,' and he will give you information that will help you to make a get-away. Don't allow yourself to be shadowed, or tell anybody where you are going."

It was unsigned, and Larry folded the letter and was about to give it to Fred.

"Do you mind if I keep this?" he asked.

"No sir, I don't mind. But, Mr. Holt, will you tell me," he demanded nervously, "is there any truth in that yarn of my being pinched?"

Larry shook his head.

"So far as I know you are not on the list, and certainly I have no warrant for you, Fred," he said. "In fact, you have such a good record just now that if you ran straight you could pretty well live without fear of the police."

"Sounds damned uninteresting to me," said Flash Fred as he slouched off, and Larry let him go.

Fanny Has a Visitor

NO. 280 CORAM STREET was an apartment house, and Mrs. Fanny Weldon occupied two rooms, one facing Coram Street and one a side turning. She lived well and she paid well, gave little or no trouble, and the breath of scandal did not touch her name. Not noticeably. She was in truth the star boarder, and her landlady would have gone very far to oblige Fanny, always providing that the fair name of 280 was not assailed.

This woman crook had spent a busy night, yet sleep refused to come to her in the day, and she rose at three in the afternoon and busied herself with those occupations which women of all kinds find interesting. She had a hat to trim, some dainty silk to iron, a little mending and a little darning.

"You were up late last night, Mrs. Weldon?" said the landlady, bringing her tea with her own hands.

Fanny nodded.

"To be exact, I wasn't in bed all night," she said, "I went to a dance. What time is it?"

"Six o'clock. I thought you were sleeping, and as you didn't ring, I didn't disturb you."

"I'm going to bed early to-night," said Fanny, yawning. "Is there anything fresh?"

"No, my dear," said the landlady, professionally maternal. "We've got a new young gentleman in the opposite room," she jerked her thumb at the door. "A gentleman from Manchester, and very quiet. Mrs. Hooper made some trouble about the dinner." She retailed grisly gossip of the boarding-house.

"Send me up something cold on a tray," said Fanny. "I am going to bed early. I have a very important appointment to-morrow."

She was looking forward to her appointment with Larry Holt in no great spirit of enthusiasm.

It was half-past seven when the woman undressed slowly and went to bed. She was deadly tired, and she fell asleep almost before her head touched the pillow. The dreams of evil-doers are no more unsound as a rule than the dreams of the pure and virtuous. But Fanny was over-tired and dreamt badly—ghastly dreams of monstrous shapes; of high buildings on the parapet of which she was poised, ready to fall; of men who chased her armed with long bright knives—and she turned and twisted in her bed restlessly. Then she dreamt she had committed a murder: she had murdered Gordon Stuart. She had never heard of Gordon Stuart until Larry had mentioned his name, but she pictured him as a weak youth.

And now the day of doom had come, she dreamt, and they brought her from the cell with her hands strapped behind her, and she paced slowly by the side of a white-robed clergyman into a little shed. And then a man, an executioner, had stepped out, and he had the mocking face of Blind Jake. She felt the rope about her neck, and tried to scream, but it was choking her, choking her. She woke up.

Two hands were about her throat, and in the reflected light from a street lamp outside, she looked up into the sightless face of Blind Jake. It was no dream, it was reality! She tried to move, but he held her so that she was powerless. One of his knees pressed on her and he was talking softly, a sibilant whisper, meant only for her ear.

"Fanny, you gave me away," he whispered. "You gave me away, you devil! Poor old Blind Jake! You tried to put him into jug, you did! I know all about it. I've got a little pal at Todd's who told me. And now you're going out, d'ye hear?"

She was choking, choking; she could not articulate, she felt her face going purple and the cruel hands tightening. And then the light switched on, and the "man from Manchester" who had occupied the bedroom on the opposite side of the landing, and who had waited throughout the night listening for the stealthy tread of Blind Jake, knowing that he would come after he had learnt he was betrayed—Larry Holt, a long Browning in his hand, covered the strangler.

"Put up your hands, Jake," he said, and Blind Jake turned round with a low growl like the snarl of a tiger at bay.

The Fight in the Dark

FOR a moment they stood thus, neither man moving, then Jake put up his hands slowly.

"Got a little gun, have ye?" he growled. "You're not going to hurt a poor old man, Mr. Holt?"

"Come forward steadily," said Larry, "and don't try any tricks or you'll be sorry for yourself."

"Sorry enough now, Mr. Holt," grumbled the man.

It was wonderful to watch him. He moved as lightly as a girl, and his extraordinary sixth sense enabled him to avoid every obstacle which stood in his way.

Larry was in a dilemma. The man's advance toward him brought the half-fainting woman on the bed in the line of fire. But for that he undoubtedly intended to shoot if the man showed fight, but it was impossible to fire now, even to save his life, without risking the life of Fanny Weldon. And yet it would have been unfair and asking the impossible to expect the man to advance by any other way, the furniture in the room being disposed as it was. But the real danger to Larry he never saw until it was upon him.

The big man came forward, his hands in the air, and one of them touched awkwardly the hanging electric light. And then before Larry knew or guessed what was happening, the big man's hand closed round the bulb, there was a deafening explosion as it burst under the pressure, and the room was in darkness.

To fire now would have been madness, and Larry put one foot back and braced himself to meet the shock of the body which he knew was hurtling towards him. And then he found himself in the hands of Blind Jake. Diana had not exaggerated his strength. It was terrific, and though Larry was a strong man he felt himself going under. What might have been the result of that struggle, Larry Holt has never speculated upon in cold blood. But there came an interruption, the sound of an opening door on the landing above and a man's voice, and then Blind Jake lifted the detective as though he had been a bundle of rags, and flung him to the other end of the room, where he lay gasping and breathless.

A second later the door had opened and Blind Jake was going down the carpeted stairs faster than any man with eyesight would have dared.

Larry struggled to his feet, took his flash lamp from the floor and found his revolver where it had dropped. He picked it up and, running to the window, flung it open and peered out. But Blind Jake had already gone round the corner.

Somebody brought another globe, and Larry went to look after the girl. She was still unconscious, the purple marks about her throat testifying to the character of Blind Jake's grip.

"You had better get a doctor," he said to the landlady, who was the third person in the room, and she looked at him with suspicion and distrust.

"What were you doing in this room?" she asked accusingly. "I am going to send for a policeman."

"Send for two," said Larry, "and get a doctor."

Fortunately the police station was near at hand, and the divisional surgeon had been called to examine a doubtful case of drunkenness, and he was on the spot within a few minutes.

By this time the woman had come back to life, but had subsided into a condition of hysteria, painful to witness.

"You had better get her into an infirmary or a hospital, I think, doctor," said Holt, and the surgeon agreed.

He was looking at the marks about her throat with a puzzled expression.

"No man could have done this," he said, "he must have used an instrument of some kind."

Larry laughed. It was a very rueful laugh.

"If you think that, doctor," he said, "you'd better have a look at my throat," and he showed the red weal where Blind Jake's thumb and finger had gripped.

"Do you mean to say that he did that to you?" asked the doctor incredulously.

"I do not mean to say very much about it," said Larry, "because it is not an adventure of which I am inordinately proud, but he picked me up like a tennis ball and chucked me amongst the crockery-ware under the window."

The doctor whistled. By this time the landlady had been assured of Larry's bona fides and was at once apologetic and tearful at the indignity which had been offered to her house by the presence, even for one night, of a detective officer.

Larry went out into the street to breathe the night air. He was dizzy and shaky and sore. The fact that he, Larry Holt, who had pretensions to winning the middle-weight amateur championship, had been treated like a punch-ball did not distress him. What made him grave was the knowledge that there was loose in the world, and in the city of London, a man of the criminal classes more dangerous than a tiger, with the strength of a bear and an intelligence which was little better than a monkey's.

"And that exhausts the whole Zoological Gardens," said Larry after he had enumerated the unpleasant qualities of his assailant.

Half an hour afterwards every police station received an all-stations message, and the hunt for Big Jake had begun.

Larry reached his flat at three o'clock, and Sunny was dozing peacefully in a chair. He aroused his servant with a gentle tap.

"Sunny," said he, "I have had the experience of a lifetime."

"I suppose you have, sir," said Sunny, blinking himself awake. "Will you have some coffee too, sir?"

Larry was thinking, thinking, thinking. He stood with his hands in his pockets and his legs wide apart, gazing down at the hearthrug.

"He took me by the scruff of the neck, Sunny," he said softly, "and he threw me to the other side of the room."

"He would, sir," said Sunny. "What time would you like your tea in the morning?"

Weary and sick as he was, Larry had to laugh.

"If I were brought home with my neck broken, Sunny," he demanded irritably, "what would you do?"

"I should stop the morning papers, sir," said Sunny without hesitation. "I think I should be doing right, sir."

"Haven't you got a heart?" snarled Larry.

"No, sir," was the surprising reply. "The doctor says it's indigestion, sir."

Larry made a gesture of despair, kicked off his boots, slipped off his coat and vest, followed that with his collar and tie, and loosening his braces, he lay down on the bed and pulled the eiderdown over him. He did this partly because he was very tired and partly because he knew that it would annoy Sunny.

Mr. Grogan Meets a Lady

THERE was a fashionable wedding on the Monday at St. George's, Hanover Square. A queue of motor-cars and broughams stretched in all directions and lined both sides of the streets and partly filled Hanover Square.

Amongst those present, as they say, was Mr. Frederick Grogan. Flash Fred had not been invited, for two reasons. In the first place the friends of bride and bridegroom did not know him, and in the second place he would not have been invited if they had. But a little thing like an invitation did not worry Fred. He knew that when the family of the bride and the bridegroom were meeting for the first time and were regarding one another with mutual suspicion and deprecation, and when all sorts of obscure cousins emerged from the oblivion which happily covered them and were not even recognizable to the principal actors in the great drama, that a face such as his, and a smartly tailored figure such as he possessed, would pass muster and gain for him a prominent seat. So he arrived at St. George's in a glossy silk hat, white kid gloves, and perfectly pressed trousers, and made his way up the aisle, where he was mistaken for the bridegroom.

He had not come because he wished to break into society, but because it was a new fashion for women to wear their precious jewels in the early hours of the morning at such functions as these. He had no particular piece of villainy in view. He was merely surveying the land as a good general might survey a possible battlefield.

Marriages did not interest him. He regarded them as superfluous ceremonies indulged in by the idle rich and the hopeless bourgeoisie. The ceremony, which was long, bored him to extinction, and he heartily regretted having taken so prominent a place and being prevented, in consequence, from stealing gently out, or from watching the people who were in his rear. At last the service ended, the organ pealed a triumphant note, and the bride and bridegroom, looking extremely ashamed of themselves, processed solemnly down the aisle, and Fred fell in, in the ranks of the near and dear, and came out on to the steps.

He was wondering whether it would be politic or advisable to go on to the reception, having discovered where that reception would be held, when somebody touched his arm, and he turned quickly.

"Hallo, Dr. Judd!" he said, relieved. "I thought it was that fellow Holt. He follows me about until he's got on my nerves."

Dr. Judd, a fine figure of a man in his morning dress, was eyeing him sternly.

"You told me you were going to Nice," he said.

"I missed the train," replied Fred glibly, "and my pal went on without me. I'm staying over for a few days and then I hope to get away."

Dr. Judd was thoughtful.

"Walk a little way along with me," he said. "I want to talk to you."

They walked without speaking a word to one another into Hanover Square, and turned towards Bond Street.

"You are getting on my nerves, Mr. Grogan," said Dr. Judd. "At least I thought I had the satisfaction of knowing that you were taking abnormal risks on the continent of Europe. Instead I find you living a fashionable life in Jermyn Street."

"I thought you said you didn't know I was still here?" asked Fred quickly.

"I said nothing of the sort," replied the calm doctor. "I merely remarked that I thought you had said you were going to Nice."

"Oh, you knew I was here, then," said Fred.

"I had heard you were here," said Dr. Judd. "Now, Mr. Grogan, don't you think you and I should effect some sort of compromise?"

Fred was all ears.

"In what way?" he asked cautiously.

"Suppose," said Dr. Judd, "I gave you a lump sum down on condition that you did not bother me again?"

Nothing better suited Fred's plans. Supposing the sum were a reasonable one, he would be saved the bother and anxiety of a burglary. Or he might even add that relaxation to swell his profits.

"I'm agreeable," he said, after a reasonable pause, and Dr. Judd eyed him seriously.

"You will have to keep faith with me," he said. "I do not intend parting with £12,000—"

"£12,000!" said Fred quickly. "Yes, that seems a nice tidy sum."

"I repeat," said the doctor, "I do not intend parting with that sum unless I have a guarantee that you will not molest me again. Will you dine with me at my house in Chelsea to-morrow night at eight o'clock?"

Fred nodded.

"There will be a few people to dinner," said the doctor, "but nobody who knows you, and I must ask as a personal favour that you will not endeavour to follow up any acquaintance you make to-morrow night."

"Don't you think I am too much of a gentleman to do that sort of thing?" asked Fred, virtuously indignant.

"I don't," said the doctor shortly, and parted from him at the corner of Bond Street.

Twelve thousand pounds! That was a most admirable arrangement, and Fred, whose funds were getting low, trod on air as he strolled down Old Bond Street toward Piccadilly.

In his exaltation, when his generous soul had swollen, and his whole mental system was experiencing the sensation of largeness, he saw a girl on the opposite side of the road. Hers was not a face to be forgotten. He had seen it once under an electric light between St. Martin's and the Strand, and he increased his pace, crossing the road and following behind her, not, however, without an anxious glance behind him. For once Larry Holt was invisible.

"It could not have happened better," said Fred, for he was sensible of his fine appearance.

He overtook her at the corner of Piccadilly and raised his hat with a smile, and for a moment Diana was under the impression that she knew this stranger and her hand was half-way up when he made the mistake of repeating that fashionable formula:

"Haven't you and I met before somewhere?"

She drew her hand back.

"My dear," said Fred, "you're the most wonderful thing in the world, and I simply want to know you!"

This, too, was part of the formula and had been effective on many occasions.

"Then you had better call on me," she said, and Flash Fred scarcely believed his good fortune.

She opened the little leather bag she carried and took out a card, scribbling a number.

"A million thanks!" said Fred elegantly as he took the card. "I'll give you mine in a minute. Now what about a little dinner—" He lifted the card and read: "Miss Diana Ward—a beautiful name," he said. "Diana! Room 47," and then his face underwent a change. "Scotland Yard!" he said hollowly.

"Yes, I am with Mr. Larry Holt," she said sweetly, and Fred swallowed something.

"If he ain't here you're here, and if you're not here he's here," he said savagely. "Why can't you leave a gentleman alone?"

The Insurance Money

THAT afternoon Diana made a request of her employer which disappointed him a little.

"Certainly," he said, "I shan't want you this evening. Going to a dance, do you say?"

She nodded.

"That's fine," he said heartily. "I hope you enjoy yourself."

It chilled him a little, for he was so completely absorbed by the game that he could not understand that what was fun to him was work to her. She must have read his thoughts, for she said, with a little jerk of her chin which was characteristic of her:

"I am merely going on duty, Mr. Holt. I should not have thought of going to the dance, but the man who asked me is a young underwriter to whom I was secretary for about six months," she said.

"You seem to have started work at a very early age," he smiled. "Did you go to a public school?"

"I went to a council school," she replied quietly. "My aunt who brought me up was very poor."

"You didn't know your father and mother?"

She shook her head.

"I hope you're not going to associate me with the missing Clarissa," she smiled. "I am afraid my origin is a little less romantic. I am always expecting to find my father figuring in the records of Scotland Yard, if he is alive, for Mrs. Ward never spoke of him except in uncomplimentary terms. Yes, I did begin work rather young."

"You say you are going on duty," he interrupted her. "What do you mean?"

She went to her desk and took up her handbag, opened it and produced a letter.

"It will interest you to know," she smiled, "that Mr. Gray's wife will be there to chaperon me and joins in the invitation."

It did interest Larry very much indeed. He did not say so because he thought it might be indiscreet, and he was not quite sure of how he would express the pleasure that news brought to him.

"Here is the paragraph that made me decide to go," said the girl, and read:

"We have had a pretty bad time lately. The loss of a ship in the Baltic hit my partner rather hard, and I have had to pay out a very considerable sum of money over the death of a man named Stuart."

"Stuart?" said Larry quickly. "That can't be our Stuart. By the way, the jury have just returned a verdict of 'Found drowned' in that case. We did not care to oppose the verdict, or offer any evidence which might put the murderers on their guard. Stuart, eh?" he nodded to himself several times. "I owe you an apology, Diana," he said, using her name for the first time. "I thought you were going to frivol, and I was hoping that you were sufficiently interested in this case to give your whole mind to it."

She looked at him with kindling eyes, and her face was flushed pink.

"I am giving all my mind to it," she said in a low voice. "It is lovely working with you," and then, to change the subject, she told him of her adventure with Fred.

"Poor old Fred," chuckled Larry. "You have the satisfaction of knowing that he will avoid you like the plague for the future. What time will you come back?" he asked.

"Why?" She was surprised.

"I was wondering whether you could come here, or whether I'd be waiting on the door-mat for you in Charing Cross Road. I want to know what you have discovered."

She nibbled her finger thoughtfully.

"I will come to the Yard," she said. "I'll be here soon after eleven."

She looked with narrowed eyes at the mark on his throat.

"Does that feel awfully sore?" she asked sympathetically.

"Not so bad," said Larry. "Injury to vanity doing very badly. It will take some time before that heals."

"He must be terribly strong," she said with a shudder. "I shall never forget that night on the stairs. I suppose there is no news of him?"

"None whatever," said Larry. "He's gone to ground."

"Are you watching the Home?"

"The Home?" he said in surprise. "No, I don't think that is necessary. The superintendent seems a very decent sort of man. I saw the local police inspector and he told me that every man in the Home is an honest character, and he can vouch for all of them except the fellow they call 'Lew.' He was the man I saw upstairs who seemed to be half-demented."

"I want to ask you a favour," she said. "Will you take me to-morrow to the Home?"

"Ye-es," he hesitated, "but——"

"But will you?"

"Surely if you wish to go, but I don't think you'll find any clue there to bring us nearer to the gentleman who murdered Stuart."

"I wonder?" she said thoughtfully.

She permitted him to lunch with her that day: it was a joyous meal for Larry and he was unusually incoherent. The afternoon was a more serious time for him, for his search for documentary proof that Diana's theory was correct and that Mrs. Stuart had had twin daughters had been unavailing. There was no record of the children's births, though the files at Somerset House had been diligently examined.

"Check Number Two," said Larry.

"Which will be overcome," replied the girl, "though it is curious that a woman of Mrs. Stuart's position should have neglected to register her children."

She said this and smiled, and Larry asked her why.

"Mrs. Ward had views on that subject. My aunt, whose name I bear," she said. "She hated vaccination, registration, and education!"

"What happened to your aunt? Did she die?" asked Larry.

The girl was silent.

"No—she didn't die."

She said this so strangely that Larry looked at her and the girl went crimson.

"I oughtn't to talk about her if I'm not prepared to go on," she said quietly. "I—I come from a very bad stock, Mr. Holt. My aunt stole from her employer, and I rather think she made a practice of doing so. At any rate, when I was twelve, she went away for quite a long time and I never saw her again."

Larry crossed the room and laid his hand on the girl's shoulder.

"My dear," he said, "you have succeeded in shaking loose and establishing yourself in a truly marvellous way. I am very proud of you."

When she looked up her eyes were filled with tears.

"I think she drank: I'm not quite sure. She was very good to me when I needed her most," she said. "I would like to know what has happened to her, but I simply dare not ask."

"She went to prison?"

The girl shook her head.

"I think it was an inebriates' home," she said. "Now, what are you doing this afternoon?" she demanded briskly, and Larry laid down his programme, dictated a letter or two and went out leaving her to finish them.

With every step he took, the Stuart mystery grew more and more of a tangle. Dead ends and culs-de-sac met him at every turn, and even the fact that Stuart had been murdered was no fact, but a theory based upon the eccentricity of the tide which had left his body on the steps of the Embankment, and a piece of paper, now stolen, embossed with Braille characters.

He stopped in his walk when he was half-way up Northumberland Avenue, and took out his pocket-book.

"Murdered . . . dear . . . sea . . ." he read, and shook his head.

"Why the 'dear'?" he wondered. The man who attempted to betray the murderers would not go to the trouble of writing 'dear sir,' and, anyway, it occurred in the wrong place. For the girl had pointed out the characters at the end of the second line.

"Dear, dear, dear," he repeated as he strolled along, and then, for no reason at all, a name came into his mind. Dearborn! He laughed quietly. That good soul of a clergyman, labouring amongst the men who lived in everlasting darkness! He shook his head again. It is a fact which all people can verify that if you see an unusual name for the first time you meet with it again in the course of twenty-four hours. His walk carried him beyond Shaftesbury Avenue, and in passing a theatre the name caught his eye. He checked himself and stooped down to read the play-bill of a theatre.

"John Dearborn," he read.

Dearborn was apparently the author of the play which was being performed here. What was the theatre? He stepped back in the roadway and looked up at the name in coloured glass on the edge of the awning. The Macready! It was from the Macready Theatre that Gordon Stuart disappeared!

Without hesitation he walked into the vestibule to the booking-office and his quick eyes fell upon the plan which the office keeper had before him. There were precious few blue marks, indicating that seats had been taken.

"Can you tell me where I can find Mr. John Dearborn?" he asked.

The office keeper looked at him with an air of pained resignation.

"You're not a friend of the management's, are you?"

"No," admitted Larry, "I am not."

"You're not a friend of Mr. Dearborn's, by any chance, are you?" asked the clerk carelessly, and Larry shook his head. "Well," said the man, "I'll speak my mind. I didn't want to hurt your feelings. I don't know where to find Mr. Dearborn, and I wish the management didn't know where to find him either! I'm leaving this week," he said, "so it doesn't matter very much what I say. He's about the rottenest playwright that the world has ever seen. I'm not choking you off buying a seat, am I?" he asked good-humouredly.

"No, no," said Larry with a smile.

"Well, I won't persuade you to buy one," said the box-office keeper. "I haven't any grudge against you, anyway! We had six people in at the Saturday matinee, and we look like having three to-night. The only people who take any interest in this play are the Commissioners in Lunacy, who come along and watch the audience, and whenever a lunatic breaks out of Hanwell they send the keepers here to search the house."

"You haven't answered my question. Do you know where I can find the author of this unfortunate play?"

The clerk shrugged his shoulders.

"He runs a mission for something or other in the West End. Poor chap, he's blind and maybe I oughtn't to slate him. But he writes rotten plays."

"Is he continuously writing plays?" asked Larry in surprise.

"Continuously," said the other glumly. "I think he writes them in his sleep."

"And they're all produced?"

The man nodded.

"And they're all failures?"

Again the man nodded.

"But why? Surely the management would not produce successive failures from the same pen?"

"They do," said the clerk in despair, "and that is why the Macready is a byword—"

"How long has John Dearborn been writing?" asked Larry.

"Oh, about ten years. Mind you, it's not bad stuff in parts. It's more mad than bad."

"Does he ever come here?"

"Never," said the man, shaking his head. "I don't know why, but he doesn't, not even to rehearsals."

"One more question. To whom does the theatre belong?"

"To a syndicate," said the clerk, who was now growing restive under the questions. "May I ask why you're making all these inquiries?"

"I'm just asking," said Larry with a smile, and seeing that no more information could be got, he went out.

It was rather an amazing situation, he thought. But to connect that one word "dear" with the author of bad plays, or give to Mr. Dearborn, an obvious philanthropist, any evil significance, was absurd. He was outside the theatre when he suddenly remembered and went back.

"As a great personal favour," he said, "could I see the house?"

The clerk demurred at first, but eventually summoned an attendant.

"You'll find it pretty dark," he said. "The house lights are not on."

Larry followed the attendant into the dress-circle and surveyed the little theatre. It was in gloom. The curtain was down, and the seats were sheeted in holland.

"Which is Box A?" asked Larry, for that was what he came to see.

The man led him along a passage through a heavy curtain and down a narrower passage which ran at the back of the boxes, and at the end he stopped and opened a door on his right. Larry stepped in. The box was in darkness, and he lit a match.

There was nothing peculiar about Box A, except that the carpet on the floor was thick and rich and the three chairs which formed its furniture were beautifully designed.

"Are all the boxes furnished like this?" asked Larry.

"No, sir," said the man, "only Box A."

Larry came out and examined the passage. Opposite the door of Box A, a thick red curtain was draped on the wall. He drew it aside and found an iron door on which in red letters were the words, "Exit in case of fire."

"Where does this lead to?" he asked.

"To a side street, sir," said the man. "To Cowley Street. It is not really a street, but a passage which is the property of this theatre and is blocked up at one end."

Larry tipped the man and went out. He was nearer to the solution of Gordon Stuart's disappearance and murder at that moment than he had ever been before. And he knew it.

He was in his office at half-past ten that night, waiting impatiently for the

The Dark Eyes of London

arrival of the girl, and endeavouring by self-analysis to discover whether his eagerness to see her was due to his professional zeal or to his personal interest in the girl herself.

She came at ten minutes to eleven, and he, who had never seen her before save in her working dress, was stricken dumb at the sight of this radiant beauty. He could not know that the black tulle dress she wore cost her something less than £5, or that the bandeau of black leaves about her golden hair cost something short of ten shillings. To him she was magnificently arrayed, and a creature so divine and ethereal that he hardly dared speak to her.

"Come in," he said; "you're making the furniture look shabby."

She laughed, dropped her cloak on her chair, and Larry forgot the official and important side of her visit and would have continued in oblivion if she had not brought him to earth with a triumphant:

"I've got it!"

"Got it?" he stammered. "Oh, yes, you saw your underwriting friend."

She opened a little satin bag and took out a piece of paper.

"I've made some notes," she said. "My friend was very hard hit by Stuart's death, and it is this Stuart."

Larry whistled.

"How did it happen?" he asked.

"My friend is an underwriter. He's in the insurance business," she explained. "When a man has his life insured for a very large sum, as you probably know, the company that issues the policy does not retain all the risk. It sends round to other offices and to various underwriters offering each underwriter some of the responsibility. It appears that my friend, the underwriter, underwrote three thousand pounds' worth of the reinsurance."

"Three thousand pounds' worth?" said Larry in astonishment. "Then, in the name of Heaven, for how much was Stuart insured?"

"I asked that," she nodded and lifted her paper. "On the policy which was endorsed by Mr. Gray the sum of £50,000 was mentioned, but Mr. Gray says that there was another policy for a similar amount."

Larry sat down, his eyes gleaming.

"So that was the business end of Stuart's death, was it? Insured for £100,000! Did your friend pay?"

"Naturally he paid," said the girl, "the moment the company which had accepted the insurance had sent in its claim. He had nothing else to do but to find the money."

"What is the name of the company?"

She paused and looked at him.

"The Greenwich Insurance Company," she replied slowly, and he jumped to his feet.

"Dr. Judd," he said softly.

At the Pawnbroker's

HE ESCORTED the girl downstairs, and they stood talking in the hall. There was a car at the door, a luxury which she easily explained.

She was using the Gray's car, which was to go back and pick up the underwriter and his wife at two o'clock.

"I hate declining your invitation," said Larry, "but I am hanging on to the end of a wire. I sent Harvey on a tour of investigation to-day, and he promised to 'phone me round about midnight."

She was looking at him in some concern.

"Aren't you rather overdoing it?" she said. "You don't get any sleep?"

He laughed.

"I am one of those fortunate people who can do without sleep," he said boastfully, and then an official came out of one of the ground-floor rooms.

"There is a call through for you, sir," he said.

"Come along," said Larry. "I may get this business off and then I shall be able to revel in that millionaire feeling."

He went back to his room and the girl followed. It was not Sergeant Harvey who had called him, but the inspector in charge of the Oxford Lane police station.

"Is that Inspector Holt?" he asked.

"That's me," said Larry ungrammatically.

"You circulated a description of a sleeve-link of black enamel and diamonds."

"Yes," said Larry quickly.

"Well," said the man, "Mr. Emden, of Emden and Smith, pawnbrokers, brought a pair of links exactly tallying with the description published in the Hue and Cry."

"Have you got them there?" asked Larry eagerly.

"No, sir," said the inspector. "But Mr. Emden is here, if you would like to interview him. He can get the links in the morning. He happened to be reading the Hue and Cry to-night after dinner and he came upon the description, and immediately walked over to the station. He lives close by."

"I'll come down," said Larry.

"What is it?" asked the girl. "Have they found the links?"

Larry shook his head.

"They've found a pair of links exactly like the one which was found in Gordon Stuart's hand," he said, a little puzzled. "I can't understand that. If it had been half a link, or a link and a half, that would have been clearly a clue."

He looked dubiously at the switchboard and the operator.

"If Sergeant Harvey comes through," he said, "tell him to ring me again, or if he is in reach of the office to come back and wait for me. I am going to the Oxford Lane police station. Incidentally," he said to the girl as they came out, "I will accept a lift in your palatial conveyance."

He dropped her at her flat. There was a lounger outside who saluted Larry.

"You are not putting a guard on me?" said the girl in surprise. "I think that's unnecessary, Mr. Holt."

"My own experience tells me that it is very necessary," said Larry grimly. "The gentleman who tossed me about as though I were a feather is not wanting in courage. There is no other way into the house except by this front door, is there?" he asked the detective on duty.

"No, sir, I have had a good look round, and I've also been into the lady's rooms."

She gasped.

"How?" she asked.

"I had a duplicate key made from yours," said Larry. "I hope you don't mind. And talking of keys," he added, "the appearance of Blind Jake in Fanny Weldon's room is now no mystery at all. She had given him a key of the house in case she missed him with the swag on Saturday night. He was to come up and take it from her. She was in such terror of him that she did not dare refuse the key, but she must have forgotten she had loaned it, for she would never have slept."

He said good night to her and went on to Oxford Lane, on foot.

Mr. Emden proved to be a mild little man in pince-nez.

"I happened to be running through the list of properties stolen," he said, "and I came upon this description of yours, Mr. Holt."

He showed a fold of the paper on which a drawing of the link, whose fellow was sought, appeared.

"You say you have a pair?"

"Yes, sir," said the man. "It was pledged with me this morning. As a matter of fact, it happened to be me who took the pledge. I don't as a rule work behind the counter, but one of my clerks had gone on a message, and when the man came in I took the links and gave the pledger £4 for them."

"They are not of a usual pattern, are they?" asked Larry, and Mr. Emden shook his head.

"They are very unusual," he said. "I don't remember having seen a pair exactly like those before. I think they must be of a French make. They were slightly damaged. Three of the diamonds on the rim were missing or I should have given him a great deal more."

"Do you know the man who pledged them?"

"No, sir. He was a smart-looking fellow who told me he'd got tired of them. My impression was—" He hesitated.

"Well?" said Larry.

"Well, I thought, in spite of his good appearance, that he looked like one of these smart thieves that abound in the West End, and I had an idea that he was pledging them, not so much because he wanted the money, but because he wanted to put them in a safe place. A thief will often do that and take the chance of the pawnbroker discovering that the property is missing or wanted by the police."

Larry nodded.

"Smartly dressed," he said thoughtfully, and then quickly: "Did he wear any diamonds?"

"Yes, sir," said the pawnbroker, "that is why I thought he was planting the stuff. Four pounds isn't much to advance on property of that value, but he didn't make any fuss."

"What name?" asked Larry.

"He gave the name of Mr. Frederick, and I think an accommodation address."

"Flash Fred!" said Larry. "Is Jermyn Street in your district?" he asked the inspector.

"Yes, sir," said the officer.

"Send a couple of men out and pull in Flash Fred. Bring him here first, and afterwards, if it is necessary, I'll take him to Cannon Row."

"Is it an arrest?" asked the inspector.

"A detention merely. He may be able to explain, but I think he'll have to be clever if he gets out of this. Now, Mr. Emden," he said, turning to the pawnbroker, "I'm afraid I can't wait until the morning and I must ask you to accompany me to your shop and let me have the actual links."

"With pleasure, sir," said the pawnbroker. "I expected something like that and I brought my keys over. My shop is only about five minutes' walk away."

Accompanied by a plain-clothes officer they went to the shop and Mr. Emden fitted the key in the side door, but as he pressed the key into the keyhole the door gave.

"Why, the door's open," he said in surprise, and went quickly down the side passage. He tried another door, but there was no need even to go through the formality of putting a key in the lock. The door was ajar and

Larry's pocket lamp revealed the mark of the jemmy that had opened it. The pawnbroker hurried into his main premises and switched on the light.

A book lay on the counter, open at the page of that day's transactions.

"Where did you put these links?" asked Larry quickly.

"In the safe, in my private office," said the man. "Look," he turned to the book, "there is the number."

"Also the word 'safe,'?" said Larry, "and somehow I don't think you'll see your safe intact."

And his words proved prophetic. The big "burglar-proof" safe presented a somewhat untidy appearance, for a hole had been burnt in the steel and the lock had disappeared. Articles of value there were none. Every package had been cleared out.

"I think they have got those links," said Larry grimly.

In Flash Fred's Flat

AFTER the discovery in the pawnbroker's shop Larry went back to the police station to make yet another discovery. Flash Fred was not in his lodgings.

"I wish you would come down and see his flat, sir," said the officer who had gone to make the arrest. "I think that something queer has happened."

"If there has been anything in this case which has not been queer," said Larry with asperity, "I should like to hear about it!"

Flash Fred lived in Modley House, Jermyn Street, a block of service flats, and the porter had a strange story to tell.

"Mr. Grogan came in at about eleven o'clock to-night," he said, "and went up to his flat. I took him a syphon of soda he ordered, and said good night to him.

"Afterwards I went round seeing that the service doors were shut and that the lights had been out in the kitchen, then came to my cubby-hole to have my supper and read the evening newspaper."

The "cubby-hole" was a space under the stairway which had been converted into a little office where the tenants left their keys.

The Dark Eyes of London

"At about half-past twelve I thought I heard a sound like a shot and a man's voice shout something and I came out into the passage and listened. There was still a sort of disturbance going on, so I went up to the second floor where the sound came from and listened again. There was a light in Mr. Grogan's flat. I could see that through the transom. It was the only light visible. I knocked at the door and after a while Mr. Grogan came to the door, and I tell you he was a most terrifying sight. He had a big knife in his hand and his clothes were smothered with blood.

'Oh, it's you, is it?' he said. 'Come in.'

"I went into the sitting-room and a pretty sight it was! Chairs thrown over, the table upside down, and glasses and bottles scattered over the floor. Outside Mr. Grogan's window are the stairs of the fire-escape, and the window was open.

'What's wrong, sir?' I asked.

'Nothing particular,' he said, 'only a burglar broke in. That's all. Give me a whisky-and-soda.'

"He was trembling from head to foot and was very excited. He kept muttering to himself, but I didn't hear what he said. When I came back with the whisky-and-soda he had cleaned the knife and was more calm. I found him standing at the open window, looking down into the yard, where the fire-escape leads, and then I noticed that one of the pictures hanging on the wall was smashed by a bullet. I knew it was a bullet because I was in the Metropolitan Police for some years, and I've seen a similar mark. I told him there would be serious trouble over this disturbance because the other tenants would complain, but he asked me not to worry about that, and gave me £50 to pay his rent and any expenses that we had been put to, and asked me to keep the flat until he returned. He said he was going abroad."

"What happened then?" asked Larry when the man paused.

"Well, sir, he came out with a bag, got into a cab and drove off, and that's the last I saw of him."

Larry made an examination of the room and he found that the porter's description had been a faithful one. The room was illuminated by a cluster of three lights hanging from the ceiling and covered by a shade. One of the globes was smashed, and Larry drew the attention of the porter to this.

"Yes, sir, these lights work on two circuits: one switch turns on one and the other switch turns on two. As a rule Mr. Grogan only has the single light on."

Larry nodded.

"I pretty well know what happened," he said.

He could picture the scene in the room: the intruder coming through the window, Flash Fred covering him with his revolver, and the big man advancing with upraised hands until he could reach the globe and crush it in his powerful paw. And then Fred had fired and the man was on him, but Fred was too slippery. Fred had been cleverer than he. These continental crooks who take enormous risks do not depend so much upon their guns as upon their knives, and to Blind Jake's surprise—for Blind Jake it must have been—Grogan had met the onrush and the suffocating hug of this animal-man with a steel blade, and, releasing his hold, Blind Jake must have made his escape through the open window. But where was Fred? In that moment Larry felt an unexpected wave of sympathy for the crook. He too, then, had stumbled by accident or design upon the murderer of Gordon Stuart.

What was that clue? He must find Flash Fred, and find him at once, for this thief might have in his hands a solution to the mystery.

He went home, 'phoned to head-quarters, and discovered that Harvey had made a negative report, took a bath and went to bed. He slept for four hours; and then by his instructions Sunny, who seemed equally able to dispense with the recuperation of sleep, brought him his tea and toast.

"What time is it?" asked Larry, blinking himself awake.

"Nine o'clock, sir," said Sunny. "The postman has come and the papers have been."

"Bring me my letters," said Larry, jumping out of bed.

He looked them through as he sipped his tea.

One had come, evidently delivered by hand, for there was no stamp upon the envelope.

The Dark Eyes of London

"When did this arrive?" he asked the valet when Sunny returned to the room.

"It was in the box when I got up, sir," said Sunny. "I think it must have come by hand."

"You're a fool, Sunny," snapped Larry. "Of course it came by hand."

"I'm glad you agree with me, sir," said the imperturbable Sunny.

Larry ripped open the envelope and took out a sheet of paper. It began without any polite preliminary:

"You had better interest yourself in another case, Mr. Holt. You will get into serious trouble if you do not heed this warning."

"Oh, yes," said Larry, and rang the bell.

"Sunny," he said, "bring me my coat and the papers that are in the inside pocket."

Larry searched for and found the letter which Flash Fred had received inviting him to call at Todd's Home at six o'clock in the morning and to avoid attracting attention.

He put the letter of warning by its side and compared them. They were in the same handwriting!

The Woman Who Drew the Insurance Money

DIANA WARD, I'm a greatly rattled man," said Larry.

The girl stopped working, her fingers poised above the keys of her typewriter; then she swung round in her chair.

"The case is growing a little clearer to me," she said quietly.

"I wish to heaven it would grow clearer to me," grumbled Larry. "Here is the situation. Let me recapitulate." He ticked off the points on the fingers of one hand as he leant back in his chair. "A rich Canadian, who comes to London apparently to visit the grave of his deserted wife and child, is murdered after seeing a play at the Macready Theatre. The author of that play is John Dearborn, who admittedly writes the worst trash that has ever been seen on the stage. But that doesn't make him a murderer. And, moreover, he is a respectable clergyman engaged in a great humanitarian work amongst the

90

blind. The murdered Stuart leaves, written on the inside of his shirt-front, a will leaving the whole of his property to a daughter, who apparently has no existence, so far as we can discover. Certain clues are found, one a piece of Braille writing, another a black enamel and diamond sleeve-link which is found in the dead man's hand. The Braille writing is stolen from Scotland Yard; the sleeve-links, when they fall into the possession of Flash Fred and are pawned by him for security, are regarded by some person or persons unknown as being of such importance that a burglary is committed at the pawnbroker's shop in which they are pledged, with no other object, I should imagine, than to recover those links. Moreover, the agent of the enemy proceeds first to attempt your abduction, then the murder of Fanny Weldon, who committed the burglary at Scotland Yard, which is understandable, and then the destruction of Flash Fred, which is also within my understanding. As a matter of fact, the only inexplicable point in the whole case," he said with a smile, "is their attempt to strafe you."

She nodded.

"That is a mystery to me too," she confessed.

"We have now discovered," said Larry, ticking off the point on another finger, "that Stuart was heavily insured, at the office of Dr. Judd, of the Greenwich Insurance Company. Dr. Judd makes no secret of the fact that this insurance was effected."

"Have you seen Dr. Judd?" she asked in surprise.

"I have telephoned to him," he said, "and I am seeing him this morning. Perhaps you will come along with me—we can postpone our visit to the Home until this afternoon."

He saw her face brighten up.

"You like to be in this game, don't you?" he bantered her.

"I think it's wonderfully fascinating," she replied, "and I like to be close to things. I had a feeling yesterday that you thought I wasn't keen."

Larry blushed guiltily.

"It was only for a second," he admitted, "and it was very unworthy, and after all, why should you elect to work all the hours that Heaven sends?"

The Dark Eyes of London

"Because I want to see the murderer of Gordon Stuart brought to justice," she answered steadily, and Larry experienced a little thrill.

Dr. Judd expected one visitor, and was to all appearances surprised agreeably when Larry's companion came into the big managing director's office on Bloomsbury Pavement.

"This is Dr. Judd. My secretary, Miss Ward," introduced Larry. "Miss Ward has a very excellent memory, and it may be necessary for me to have a shorthand note of our talk."

"I should prefer that," said Dr. Judd. Yet he seemed ill at ease at the presence of the girl. If Larry noticed this fact, it did not alter his plans.

"I am glad you have come," said Dr. Judd slowly. "I wanted to talk to you about the man with whom you saw me the first time we met. I am afraid that you received an altogether wrong impression, though as to this I cannot blame you, for the man is a disreputable scoundrel. Have you seen him lately?"

"I have neither seen nor heard of him for weeks," said Larry untruthfully, and the girl found that she had to exercise all her self-control to prevent her looking up in surprise.

"Well," said the doctor, "we can talk about that at some other time. Do you mind my smoking. Miss Ward?" She shook her head with a smile. "I am an inveterate smoker of cigarettes," said the doctor. "I have smoked a hundred a day for twenty-five years, and my robust health gives the lie to all the anti-tobacconists!"

He laughed, and he had a very hearty and pleasant laugh. It was a gurgle of genuine merriment, which was so infectious that Diana found herself smiling in sympathy. The doctor lit a cigarette, then took a folder from his desk and opened it.

"Here are the policies," he said. "You will notice that they are made payable to a nominee who shall be afterwards named. That authorization came to us on the day of Stuart's death. I will show it to you presently. The matter was not brought to my attention until yesterday morning, when my clerk reminded me that we had issued these policies. Simultaneously we received a demand for the money, accompanied by a certificate of death—or rather, a copy of the certificate issued by the coroner."

"Which can be obtained for about five shillings," said Larry, and Dr. Judd inclined his head.

"It was sufficient," he said quietly, "and at any rate, when the legatees called, there was no reason in the world why I should not pay the money, and that payment was made."

"How was it paid? By cash or cheque?"

"By open cheque, at the lady's request."

"At the lady's?" said Larry and Diana together, for she had been surprised into this ejaculation.

Dr. Judd looked at her with a little smile and rubbed his hands gleefully.

"I like a secretary who takes a keen interest in affairs," he chuckled.

"But who was the lady?" asked Larry.

The doctor took two slips of paper from the folder and laid one before the detective.

"Here is the receipt," he said. "You see it is for one hundred thousand pounds."

Larry took up the paper and examined it. It was signed "Clarissa Stuart"!

When Diana Fainted

LARRY could not believe his eyes. He handed the slip to the girl, but she had already seen the signature over his shoulder.

"Clarissa Stuart?" he said slowly. "Do you know her?"

"Never heard of her before," said the doctor cheerfully. "But she was the person nominated to receive the proceeds of the policy."

"What is she like?" asked Larry after a pause.

Dr. Judd was lighting a fresh cigarette from the glowing end of another, and he threw the butt into the fireplace before he replied.

"Young, pretty, fashionably dressed," he said briefly.

"Did she seem—distressed at all?"

"Not at all," said the doctor. "On the contrary, she was rather amusing."

The Dark Eyes of London

They looked at one another, Diana Ward and Larry Holt, and there was blank astonishment in each pair of eyes.

"Did this lady give any address?"

"No, it was not necessary," said the doctor. "I told you I gave her an open cheque. Well, she seemed a little perturbed at first. She did not want a cheque; so I sent my clerk to the bank to draw the money, and when he brought it back I delivered it to her."

"So it was in cash?" said Larry.

"Literally it was in cash I paid her," said Dr. Judd.

"You have never seen her before?" persisted Larry.

Dr. Judd shook his head.

"She came from nowhere so far as I am concerned," he said. "She was undoubtedly the daughter of Mr. Stuart, or at least, she told me so, and I have no reason to disbelieve her word."

Larry and the girl were out in the street again before he spoke to the girl.

"It is amazing," he said. His cab was waiting and he ushered the girl in. "304 Nottingham Place," he said.

"Where are we going?" asked the girl in surprise.

"We're going to the lodgings that Stuart had," replied Larry. "I left the investigation at that point to Sergeant Harvey, and he is a particularly thorough man, but may have missed something. Surely, if Gordon Stuart learnt on the day of his death that he had another daughter, he must have had some visitor?"

"Do you think the girl saw him?" asked Diana quickly. "Clarissa, I mean."

"It is possible," replied Larry, "but that is to be discovered."

No. 304 Nottingham Place was a big and sedate-looking mansion, of the type which is patronized by American visitors of the better class, and Larry and his companion were shown into a comfortable drawing-room. A few minutes after, a little lady with white hair came in.

"Mrs. Portland, isn't it?" said Larry. "My name is Holt. I am from Scotland Yard."

A look of dismay came to the lady's face.

"Oh dear," she said, evidently distressed. "I did hope that the police had finished with me. It gets this house such a bad name, and I've already suffered in consequence. The poor gentleman committed suicide, didn't he? Why he should I don't know," she said, shaking her head. "I have never seen him so cheerful as he was the night just before he went to the theatre. As a rule he was so glum and sad that it depressed me to see him."

"Cheerful before he went to the Theatre?" said Larry quickly. "Unusually so?"

She nodded.

"Had he any visitors in the afternoon?"

"None sir," replied the lady, and Larry's face dropped. "None at all. I told your detective officer who called that he never received visitors. He had been out in the afternoon, and I must confess that he came back a little before we expected him. We had a charwoman in, and she was making his room tidy, and the first I knew about his room was when I passed his door and I heard him having a long conversation with somebody. It was so unusual that I spoke to my head waitress about it."

"Who was the somebody?" asked Larry, and the landlady smiled.

"It was the charwoman," she said. "A woman I used to get in to do odd jobs. I thought it was extraordinary, because he never spoke to anybody."

"How long was the woman with him?" asked Larry.

"Nearly an hour," was the surprising reply.

"An hour?" said Larry. "He was talking with a charwoman for an hour? What did he talk about?"

She shook her head.

"I don't know. I remember it well, because the charwoman left without drawing her wages. In fact, she must have gone straight out after leaving Mr. Stuart's room—and she never came back."

Larry frowned.

"That is important," he said. "Did you tell Sergeant Harvey?"

"No, sir," said the lady in surprise. "I didn't think it was worth while reporting a little domestic incident like that. He asked me if Mr. Stuart had

had any visitors, and I replied truthfully that he had not."

"What was the woman's name?"

"I don't know," said the landlady. "We used to call her Emma. I am surprised she didn't come back, because she left her wedding ring here. She used to take it off before she started scrubbing. It is a peculiar ring for a woman of her position—half platinum and half gold, and—Catch that young lady, sir," she said suddenly.

Larry turned quickly and caught the girl as she fainted.

The Man Who Was Deaf

HE CARRIED her to a sofa and laid her down, and presently she opened her eyes.

"I am an awful idiot," she said trying to rise, but he laid his hand on her shoulder.

"You must lie there a little while. What is the trouble?"

"The room is a little close, I think," she said.

The room was stuffy: Larry had noticed it when he came in, and as the landlady pulled up the window, she apologized.

"I'm always telling the servants to keep this room aired, and they never do," she said. "It's like a furnace. I am very sorry."

Larry had seen many fainting women, but never before had such a phenomenon occasioned him so much alarm.

"I don't remember doing such a stupid thing before," said the girl at last sitting up.

"You had better go home," said Larry solemnly.

She was still very white, but the cup of tea which the landlady brought in revived her.

"I'm not going home," she said firmly. "I am going with you to Todd's. You promised me I should, and as soon as I get into the air I shall be all right. If you were to take me a drive around Regent's Park—it's quite near—I should be as well as ever."

They made the slow round of the outer circle and the colour came back to her face.

"Was it this morning you told me I was overdoing it?" smiled Larry. "My young friend, you are in danger of a breakdown."

She shook her head.

"I shall be very hurt if you insist upon that. I am not so stupid that I would go on if I wasn't fit," she said. "That undignified collapse into your arms will not occur again. Besides," she said mischievously, "if I am liable to having a fit on the mat, don't you think it would be better if you were with me than if I were by myself in my room?"

"There's something in that," said Larry. "But I'm not so sure that visiting Todd's is the best way of spending an afternoon. It's very smelly, and the sights are not quite pleasant."

"They will not worry me," she answered quietly. "Please, please let me go!"

He reached over and took her hand and she did not resist this attention.

"You can go just where you like, Diana," he said, "and—and—as far as you like!"

By now his own flustered feelings had calmed, and he remembered that he had not asked to see the novel wedding ring of Emma, the charwoman. Nor had he made the inquiries which he would have made but for the dramatic interruption of Diana's collapse.

He drove the girl back to Piccadilly, and they lunched together, and then they went on to Scotland Yard. In the restaurant he had telephoned to Harvey, and Harvey had renewed the distress of Mrs. Portland by another visit. He was waiting for Larry at the Yard in Room 47 when they returned.

"I've traced Emma," he said, and his tone was so serious that Larry knew that he was not wrong in giving importance to the interview which the charwoman had with Stuart. "She lives, or lived, in Camden Town," said Harvey. "She lodges with an Army pensioner and his wife."

"Well, have you seen her?"

"No, sir, I haven't seen her. She's no longer there," said Harvey. "She has not been home since the night following the Stuart murder."

Larry made a little grimace.

"That is the real end and the real clue of this crime," he said. "Emma the charwoman is going to supply us with a considerable amount of information. Did she take away her things from her lodgings?" he asked.

"No, sir," replied Harvey. "That is the curious circumstance. The woman neither told her friends that she was leaving, nor did she take any of her clothing or her belongings with her."

"Put her on the list," said Larry, "and warn all stations. No news of Blind Jake?"

"No, sir."

"Nor Fred?"

"No, sir."

"To the already overburdened vigilance of the Metropolitan Constabulary—poor chaps!—" said Larry with a smile, "we will add the name of Miss Clarissa Stuart. Young, pretty, and smartly dressed, probably staying in a good-class hotel. Put a comb through those places where a woman of wealth is likely to be, and report."

Harvey lifted his hat and went out, and Larry walked slowly to his desk and stood for a while looking down at it disapprovingly.

"I don't know why I am given a table in this office," he said. "I never sit at it." Nevertheless he dropped down in his chair and glanced across at the girl. "Well, Miss Ward," he said, "you have a further mystery to add to the others. Emma has disappeared as unexpectedly as Flash Fred or as Stuart, and the man who persuaded Emma to go was the man who nearly persuaded Mrs. Weldon to depart this life."

"Blind Jake?" she asked.

"That is the lad," he replied. "A terrible figure. I can't think of him without a shudder."

"What a confession for a detective to make!" she scoffed. "Of course you can think of him—he's human!"

"And a very sore human, too," smiled Larry. "For Flash Fred was fairly useful with a knife in the days when I was trailing him for carving up Leroux, a rival of his."

"Do you think they have caught him?" she asked.

He shook his head.

"No, Fred has gone to earth. He's gone because he's afraid they'll catch him."

"Then he is not in with them?"

"Fred?" He laughed. "Not Fred. Fred's a lone wolf and plays a lone hand. He preys upon the virtuous and the wicked alike. One of his many boasts is that he has never been a member of a gang, and I dare say that is why he has so far escaped, or partially escaped, the consequence of his rascality. He is in London," he mused, "and I have an idea we shall see him again very soon."

How soon he could not guess.

He worked for an hour, and seemed oblivious both to Diana's presence and the looks she shot across at him—glances which were intended to remind him that he was taking her to Todd's.

He covered sheet after sheet of paper, for it was his practice to write down his cases in narrative form, dovetailing the cause to the effect. They were curious-looking documents, these "statements" of his, abounding in marginal notes and interlinear corrections. Presently he finished writing, dropping the last sheet and slipping the paper into a drawer. Then he got up and stretched himself. He walked to the window and looked out. It was late afternoon and he could glimpse a wonderful picture of the Thames Embankment, a vista of blue bridges spanning a leaden stream, of dim spires looming through the eastern haze, of a long line of green where the trees shaded the broad sidewalk, of chocolate-coloured tram-cars that flashed to and fro—a fragment of London, recognizable even to those who had never seen the great city, or throbbed to its ceaseless pulsations.

Larry Holt scratched his nose unromantically and turned a dubious look to the waiting girl.

"If you still want to go to Todd's, I'll take you," he said. "This is the hour I'd promised myself the pleasure of a visit."

A car took them to the end of Lissom Grove, and they walked down Lissom Lane, which was a cul-de-sac opening from the bigger thoroughfare. Two plain-clothes police officers, who were waiting, joined them, and the party stepped to the side of the street opposite that on which the Home was situated.

"What is the place next door?" asked Larry, nodding at a black-looking house with shuttered windows.

"It used to be a laundry," said the policeman. "There's a yard and a shed at the back."

"Laundry?" said the girl thoughtfully. "Do you remember that it was a laundry van that was outside my flat that night they tried to carry me off?"

"By Jimmy!" said Larry. "So it was!"

"It couldn't have been this laundry, miss," said the policeman. "It has not been doing business for twelve months. They went bankrupt, and somebody bought up the business, but doesn't seem to have made a start yet."

"Those gates lead to the yard, I presume?" said Larry pointing.

"Yes, sir. I haven't seen a motor-van come out of there, and I don't even know that they have one," said the policeman. "But nowadays, when there are so many motor vehicles about, it is impossible to keep track of them."

Larry went up the steps and knocked at the door, and the same little old man opened.

"Four people!" he yelled. "All strangers! What do you want?"

"I want to see Mr. Dearborn," said Larry.

"Oh yes, sir, you were the gentleman that came on Sunday morning at six a.m.," said the little man, and went pattering down the long passage. "Come this way!" he bawled. "All of you. Four of them, sir!"

The Rev. John Dearborn came out of his study to meet the party, and ushered them in.

"Mr. Holt? I think I recognized your voice," he said. His little dictating machine was spinning, and there was a thick pad of typed manuscript on his table. He put his hand lovingly upon it as he passed to his chair. "I have a gentleman who comes in to read for me in the evening," he said, as though guessing Larry's thoughts. "Now what is the object of to-night's visit?" he asked. "Have you found your Blind Jake?"

"I have met him without finding him," replied Larry grimly. "I merely want to see over the house. I have brought a lady with me."

"How interesting!" said the Rev. John Dearborn, rising.

The girl held out her hand instinctively, and the man took it.

"I shall be most happy to show you round. You have some other friends?"

Larry introduced them, and together they went up the stairs, John Dearborn leading the way.

"We will start at the top of the house this time," he said humorously. "Our friend Lew is still in his cubicle."

"Aren't you afraid to keep a man here who is not quite right in his head?"

"He is very weak," said John Dearborn, "and I haven't the heart to send him to the infirmary. I fear that I must do so sooner or later."

Larry had the girl by his side on the landing, and lowering his voice he asked:

"Do you want to see this old man? He is rather——" He did not finish his sentence.

"I want to see him—yes," she said. "You forget that I was nurse in an institute for the blind."

Dearborn led the way to the cubicle. No lights shone, though there were electric globes on every landing. The blind needed no lights, thought Larry.

The old man in the cubicle lay quietly on his back, his hands folded patiently. He was no longer talking, and was, indeed, much calmer than when Larry had seen him last.

"How are you to-day?" asked Larry.

The man made no reply. It was the girl who laid her hand upon his shoulder.

"Are you feeling better?" she asked, and the man started round.

"Who's that? Is that you, Jim?" he asked. "Have you got my supper?"

"Are you feeling better?" said Diana.

"And bring me a mug of tea, will you?" said Lew, and lay over on his back and resumed the same attitude of resignation in which they had found him.

The girl stooped and looked closely at the old man; and, sensing her presence, he put up his hand and touched her face.

"Is that a lady?" he said.

And then Dearborn pressed past them and caught the man's hand in his.

"Are you better to-day. Lew?" he said, and the man winked.

"All right, sir," he replied. "I'm feeling fine, thank you."

Diana Ward walked out of the cubicle, her eyes fixed absently on space, and Larry joined her.

"What is the matter?" he asked.

"That man is dead," she said.

"Dead?" he repeated in amazement. "Of course he's not dead."

She nodded her head.

"Diana, I don't understand you," said Larry. He thought for a moment that her fainting fit had affected her mind and that she was talking lightheadedly.

"Dead," she repeated, and her voice had a passionate thrill which made him gasp. "As effectively dead as if he were lying cold and lifeless on that bed. Oh, it's cruel, cruel!"

John Dearborn and the detectives were still in the cubicle discussing the invalid.

"What do you mean, Diana?" he asked.

"Don't you see? I've seen it happen once before," she said in a low voice that shook. "There were little black marks on the man's ear. Those are powder marks. He has been deafened."

"Deafened?" he whispered, still not grasping the significance of the revelation.

"You told me something of what this man said when you saw him on Sunday," she said, speaking rapidly and almost in a whisper, "and now I see what has happened. This man has had a shot-gun discharged near both ears, and he is dead."

"But, I don't understand."

"Do you realize," she asked, and she spoke slowly now, "what it means to be blind and deaf?"

"Good God!" he gasped.

"That is what has happened to the man they call Lew. Some persons, who for their own purpose desire to spare his life, have made him incapable of testifying against them."

"What do you mean?"

"I mean," she said, "that he was the man who wrote the Braille message found in Gordon Stuart's pocket."

The Disappearance of Diana Ward

WAS IT guess-work? Was it sheer deduction? Was it knowledge? These three questions flashed through Larry's mind, but before he could ask her any further questions, John Dearborn had come from the cubicle and was feeling his way down the stairs.

On the next landing he opened the door of a dormitory which Larry had seen before. It consisted of three rooms which had been knocked into one at some previous period.

Obedient to Larry's instructions, the two detectives did not follow the party in. One strolled down and took his place on the lower landing; the other sat upon the stairs that led to the cubicles above and waited.

"Is it light?" asked Dearborn as he walked into the inner room.

"Quite light," said Larry.

"I am told there is rather a good view from this window," said Dearborn, and pointed unerringly to a view which was neither picturesque nor extensive.

Larry did not reply. It was possibly a polite fiction that the views from the Home were lovely, and he did not desire to hurt, even in the slightest degree, the man who was so proud of a prospect which included six roofs and a hundred chimney pots.

"Is the window closed? I think it is," said John Dearborn. "Will you open it for me?"

Larry pulled up the noisy sash, and a breath of cool, sweet air came into the stuffy dormitory.

"Thank you," said Mr. Dearborn. "Now, perhaps the young lady—"

The Dark Eyes of London

Larry was looking about the room. The girl was not in sight. He walked quickly to the door and the officer on duty stood up from the stairs on which he had been sitting.

"Which way did Miss Ward go?"

"She didn't come out, sir," said the man in surprise. "She went in the room with you."

Larry stared at him.

"Didn't come out?" he repeated in amazement. "Are you sure?"

"Absolutely sure."

He called to the man on the lower landing.

"Did you see Miss Ward?"

"No, sir," said the officer, "she hasn't come out of that door. I can see it plainly from here, and I haven't taken my eyes off it."

Larry went back into the room. It was empty. There were half a dozen plain iron beds, but there was no place of concealment save a cupboard which stood against the wall opposite the fireplace. He was in a panic, and his heart was beating wildly as no danger to himself could have made it beat.

He pulled open the cupboard door. It was empty, except for some old clothing which was hanging on a line of pegs. He flung these out and struck the back of the cupboard. It was solid.

"Have you found the young lady?" asked Dearborn presently.

"No, I have not," said Larry quickly. "Is there any other way out of this room but these doors?"

The clergyman shook his head.

"No," he said in astonishment, "Why do you ask? Oh, perhaps you are thinking we should have a means of egress in case of fire. We have been thinking over that matter—"

Larry was white of face, and he was trembling. He called in one of the police officers.

"You will remain in this room until you are relieved," he said. Then he summoned the other. "Call Scotland Yard in my name and tell them I want twenty plain-clothes men here at once. There's a constable on point duty at the end of Lissom Grove. Bring him here and station him outside the house."

"What has happened?" demanded the Rev. Dearborn anxiously. "These are the only times when my malady distresses me, when I feel that I cannot help."

"Perhaps it would be better if you went to your study," said Larry gently. "I am afraid a crime has been committed under my very eyes."

How could it have happened? He had heard no sound. He thought the girl was behind him. He knew she had gone into the room because he had pushed her in before him; he remembered that distinctly. He remembered her turning to the left to inspect the lower end of the room when he had gone to open the window—that was when it happened!

When he had pulled up the window he had made a noise which had drowned any sound which may have occurred at the further end of the room. But it had all passed so quickly, and she had not left the room.

He began a systematic examination of the walls, looking for secret doorways. The coco-nut matting on the floor was pulled up, but without result. Diana Ward had disappeared as though an earthquake had swallowed her, as though she had dissolved into minutest atoms and had floated out of the window in invisible vapour.

The Laundry Yard

LARRY paced the dormitory, sick with fear, terrified as he had never been before. He had searched the house from roof to cellar, had explored dusty and dark corners of which the occupants of Todd's Home were unacquainted; but searchings and questionings produced nothing—nothing!

Within half an hour a cordon of plain-clothes men had been drawn round the house, and Larry had been relieved from the dormitory and set free to conduct his search elsewhere.

"There is no communication between this house and the next?" he had asked the clergyman.

"None whatever," said John Dearborn without hesitation. "In fact, some years ago the noise from the laundry was so great and disturbing to my men that I compelled the proprietors of the building to put up a new wall, a sort of inner lining, to deaden the sound. It is no longer in the occupation of the company," he said. "They went bankrupt, and the premises were taken over by a firm of provision merchants. I understand that they intended storing their goods in the laundry building."

"That is the small building one can see over the gates at the end of the yard?" said Larry.

"That is so," replied the superintendent.

Larry went up to the door of the empty house and examined it carefully; and a sergeant from Scotland Yard made a close inspection.

"I can tell you this, sir, that nobody has been in or out of this door for a very long time," he said. Over the railings which enclosed a narrow area they could see through the dusty windows into a room which was the quintessence of dinginess. It was quite bare and innocent of furniture. Larry felt his heart sinking with every minute that passed. If he should lose her, if he should lose her!

Only then did he realize what this girl meant to him. She was a friend of less than a week, and yet all other matters and interests—friends, profession, success—none of these meant anything to him, compared with that one slim girl. He would willingly have sacrificed every prospect he had in life to hold her hand once more, or to exchange with her a dozen words. In the power of Blind Jake! He reeled under the thought. It was maddening—grotesquely horrible!

He pulled himself together with a jerk. He would go mad if he allowed his mind to dwell upon that hideous possibility.

He had no time to think upon the Stuart case or its bearing on this disappearance. All his energy and agony of endeavour were concentrated upon one object, one discovery—Diana Ward.

He climbed over the wooden gates and explored the yard of the laundry; and here he found something which set his eyes on the trail again. There were wheel tracks, and they were comparatively new. The tracks of a motor-car, possibly two cars. He looked round the littered yard for a garage, and saw a black-looking door which had the appearance of closing some such building.

Sergeant Harvey, who had followed him over the gate, tried a pick-lock on the door, and after two attempts succeeded in forcing back the bolt of the lock. The doors were fixed on slides, and they went back easily and noiselessly, almost at a touch.

"They have been used recently," said Larry.

There were two cars in the garage—a long-bonneted limousine and a small motor-van. Larry walked in, and there was light enough to see, for the day had not yet failed.

"Look!" cried Larry suddenly, pointing to the hood of the motor-van.

It had been newly painted; but clearly underneath the white paint which covered it was the faint impression of a word, badly and awkwardly painted by an amateur hand—the word "Laundry."

"Do you remember, Harvey, Miss Ward telling us that there was a laundry van outside her flat the night they tried to abduct her? If she can identify this——" He stopped suddenly with a twinge of pain. If she were there to identify anything!

The limousine had recently been cleaned, and he took the precaution of jotting down the numbers of both cars. It might be, of course, that these machines were the legitimate property of the new owners of the building, and had been engaged only in perfectly innocent business. It might have been a coincidence that such a car was waiting in the Charing Cross Road the night Blind Jake tried to abduct the girl.

He closed the doors, and Harvey re-locked them.

'Phone these numbers through to the Yard," said Larry. "Ask the Registration Department to identify them!"

Harvey went off and Larry was left alone in the yard. He went again to the wheel tracks. They had been made that morning, for a shower of rain had fallen in the night, and the newness of the markings was obvious.

He walked along to the laundry building proper—a new erection of brick, with ground-glass windows. Here, too, was a sliding door, and on the stone steps leading up was a foot-mark. He bent suddenly to look at the print.

Larry, in moments of excitement, was wont to act jerkily. And now his movements to an observer would seem sudden and unexpected. As he bent his head——

"Plok!"

It was a sound like a cork being discharged from a gaseous champagne bottle, only a little louder, a little more metallic. There was an answering crash near at hand, a splinter of wood fell upon Larry's neck, and he jumped up with a start. A panel of the door was smashed as by a bullet. If he had not dropped his head at that moment to examine the foot-print—Sunny would have stopped the morning papers! That, strangely enough, was the first thought that struck him.

Larry looked round quickly; he had recognized the sound as soon as he had heard it. There had been no report, but he had been fired at with a rifle or pistol fitted with a Maxim silencer. He had heard that "Plok!" before. His keen eyes ranged the windows of the building behind for a sign of smoke, but whatever there might have been must have been instantly dissipated. Then he noticed for the first time that the dormitory from whence the girl had disappeared commanded a view of the yard. He saw the open window, and with his exact sense of topography located the room. No other shot was fired, and he crossed the yard, keeping his eyes upon the backs of the two houses, ready to drop at the first flash of a rifle.

Harvey, on his way back, had opened a wicket in the bigger gate, and Larry stepped out into the street in a thoughtful frame of mind. He went straight back to the Home. The blind hawkers who used the Home were beginning to arrive. They came in ones and twos, tapping their way with their iron-shod sticks, and as they passed him on their way to the common room, a local officer identified them.

"They're all decent citizens, eh?" said Larry. "None of them is on the crime-index?"

"None, sir," said the man. "They're all quite law-abiding people, and we've never had a complaint against any of them."

Larry went up to the dormitory from whence he believed the shot had been fired. To his surprise, the door was locked and the officer was on duty outside.

"What is the meaning of this?" he asked sternly.

"The superintendent sent a message up, telling me that you wished to see me, sir," said the detective. "I went down and found that he had sent no such message. When I came back, the door was locked."

"From the inside?" asked Larry.

"Apparently, sir. There is no key in the lock."

"Who brought the message?"

"The little fellow who opens the door of this place."

"I know him," nodded Larry. "What explanation did he give?"

"He said that somebody with the superintendent's voice told him to go upstairs with the message."

"Stand on one side," said Larry, and with his foot kicked open the door.

The room was empty, but he sniffed.

"A rifle has been fired in here, probably when you were downstairs," he said. "You understand that you are not to leave this room unless I personally or Sergeant Harvey come to you and bring a man to take your place."

"Very good, sir," said the crestfallen worker.

"But in the circumstances I'm not blaming you," interrupted Larry with a faint smile. "We are dealing with an extraordinary gang, and they will use extraordinary methods—you cannot be expected to meet every move as it comes, let alone anticipate what their next will be."

There was no doubt that the rifle had been fired in this room; he could smell the exploded cordite; the proof came when he found under the bed near the window, the exploded shell of a cartridge. He descended to the superintendent's office and found the Rev. John Dearborn a little perturbed.

"How long do you intend keeping your men here, Mr. Holt?" he asked. "Some of my fellows want to go to their dormitory to sleep."

"I am keeping my men here until I get some proof that Miss Ward is not on the premises," said Larry shortly, "and until I have found the gentleman who shot at me from the very dormitory in which she disappeared.'

"Shot at you?" said the other in surprise. "You don't mean——"

"I mean just what I say," said Larry. "Forgive me if I am brusque. Whilst you were talking to the detective who had been brought downstairs by a ruse, I was shot at from that room and the door was locked."

"It is most amazing," said the Rev. John, shaking his head. "I cannot imagine a situation more trying to myself or more exciting for you."

"Exciting!" repeated Larry, and laughed bitterly. "There will be excitement all right," he said grimly, "but it will come later, when I have unravelled this tangle."

And then his mordant humour asserted itself.

"You should put this situation into one of your plays, Mr. Dearborn," he said, and he thought he saw the colour come to the man's pale face.

"That is quite an idea," replied the superintendent thoughtfully, "and I thank you for it. Have you ever seen any of my plays?"

"No, I have not seen them," said Larry, "but I am going at the first opportunity to pay a visit to the Macready."

The superintendent shook his head.

"I sometimes fear," he said, "that they are not as good as some of my friends think they are, and I am disappointed that you have not seen one. But they go on producing them, and money comes in for the Home."

"Who pays the cost of production?" asked Larry curiously. He welcomed any diversion from the overwhelming misery of his thoughts.

"A gentleman who is interested in my work," replied Mr. Dearborn. "I have never met him, but he has never refused to produce a play of mine. Sometimes I think he does so because he wishes to help this Home."

"He must have some good reason," said Larry.

Conversation flagged after this. Once a telephone buzzed, and the superintendent took up a receiver from his table and listened.

"Yes, I think you had better," he said, and hung up the receiver again. "A mundane question from the kitchen," he smiled. "I have telephones fitted all over the house so far as our means allow us," he added. "It saves so many journeys."

Just then a deputation came from the common room with a grievance. The men of No. 1 Dormitory wish to go into their sleeping-places. Some of them made a practice of sleeping the clock round, and all of them, whether they wanted to retire at once or not, claimed their right to enter their dormitory.

"You hear?" said the superintendent. "It is rather difficult for me."

Larry nodded.

"They can have beds at the nearest hotel," he said, "and I will pay for them. Or they can sleep somewhere else. I don't mind the beds being taken out. But nobody occupies that room until Miss Ward is found."

He strolled out into the passage and walked to the common room. These poor men were entitled to an explanation, and he gave it, stating the case fairly and simply, and there was a chorus of approval even from the most obstreperous.

He had concluded his harangue and was standing in the passage with his back to the wall, his head on his breast, thinking, when he heard a commotion upstairs, and a cry, and leapt up the stairs two at a time. He got to the first landing and was turning, when he saw a sight that brought his heart into his mouth.

Walking slowly down the stairs towards him was Diana Ward. Her blouse hung in rags, so that the under-bodice and the snowy white of her shoulders were visible. She carried in one hand a compact Smith-Wesson revolver, and on her white face was a smile of triumph.

For a second Larry looked at her and then leapt up the remaining stairs to meet her, and caught her in his arms.

"My dear, my dear!" he said brokenly. "Thank God you have come back!"

What Happened to Diana

DIANA WARD had strolled to the farther end of the dormitory and was feeling the texture of the rough sheets. The housewife instinct in her was a strong one, and her nurse's training had given her an additional interest in the means which were adopted to give comfort to these poor blind beggars—for beggars most of them were. She had heard the superintendent ask Larry to open the window, and she was watching idly, when the door of the cupboard behind her opened without a sound and a barefooted man crept out.

The first thing that Diana knew was that something like a piece of wet chamois leather was over her face, and she was being lifted bodily. For a second she was paralysed, and in that second she had passed through the cupboard and the wall behind. Both doors fastened—for the back of the press, as Larry had suspected at first, was a door that moved, pegs and all, outwards. What he could not know was that it was literally a brick door.

She heard its thud as it closed, and, wriggling her face clear of the wet leather, she screamed. Again a hand that was big enough to cover the whole of her face came over her mouth, and she was dragged along in the darkness; another door opened, and she was thrown in. There was a click, and an electric light blazed from above, and she saw her captor and shrank back in terror.

He was tall, bigger than any man she had seen. She guessed he was seven feet in height, and his breadth was in proportion. He was dressed in a shirt and a pair of trousers. His feet and his arms were bare, and she had no need to study that hairy forearm to appreciate its strength. It was as massive as an average man's thigh, and the muscles stood out in swathes. His face was red and large and curiously flat.

His eyes, which did not move when he spoke, were of the palest blue, and a mane of grey hair swept back from his forehead and hung untidily behind. The mouth, heavy and gross, was covered by a short unkempt beard which was neither grey nor yellow, but had something of each in its hue. His enormous ears stuck out from his head almost at right angles, and she thought she had never seen so terrible a creature in her life.

"I'll let ye have a look at me so that ye'll know me again," he giggled. (There was no other word that Diana could think of that so described that shrill laugh of his.) "Where's your gun?" he bantered. "Why don't you fire it at poor old Jake—he told you all about me, I'll bet!"

She knew that he referred to Larry Holt, but made no reply. Her eyes were searching the room for some weapon, but the rough plastered walls were bare and there was not a stick of furniture in the place. The only window was a long narrow slip of toughened glass near the ceiling, flanked on each side by two wall ventilators. She searched her bag, but there was nothing there. She was even without hat-pins, though they would be practically useless against this brute.

"Looking for something to kill me with, are you?" he giggled again. "I hear you! Now you sit down and be patient, young woman," he said. "There's a good time coming, and nobody wants to hurt you."

He did not attempt to approach her, and she had that relief, but his next words told her that the real danger was but postponed.

"Ye're pretty by all accounts," he chuckled. "And them as likes pretty ones might give the world for you. It's a wonder to me that They ain't took ye, my dear, but They haven't any use for women or marriage and the like, so They've given ye to Old Jake."

He giggled again and the girl went cold at the sound. He had a trick of pausing before and emphasizing "They" as though the word stood in capitals in his dark mind.

"I can't see ye, so prettiness don't mean much to me, my little darling. And if your face was like hers"—he jerked his thumb to the ceiling—"it wouldn't make no difference to me."

"You'll never get out of this building," she said, realizing that it was best to show a bold attitude. "Mr. Holt is in the house next door, and by this time the place will be surrounded."

This time his chuckle had a deeper note.

"There are ten ways out of the house," he said contemptuously. "That's why They bought it. There's a hole underneath the cellar where you can walk for miles, and nobody there to stop you but the rats. Rats are afraid of blind men."

There was the hint of a curious, childlike simplicity that ill fitted his monstrous shape.

"Sooner or later he will get you," she said quietly, and then, with a sudden inspiration: "He has already got Lew."

He was on the point of leaving the room, and he spun round, his face working.

"Lew!" he roared. "He's got Lew!"

Then he was silent, and the silence ended in a shout of laughter that seemed to shake the room.

"Lew will tell him a lot!" he said. "How's he going to ask Lew for information when Lew doesn't know where he is, or who he's talking to? He can't read or write. He'd have been dead, too," he nodded sagely, "dead as a door nail, Lew would have been, for the dirty trick he played upon Them. He was the man who put the paper into the pocket of the feller They croaked!"

"We know that," she said boldly, and he seemed to be impressed.

"You found that out, did you?" he said. "But Lew didn't tell ye. He'd have been dead, as dead as a door nail, Lew would, only They didn't want no dead men knocking about. Me and Lew carried him down the steps," he said, nodding his great head. "I can tell you that, because I know the lor. I know the lor properly, I do. You can't tell Old Jake anything."

She was wondering what he meant by this boast of his knowledge of the law.

"A wife can't give evidence against her husband," he said with a little leer. "That's why I tell you all this, little darling."

"A wife!" she gasped, sick at the ghastliness of the suggestion.

"Mrs. Jake Bradford," he chortled. "Bradford is my name, my darling, and you'll be married by his reverence too, proper and in order."

"You fool!" she burst forth in her anger and fear. "Do you think anybody could marry me to a horror like you? Do you think I should stand without protesting and telling all I know, by your side? You're mad."

He bent his head forward and his voice came lower as he spoke, until it was little more than a whisper.

"There's worse than me in this house," he said slowly, "and maybe you won't mind me if you don't see me, young lady. And you may be blind as I am, and deaf too, like Lew." He paused, and she shrank back, holding on to the walls for support. "And dumb, if you're going to talk!" he roared in a sudden fury. "There's nothing I wouldn't do to you if They told me to."

The door opened and closed. A key turned and a bolt was shot, and looking up she saw he was gone, and slid to the floor half conscious, half fainting. Then with an effort she drooped her head low and felt the blood coming back, and presently she was able to stand.

No power of will could stop her hands from shaking, and it was not until she had paced the room for ten minutes that she came back to anything like normal. She knew that it was no idle threat this man had uttered. He would be merciless if his unknown superiors gave the order. He would crush out the youth and the beauty of youth, the sweet senses of life, without compunction at the word of They. He would mutilate and torture, and pity would not come to him. She had to think clearly and think quickly.

She went to the door, but she knew that escape that way was impossible. There was no chair by which she could reach the window, and she could not make her escape without even attracting attention through that slit of wall. There was nothing in the room but the electric light.

She remembered Larry's story of how this man had come toward him with his hands up, and how he had crushed the bulb in his powerful fist. He must be animal strong, she thought. Wasn't there a danger of his being shocked by the electric current?

At that thought she looked up quickly. The light had been fixed without any regard to appearance. The long wire came from the ceiling at one end of the room and was loosely tacked to the ceiling as far as the centre, where it passed over a hook and hung downwards, with a little tin reflector over the pear-shaped lamp. She reached for the lamp and turned it round.

"Two hundred volts," she read, ground upon the crystal glass.

She tried to unhook the wire by throwing up the loose end, but it was some time before she succeeded, and at last the loose part fell and the lamp jerked to the floor and almost touched it. She caught the loose flex in her hand and pulled gently, and the thin wire brackets which held the flex to the ceiling came away without any difficulty. The switch was near the door, and she walked across and turned it off. Putting one foot upon the flex, near to where it entered the aperture of the shade, she pulled with all her might and after several attempts it snapped.

She was in darkness, but her nimble fingers plucked at the loose end of the wire, and with her fingernails she cleared away the rubber casing which enclosed the tiny thread-like strands of copper. Soon she had something that felt like a loose-haired broom in her hands, and she was satisfied. She thought she heard a noise in the passage, and, running to the switch, turned the current on again. She groped in the half-darkness for her bag and found it, took out her gloves and put them on, then felt gingerly for the hanging strands. She took them in her hands and held the "brush" before her, being careful not to touch one exposed strand. Pushing away the shade and the globe with her foot, she waited in the centre of the room. And then the door opened.

"Here I am again, dearie," and her breath came quickly as she heard the door locked from the inside. "You think I'm a funny-looking fellow, don't you?" He did not know that the light was out, for he lived in everlasting darkness.

For a time he made no attempt to come near her. She could just see the shape of him by the evening light which filtered through that narrow window.

"Tony missed him," he said, by way of conveying information. "Missed him!" he said contemptuously. "If I'd had my eyes, I'd have got the devil! I'd get him now with this little gun of mine, blind as I am, if I could hear him move. But we'll have Holty yet, my darling. We'll have him and cut his heart out. He'll wish he was never born."

He lowered his voice, and said something which was not intelligible to the girl. Then he seemed to recall the object of his visit.

"Come to Old Jake, my dear," he giggled, as he walked stealthily toward her, both of his huge arms outstretched. "Come to your old husband, my pretty!"

He was as quick as a cat, and one hand had gripped the shoulder of her blouse before she realized he was upon her—gripped it and tore it from shoulder to hem. She threw herself back, and his other hand came up—and touched the outspread wire. With a yell that was half shriek, half roar, he fell back.

"What did you do?" he asked savagely. "What did you do, you little devil? Did you knife me like that swine?"

He was evidently feeling himself to discover an injury, and then he leapt at her, and this time the wire struck his face, and he fell to the ground like a log.

She heard him stir.

"What is it, what is it?" he whispered. "I can't see it! You oughtn't to treat an old blind man like that, you little—"

His hand shot out and caught her ankle, flinging her to the ground. But again his face touched the electric wire, charged with 200 volts, and he screamed and rolled over. He was mad now, a whimpering lunatic. Again and again he approached her; again and again his hand, his face, his neck, came into contact with the current. And then suddenly he fell again, and the girl thrust the cruel ends of the wire at his throat. She felt like a murderess as he shivered convulsively. But she had to kill him; she knew that nothing short of killing him would save her life.

Presently she took the wire away. He lay very still, and her shaking hands searched his pockets. She found the key, felt the revolver in his pocket and extracted it, and fumbled for the lock. Presently the door was open and she was in the passage which turned to the right, and along here she went. She was in a lighter room with two windows, but she was still in mortal terror; for now she had lost her best weapon of defence.

The door was easy to find. Cleverly concealed it might be in the dormitory of Todd's Home, but here it was well marked. She pulled a handle, and the mass of brickwork swung back and she walked through the door. A man standing in the dormitory spun round, a revolver in his hand.

"Good Lord!" he cried. "Miss Ward, where did you come from?"

Back Again

THAT sense of security, of peace, and of deep happiness was inexpressibly sweet, she thought, as she lay in Larry Holt's arms. Presently she released herself, and in a few hurried words had said enough to send a small battalion of detectives racing to the dormitory and through the brick door, which she had left ajar.

Larry handed the girl to the care of Harvey and followed his men. The room where Diana had been imprisoned was empty. He stopped long enough to switch off the current, then joined the searchers. There was no doubt that this place, for all its unoccupied appearance, had regular tenants. They found rooms that had been built within rooms, a thin wall being erected within a few feet of each window. This meant that the house might be occupied at night, and lights might blaze in every apartment without anybody outside being the wiser.

Blind Jake had said no more than the truth when he had told the girl that there were plenty of ways out of the house. They found one in the cellar that led to an old disused rain-water sewer, and here pursuit was abandoned. None of the party except Larry, who always carried a small flash-lamp, was equipped for a chase through the darkness.

Another exit led directly into the yard where Larry had found the garage. A third communicated with the kitchen of Todd's Home.

Larry, realizing that his quarry had escaped, went back to the girl. He found her sitting in the superintendent's office, the watchful Harvey embarrassingly close to her side—an attitude which was explained when the laughing girl lifted one of her arms, for Harvey, who was taking no risks, had handcuffed their wrists together!

"And very wise too," said Larry with a smile as the detective unfastened the irons. "Now, Mr. Dearborn, I want to have some sort of explanation of the mysterious happenings in this house."

"I don't think anything mysterious has happened here," said Mr. Dearborn

118

quietly. "You cannot hold me responsible for villainy which may have been perpetrated next door. I am told that there are doors communicating between these two houses, but of that I had not the slightest knowledge. If there was a man living next door——"

"There were six men living next door," said Larry. "We found their beds and some of their clothing. From the fact that there were books, some of them open, it is pretty clear that they are not blind."

Mr. Dearborn shrugged his despair.

"What can I do?" he asked. "In this house we are dependent entirely upon the loyalty of our inmates; and though it is possible sometimes to detect the presence of a stranger by his unusual footfalls, his voice or his cough, it is quite possible that these men made the freest use of the Home for the purpose of carrying on their nefarious work, without our having the slightest knowledge of such things."

This argument was so logical that Larry did not contest its truth. These cunning men who formed the gang might use the Home with impunity, if they exercised care in their movements and maintained silence. Frankly, he acknowledged the reasonableness of Mr. Dearborn's argument.

"I quite appreciate the possibility," he said. "It is rather unfortunate for you as well as for me. It might have been a great deal more unfortunate," he added with truth. Though how unfortunately this adventure might have ended he had to learn when the girl told her story on the way to Scotland Yard.

"Dreadful, dreadful!" he shuddered. "My poor, poor child!"

His own relief had been so great that he felt physically ill. But no such reaction was visible in the girl, who grew calmer and brighter as the taxi neared Scotland Yard. She wore his raincoat, and they had stopped in the Edgware Road to allow her to buy a blouse, for she insisted upon going to Scotland Yard first to make her statement.

"I'm rather sorry for Dearborn," he said. "He is a pathetic figure. Men who devote their lives to this kind of work may be excused even their feeble dramatic efforts. Did you notice how eagerly he shook hands with you?"

The Dark Eyes of London

She looked at him sharply.

"Yes, I noticed that," she said in a strange tone.

"Why, Diana," he said, "what do you mean?"

"Oh, nothing," she said lightly. "I mean that he took my hand, that is all, and shook it very heartily."

"Well, there's nothing in that," said Larry with a smile.

"There is a great deal in that," said the girl, "a great deal more than you can realize."

He leaned back in the cab and laughed softly.

"You're going to mystify me. I can feel it coming on," he said, and she squeezed his arm affectionately.

He sent her up to 47 alone, and she had changed her torn blouse for the new purchase by the time he discreetly knocked at the door.

"By the way," he said, "I forgot to ask you. Where did you dig up that deadly-looking weapon I saw in your hand as you were coming down the stairs?"

"From Blind Jake's pocket," she said. "Ugh! It was horrid touching him, but I wanted to be quite sure that I had some kind of weapon."

"Undoubtedly you have a big end of the story," he said. "We know now that Blind Jake and the man Lew——"

"Have you left him there?" she asked quickly.

He smiled a little wryly.

"I've made too many mistakes in this case to add to them," he said. "No, I have taken this man to another institution where he is being looked after. Lew and Jake were the two men who were employed, either before or after the murder of Gordon Stuart," he went on. "The gang has probably got a hold on Lew, and he was anxious to escape from their clutches or to be avenged upon them for some treachery they have committed, and he wrote the message which we found—on the strip of paper with the Braille characters. That fines the search down to one man, because we can find means of inducing Lew to understand whose hands he is in."

"And the greatest discovery of all you haven't touched," she said quietly.

Larry got up from his chair, laughing, and paced the room, a favourite occupation of his.

"You're an extraordinary girl," he said. "No sooner do I think I have got the case set, than you produce something new, something more important in the shape of clues, and something generally," he added pensively, "that upsets all my previous theories."

"I don't think this will," she said. "I am referring to the woman upstairs."

"What woman upstairs?" he asked, astounded.

"Do you remember I told you that Jake pointed with his thumb to the ceiling, and said if I had a face like hers——" She stopped.

"I'm sorry," he said gently. "I'm a brute and a forgetful brute; but things have happened to-day which have driven the Stuart case out of my mind. And that reminds me," he said, "I want to telephone."

He called a number, and she recognized it as the number of the Trafalgar Hospital.

"I want the matron's office, please," he said, and whilst she was wondering where his mind had led him, he said: "Is that you, matron? It is I, Larry Holt. Yes, how do you do? Are the nurses you send out to cases having a slack time? I mean, are there plenty to go round? There are? Well, will you send a nice motherly lady to my address at Regent's Gate Gardens? You know where I live? No, I'm not ill," he smiled, "but I have somebody with me who isn't too well—yes, a lady."

He hung up the receiver and turned to meet the girl's astonished eyes.

"Have you a lady staying with you?" she asked.

"I haven't, but I shall have," said Larry. "You're not going back to Charing Cross Road to-night except to get the things you require; you're coming up to my flat, and there you're going to stay, chaperoned by a very nice nurse, and you'll greatly oblige me if you'll pretend that you're a little bit under the weather. I must save my face."

"But I can't, it's impossible!" she said, scarlet of face. "I couldn't——"

"Oh, yes, you could," said Larry. "Now you're going to do as I tell you. Otherwise, it means that I must sit outside your flat all night catching my

The Dark Eyes of London

death of cold."

Finally she consented. They dined together, and he took her to see two acts of the Dearborn play. They came out at the end of the second act, bewildered.

"But how could anybody put such awful stuff on the stage?" asked the girl on their way to his flat.

"It is rather amazing, isn't it?"

Then Larry began to chuckle.

"You're easily amused to-day," she said.

"I'm very happy to-night," he corrected. "It just occurred to me that Sunny will have to meet the nurse when she comes."

"Whatever will he say?" she gasped.

"Well," drawled Larry, "if the nurse insists there's a lady ill in the house, Sunny will say, 'Yes, madam,' and will do his best to produce one!"

It was past eleven when they got to the flat. The elevators had stopped running at half-past ten, and they had to walk up the stairs.

"Watch your step," warned Larry. "They light these stairways abominably."

He went first, and she saw him pause on the top step of the second flight.

"Great Scott! Who's that?" he asked.

Against his door a man was lying, doubled up and still. Larry leant over him and rang the bell, and Sunny came to the door.

In the flood of light thrown by the hall lamp, Larry saw the face of the prostrate figure. He was breathing stertorously, and his face and his head streamed with blood.

"Sunny, has the nurse arrived?"

"Yes, sir," said Sunny, looking down at the figure.

"Then she'll be wanted," said Larry quietly.

"Who is it?" asked Diana, peering round behind him.

"Flash Fred," said Larry, "and as near to dead as makes no difference."

"John Dearborn Is Not Blind"

THEY carried the injured man into the sitting-room and laid him on a

122

couch. There was a doctor living in the flat above and luckily he had not gone to bed, and was down in a few minutes.

"He is badly injured," he reported. "There are one or two knife wounds, and the wound in the head looks as though there were a fracture of the skull."

"The man must have been attacked outside my door," said Larry. "He couldn't have walked far in this condition."

"No," said the doctor, shaking his head. "He might have walked two or three yards, but the chances are, as you found him outside the door, that he was there when the attack was made on him. Do you know him?"

"Yes," said Larry, "he is an old acquaintance of mine. Is there any danger of his dying?"

"A very big danger," replied the doctor gravely. "That concussion may be anything. I should send him straight away to hospital, where he can be thoroughly examined and, if necessary, operated upon."

The ambulance had come and gone, and the only evidence of Flash Fred's visit was a few dark stains about the door, before Larry began to think consecutively.

The nurse who had arrived fulfilled all his telephoned requirements. She was stout and jovial and matronly, and the first use Larry made of his freedom from distraction was to tell her in a few words just why she had been sent for.

"Obviously I could not allow Miss Ward to go back to Charing Cross Road after her terrible experience to-day," he said, and Nurse James, who was by no means dissatisfied with having so easy a "case," agreed.

She exercised her authority to the extent of ordering Diana to bed immediately, and the girl meekly obeyed. But she could not sleep. At two o'clock Larry, writing at his table, heard the creak of an opening door and looked up to see her. She was in her dressing-gown, and her hair was braided in a long golden plait.

"I can't sleep," she said restlessly, almost irritably, and he saw that she was overstrung and rose to get an arm-chair for her.

The Dark Eyes of London

She neither apologized for her attire nor her visitation, and these circumstances struck Larry as curious. But that which was on Diana Ward's mind was of so great an importance that the thought of decorum did not occur to her. She sat there, her hands folded on her lap, and there was no sound save the tick of a clock on the mantelpiece and the squeak of Larry's chair as it turned.

"What is troubling you, Diana?" he asked.

She looked up at him quickly.

"Do you think I'm troubled?" she said.

"If you're not, you're a wonderful girl," said Larry gently. "You've had an awful time to-day, my dear, but somehow I do not think that that is what is on your mind."

She shook her head.

"It isn't," and added, "it is the woman upstairs."

"The woman upstairs? Oh, you mean the woman that Jake spoke about? But, Diana, there was no 'upstairs'. You were on the top floor of that building, which is a story lower than Todd's Home."

But still she was not satisfied.

"Besides," he went on quietly, "if she had been there, the woman may have been—as bad a character as any of the other occupants of that house. The fact that she was unpleasant to look at, as Jake suggested, does not make her innocent."

"Poor soul, poor soul!" said the girl, and then to Larry's horror she began to weep softly. "I can't sleep for thinking of her," she sobbed. "They will keep her, they dare not let her go!"

"Why," he gasped suddenly, "you don't suggest that she is Clarissa Stuart?"

She looked up at that, her face stained with tears.

"Clarissa Stuart?" she repeated slowly. "No, I don't think she is Clarissa Stuart."

"Then who is she?" he asked. "At any rate, who do you think she is?"

"I don't think—I am sure," she said, speaking with painful slowness. "That woman was Emma, the charwoman of the boarding-house," and Larry jumped to his feet.

"The charwoman," he said slowly. "You're right!"

Again the tick of the little clock asserted itself as they sat, each busy with their own thoughts.

"You connect this terrible gang with the Stuart mystery?" he said.

She nodded.

"I also connect them," said Larry, "for very excellent reasons. And yet I cannot see what they gained by Stuart's death, unless they were in league with this girl who calls herself Clarissa Stuart?"

She made a hopeless little gesture and rose.

"I can connect them all," she said. "They are very distinct in their relationships, but then," with a faint smile, "I have an advantage over you."

"You have many advantages over me," said Larry, humouring her. "And now, dear, you must go back and sleep."

But she did not heed him.

"There is only one I did not connect," she went on, "and you have made his case understandable."

"Who is that?"

"Flash Fred," she replied. "He is just a criminal who has touched the fringe of the conspiracy and has been in it without knowing he was in it." She nodded as though she had only at that moment decided her point of view. "But the others? Blind Jake who works for an unknown master; the charwoman, the greatest victim of them all; poor Lew, with his deaf ears and his blistered fingers—you didn't see those. I should have told you, only the doctor interrupted us."

"Blistered fingers?" said Larry in amazement. "No, I didn't see them."

"I felt them," she shuddered, "when he touched my face. His fingers and thumbs have been blistered at the tops."

"But why?"

"So that he shall not read Braille or write Braille," said the girl quietly.

"It's impossible, impossible!" said Larry in horror. "There cannot be such villainy in the world. My child, I have been acquainted with some of the worst crimes that have ever been committed in Europe. I have seen the victims, I have tracked and hanged the criminals. Men are cruel, vicious, unscrupulous and bloody-minded, but they do not commit such cold-blooded deeds as you say have been committed upon that poor blind man."

She smiled again.

"I don't think you realize just how bad these people are," she said. "For if you did, you would never say that it was impossible. For Dearborn——" she began, and he laughed outright.

"Diana, dear, you've reached the stage which we always reach, when you're suspicious of everybody! Not of poor John Dearborn, working for the good of humanity in that slum, and amidst those fearful people?"

She nodded.

"I shook hands with John Dearborn when I went there. I shook hands with him when I came away," she said.

"That doesn't make him a criminal," he smiled.

"And when I offered my hand he took it," she said. "Please remember that I was a nurse in a blind asylum for two years—when I offered my hand he took it."

"Well, why shouldn't he?" asked Larry in surprise.

"He shouldn't have seen it," said the girl, "if he was blind. And John Dearborn is no more blind than you or I!"

Who Runs Dearborn?

SAY THAT again," said Larry slowly. "You offered your hand and he took it?"

She nodded.

"Don't you know that when you shake hands with the blind, you always reach out and take their hand, because they cannot see yours offered; but Dearborn raised his just as soon as I raised mine."

Larry was staring helplessly at her.

"If he is not blind, why is he there?" he asked. "He is a clergyman."

"There is no John Dearborn in the Clergy List," said the girl calmly. "I went carefully through the list; and he is not amongst the Congregational, the Baptist, or the Wesleyan ministers."

Larry looked at her, lost in admiration.

"You're a wonder! But don't forget that he came from Australia."

"The Australian lists are available," said the girl immediately, "and the only John Dearborn is an aged gentleman who lives at Totooma, and is obviously not our John Dearborn."

She had come to the table and had drawn a chair up close. She now leant forward, her hands clasped in front of her.

"Larry," she said—"I'm going to call you Larry out of office hours—has it not struck you as strange that John Dearborn's plays should be produced at a theatre, remembering that he has written a succession of failures?"

"I've always thought that," Larry admitted, and she nodded her head.

"I wish you would look into the directorate of the Macready," she said. "Find out what comprises the syndicate which puts up the money for producing these plays. I don't forget that Mr. Stuart disappeared from that theatre."

"Nor I," said Larry quietly. "But John Dearborn! You amaze me."

She rose.

"I feel sleepy now that I have got that off my mind," she smiled. "Are you"—she hesitated—"watching the laundry?"

"I have two men there who are instructed to stop any car coming out and discover who is the driver and what the car contains."

"Then I can go to bed cheerfully," she said with a little laugh, and passing him, she rested her hand gently on his head. "They will keep—Emma alive for some time yet. The only danger is that they may take her away from the laundry."

"You can rest your mind on that," said Larry quietly, and with this assurance she went to bed and he heard her door close.

The next day was uneventful. The police had made a further search of the laundry, and had discovered a room above that in which the girl had been imprisoned. It was a very tiny attic apartment, but showed signs of having been occupied, though it was empty when the police made their call.

Larry cursed himself that he had not made a more thorough inspection of the premises. He had been so relieved at the discovery of the girl that he had not been as painstaking as he should have been—this he told himself disgustedly.

There were two people whom he desired greatly to meet. The first of these was the man who had lost the little finger of his left hand. That curious individual who had preceded him the day he was investigating the reason for Gordon Stuart's mysterious visits to a country churchyard. The second was the mysterious Emma. In his heart of hearts he knew that Emma would supply the key which would unlock the door to great and conclusive revelations.

"I shall never forgive myself," he told Diana, "if any harm comes to this woman."

She shook her head.

"You need not fear that they will do her harm," she said. "She is much too valuable, and I shall know just when her danger period commences."

"You!" he said in surprise. "Really, Diana, you scare me sometimes."

She laughed, and her laughter was drowned in the rattle of her typewriter.

"Flash Fred has not recovered consciousness yet," he told her, "but there's a big chance that he will. The doctors say that there is no actual fracture, and that there is a possibility that the pressure which now keeps him unconscious will disperse."

"Where is he?" she asked.

"In St. Mary's Hospital," replied Larry. "I have him in a private ward with a police officer on guard. Not that poor Fred could escape," he smiled, "but there are people in this city who will probably be most anxious that he escapes by the only way which leaves them safe . . ."

She did not need to ask which way that was. He put down the pen he had been holding, though he had done very little writing.

"It wouldn't be a bad idea if we went along to St. Mary's and discovered at first hand how the man is," he said. "Will you come?"

As she put on her hat before the four-inch square of looking-glass which she had imported into the building, she asked, without turning her head:

"What are you going to do about John Dearborn?"

Larry rubbed his chin.

"I hardly know," he said. "It is not an offence for a man to pretend to be blind if he isn't. Besides," he continued, "he might have had sufficient sight to have seen your hand. There may be a dozen explanations. He could have offered his hand mechanically, almost instinctively."

She nodded.

"It is possible," she said quietly, "but he smiled too when I smiled."

"Who wouldn't?" said Larry gallantly.

In the business-like office of the senior house surgeon at St. Mary's they met the surgeon in charge of the case.

"You've come at a very fortunate moment," he smiled. "Your man has recovered consciousness."

"Can he talk?" asked Larry eagerly.

"I think so. At any rate, I see no particular reason why he shouldn't, if there is urgent necessity for your questioning him. Naturally, he is still very weak, and in ordinary circumstances I should not allow anybody to interview him; but I gather that you have particular police business."

"Very particular," said Larry grimly.

The surgeon led the way to the ward. At the door of the ward the girl hesitated.

"Shall I come?" she said.

"Your presence is necessary," said Larry, "if it is only in a professional capacity. Have you got your note-book?"

She nodded and they went into the little private ward where Fred Grogan lay. His head was swathed in bandages and his face was white and drawn, but his eyes lit up at the sight of Larry.

"I never expected to look forward to seeing you," he said. "But first of all, governor,"—his voice was earnest—"you ought to get hold of that woman in the boiler-house."

The Dark Eyes of London

"The woman in the boiler-house?" repeated Larry quickly. "What do you mean?"

"Clarissa's nurse," was the staggering reply; "and who 'Clarissa' is, the Lord knows!"

Flash Fred's Story

NOW I'M going to give it to you straight, governor," said Fred, settling himself comfortably in bed. "I won't say that I couldn't tell a lie—that's the one saying of Napoleon's that I've never believed."

"The same period, but another man," said Larry, concealing a smile; "but don't worry about your history, Fred. I want you to get this story off your mind as quickly as you can."

"I've done a lot of reading in my time," said the sick man reminiscently. "Histories and high-class novels—they've got a pretty good library in Portland Prison, but they're not so good as the books you get in Wormwood Scrubs. Anyway, I am going to tell you the truth, Mr. Holt. I might as well start at the beginning, and I know I'm going to put myself in wrong, but you'll have to forget a lot of the things I tell you, because they make me look as if I was a dishonest person."

"I should hate that impression to get abroad," said Larry without a smile, "and I promise you that anything which doesn't relate directly to the murder of Gordon Stuart will be discreetly forgotten."

"Cheerio!" said Fred, visibly brighter. "Well, this story begins about four or five years ago in Montpellier. You don't know Montpellier, perhaps?"

"I know it," said Larry. "You can cut out all the topographical details. I know it from the Coq d'Or to the Palace."

"I happened to be there," said Fred, "looking round and enjoying myself, and I drifted into a little game that was run by a man named Floquart on the quiet. It was baccarat, and I'm very lucky at baccarat, especially when I've made friends with the dealer. But this time the dealer and me weren't on speaking terms, as you might say, and for three days I never felt money that wasn't my own. And each day there was less of my own to feel. Then one night they cleaned me out proper, and I left Floquart's with just enough to get me home to the hotel if I walked.

"I was turning out of the rue Narbonne when I heard a shot, and, looking across the place, I saw a man lying on the ground and another fellow walking away pretty slick. In those days the police arrangements at Montpellier weren't all they could have been, and there wasn't a gendarme in sight. The fellow who was walking must have thought he'd got away with it, when I suddenly came up to him. There was just enough light, for the day was breaking, for me to distinguish his face. A fine-looking fellow he was, with a big yellow beard, and I think he was scared sick when I suddenly stepped out and claimed him as my own. It was not my business to butt into private disturbances, but you understand that I was broke, and I thought that here was a chance of helping a fellow creature in distress to get rid of any incriminating money he might have in his possession. He told me a yarn that the man he'd shot had done him a very bad injury, which I won't refer to in front of the young lady, and then he slipped me about sixteen thousand francs and I let him go, because I was sorry for him."

He glanced slyly up at Larry and grinned.

"Well," he went on, "seeing that no gendarme had appeared, I walked over and had a look at the lad who was shot, though I knew I was taking a risk by being seen in the company of a soon-to-croak. They say he was shot and must have died immediately, but that isn't true: he was alive when I got to him, and when I was bending over him, it was to find out if I could do anything for the poor devil before he passed out. I asked him who had shot him, and he replied"—he paused impressively—'David Judd.'?"

Larry's eyebrows went up.

"David Judd?" he asked. "Is he any relation to the doctor?"

"His brother," said Fred. "That's how I came to know him. I've always told Judd that I recognized him in the street; as a matter of fact, it was the poor guy on the ground who gave him away. I was trying to find out why he was shot, when he croaked. I knew there was nothing to be gained by being found attached to a murdered man, though fortunately I hadn't a gun in my possession and could have proved an alibi. Then I heard a gendarme's heavy feet coming down one of the side turnings, and I got away as quickly as I could. But the swine recognized me, though, and I had to go before an examining magistrate and prove that I had nothing to do with the murder and that I was going for a doctor when I was spotted. I had the good sense to go for a doctor," he added, "the moment I realized that the copper had seen me."

He paused, finding it rather difficult to explain his subsequent action in language which would be wholly creditable to himself.

"When I got back to London I thought it my duty to call on Mr. David Judd," he said. "He wasn't in his office—he used to have a room at the Greenwich Insurance—but I saw his brother, and I unloaded my trouble."

"Your trouble being to discover how much they'd 'drop' for keeping your mouth shut, I suppose," said Larry.

"You've got it at once, Mr. Holt. What a mind!" said the admiring Fred. "He was terribly upset, was Dr. Judd, and said he would see his brother as soon as he came back from the country. And then happened an event which looked like spoiling all my beautiful prospects. Dr. David died. He caught a cold coming down from Scotland and died in twenty-four hours. I went to the funeral," said Fred, "as a mourner, and I bet that nobody mourned more than I did. Anyway, I must say that Dr. Judd acted like a gentleman. He sent for me after his brother's funeral and said that he wanted to save his brother's memory from disgrace, and offered me a yearly income if I would keep my mouth shut."

"The man who was killed was a clerk, was he not?" asked Larry.

"He was a clerk," said Fred slowly, "a clerk in the employ of the Greenwich Insurance Company, who had blackmailed David Judd."

Larry whistled softly.

"The Greenwich Insurance Company," he said; "and blackmailed David! Why, what crime had David committed?"

Fred shook his head.

"I can't tell you that, Mr. Holt. If I could, I would. But it was something pretty bad, you can bet. Dr. Judd said that this clerk had pinched a lot of money, and I think that's true, because I remember his playing, and playing very high, at Floquart's.

"Well, to cut this story short, I've drawn about four years' income from Dr. Judd. I'm not apologizing or trying to prove to you that I acted like a little gentleman; that doesn't interest you, anyway. The other day I met the doctor at a wedding. He was invited, but I wasn't," explained Fred shamelessly, "but that didn't make any difference: I went. He asked me if I'd go to dinner with him last night at his house in Chelsea. He's got a real fine house, has Dr. Judd, full of wonderful pictures and sparklers. And as he was going to pay me a lump sum to get rid of me, I decided to go.

"There is a man at the doctor's," he said after a pause, "a valet. I don't want to give him away, Mr. Holt, but he's an old lag and was in the next cell to me at Portland."

"His name is Strauss," said Larry. "He takes drugs, and has had three convictions."

"Oh, you know that, do you?" said Fred in surprise. "Well, anyway, I know him. I met him in Piccadilly the other day. He was going to fence a few articles that he'd pinched from his boss, and he dropped me a pair of sleeve-links——"

Larry gasped.

"Oh, that is where they came from; they were Dr. Judd's?"

"I ain't so sure that they were Dr. Judd's," said Fred. "From what I have heard, the doctor has people who stay with him over week-ends, and Strauss may have pinched them from one of these. Anyway"—again he hesitated, finding it difficult to express his plans in such a manner as would save him from the charge of ingratitude—"I had an idea of helping myself to a few souvenirs of Dr. Judd before I went," he explained, "and I'd fixed it up with Strauss so that I could just look over the premises and pick a few things that would remind me of my old friend. So when I was asked to dinner, naturally I jumped at the chance. I don't say that I'd have gone alone to dinner, because the doctor and me aren't quite bosom companions; but he told me

The Dark Eyes of London

that there was a lot of people coming, so I went. I was supposed to go at eight, which is well after dark, but I went at seven, and not to the house but to the opposite side of the street, because I was anxious to see Dr. Judd's guests arrive before I got in. I waited till eight and nobody came. I waited till half-past eight, and then I saw the doctor come out and look up and down the road. I was so hungry that I nearly went over to him, but I didn't see myself dining alone with a fellow that I've been swindling. So I waited and waited, and presently a motor-car drove up and went straight to the gates at the side of the house. I thought he was going to push them in, but the moment the head-lamps touched the gates they opened. 'That's funny,' says I to myself, and I crossed the road and had a look over the top of the gate. It meant a bit of a climb, but I did it without making any noise; and the first fellow that got out of the car was that big stiff who tried to croak me in Jermyn Street."

"Blind Jake?" said Larry.

"I've never been introduced," replied the other sardonically. "I saw him plain for a minute because he passed in front of the head-lamps, and then the lights went out and I saw nothing more. At ten o'clock the gates opened—like magic it was, for there was nobody near them—and a car came out. It passed me, going slow, and I ran behind and jumped on to the luggage-carrier, which was down. I got off as it went into the King's Road, Chelsea, because there is a lot of light there and a copper might have seen me and given me away. But there were plenty of taxis about, and I hired one and told him to keep the car in sight. I wanted to know where Blind Jake—that's his name, is it?—was living, and I didn't have much difficulty in keeping the car in sight. We went up past Victoria, along Grosvenor Place, up Park Lane. I was afraid the car would turn into the park, for private cars are allowed there but taxis aren't, and I should have lost him. But, luckily or unluckily, it didn't. The car went up Edgware Road—Tyburn Tree, where they hanged them in the old days, used to be there," he said, apropos of nothing. "I read that in a book when I was in stir."

"Cut out those memories of Old London," begged Larry.

"I followed up close behind, and then the machine turned into some side-streets," said Fred, "and I took the risk of paying off the cabman and following on foot. I know that district pretty well, and I hadn't been searching for ten minutes before I saw the car pulling up against a gate which was set into a high wall. The driver must have missed the way, because I was there almost as soon as the doctor."

"Dr. Judd? Was he there?" asked Larry.

Flash Fred nodded, and was very sorry for himself that he had done so. It was some time before he could speak again.

"If I don't keep my blinking head still," he said good-humouredly, "I shall lose it. Yes, the doctor was there. I was close up to them; as a matter of fact, I was standing behind the car when they all three got out. Blind Jake was one; a fellow I didn't recognize was another, and the doctor was the third. He had a bag in his hand, and he seemed to be a bit put out.

'I protest against being sent for at this hour of the night,' he said.

"The other man, not Blind Jake, said something in a low voice which I didn't catch.

'Why couldn't you have got another doctor? Remember that you have forced me to come here, and I come under protest. Where is this woman?' he asked, and I don't think the reply was intended for my ears, for the big blind man said, 'In the boiler-house,' and laughed, and the other fellow turned to him with a curse and told him to keep quiet.

"They went through the gates, and presently the car moved on. I think it had to turn, and the street wasn't wide enough. The gate was locked and it had been painted black, but I saw that the word 'Laundry' had been there before the new coat had been put on."

"Did you notice the name of the street?" asked Larry.

"Reville Street," said the other, to Larry's surprise, and then he remembered.

"That is the street behind and running parallel with Lissom Lane," he said. "Go on, Fred."

"Well, I had to slip away; otherwise I should have been seen. I went all round the houses and came back behind it, just as the doctor came out, and this time there were only two of them; the big blind man had gone. I couldn't hear what they were talking about, but presently I heard the doctor say good night and the car drove off. The other man was looking after the tail-lights, and I had nothing to do but to slouch past as though I had been coming along, walking all the time. If there's one bad habit that's worse than another," said Fred reflectively, "it's talking to yourself, whether you talk in your sleep or while you're awake. But there are some men who can't help it. There was a pal of mine in Barcelona—however, I won't talk about him, Mr. Holt. Well, this man that was left standing was one of that kind. A brooder, I should think. And before I got opposite to him, I heard him muttering, as he stood stock-still, his hands behind him, looking after the car; and the words that I heard as I passed were these. I remember them—sort of committed them to memory. And the words were: 'Clarissa's nurse.' He said it twice. I walked on, never dreaming that he'd spotted me, and as I walked I thought: 'Now the best thing you can do, Fred, is to go straight to Mr. Holt and tell him what you've seen and what you've heard.'?"

Larry nodded.

"I was only a few hundred yards from your house, so I made up my mind I'd do it. I hadn't gone very far when I got an uncomfortable feeling that I was being followed. I couldn't see anybody, but I had that creepy sensation that you get when the splits are after you, and I couldn't shake it off. I got into your street and began looking for the block where your flat was. I passed it once and was directed back here; and I think that the people who were following me must have slipped in and got upstairs and were waiting for me when I came up. I remember putting my hand up to the knocker of your flat, and then I don't remember anything more."

The girl had been writing rapidly, and now she closed her book.

"I think that's about all," said Fred weakly. "I'd like a drink."

Ten minutes later two motor-cars laden with plain-clothes officers were on their way westward, and the inhabitants of the little street upon which the laundry backed were interested spectators of another raid.

"What is this wall?" asked Larry of his assistant.

"It is the wall of the laundry building proper," said Harvey. "I inspected it very carefully, but there was nothing there."

"Did you see the boiler-house?"

"Yes, sir, it is a very ordinary underground room with one large boiler and a steam engine."

"Get that door open," said Larry. "You have got some men in Lissom Lane to watch the other gate?"

"Yes, sir," reported the sergeant, and with an expert hand he manipulated the lock and presently the door swung wide.

The room into which the door directly led was in darkness. It proved, when lights were obtained, to be a long brick shed, with a concrete floor, and four rows of trestles down the centre, where, in the days of the laundry, the washerwomen worked. A flight of steps, guarded by a rail, went down to a lower floor, and Larry led the way into the boiler-house.

In the Tubular Room

YOU OUGHT to be ashamed of yourself," said Blind Jake, shaking his huge head.

He sat huddled up at one side of the tubular room, and his remarks were addressed to a wretched-looking woman who sat on the other side, her arms folded on her knees, her head bent in dejection. She was miserably clad; her hanging hair was streaked with grey, and her hands and face were grimy.

The room itself could hardly be described as a room. It was like an enlarged gas main. The floor was littered with fragments of rubble and broken concrete. One end was a steel door, just large enough for a medium-sized person to squeeze through, and the other was a jagged hole torn in the steel wall, and disclosing beyond a black void which, in the light of the candle, was also littered with rubbish.

"You ought to be ashamed of yourself," reproved Blind Jake. "Here are They doing all They can for ye, ye ugly old devil, and ye're whining and snarling! Like a pup who's had his tail bit!"

The woman moaned and said something.

"You'd have something to snivel about if I had my way," said Blind Jake. "Don't we feed ye? Didn't we give ye a good bed to lie on, till that dog came nosing about?"

"I want to go away," said the woman. "You're killing me here."

"Not yet," said Blind Jake with a chuckle. "Maybe. They'll want ye killed, and then ye'll be killed, sure."

"I want to go out of this horrible place," cried the woman with a sob. "Why am I here?"

"Do ye want to be down with the rats?" growled Blind Jake. "Didn't ye squeak and squeal when I took ye down in the long passage under the street, because the little fellows squeaked at you? And now ye're safe and sound where a rat couldn't get ye, and to-morrow you're going into a nice house to live, with fine sheets on your bed. You ungrateful old devil!"

She raised her woebegone face and looked at the blind man curiously.

"You talk about 'em as though they were gods," she said. "One of these days they'll betray you——"

"Shut up!" snapped the man. "You don't know 'em! What have they done for me? They've given me a lovely life—all the money I want, everything I can eat and drink. They gave me a young wife," he chuckled, but the chuckle ended with a hideous distortion of face. "I'll have her yet; she nearly killed me, that wench."

"Who was she?" asked the woman.

"Never ye mind. Nobody ye know," said Jake, but did not seem disinclined to talk on the matter. "A young, white, sleek girl she was," he said. "They wanted her because she's police too."

She was silent for so long that he leant forward and touched her with his big hand.

"You're not having a fit, are ye?" he said with a note of anxiety. "Not another one of them fits? We can't always bring a doctor. The next time I'll rouse ye," he said menacingly. "I'll make ye wake." He shook her savagely.

"I'm awake, I'm awake," she said, terrified. "Please don't do that; you will break my arm."

"Well, behave yourself," he grumbled, and then began to crawl slowly towards the farther end of the tubular room. Even the woman, though she was far from tall, could not have stood upright in that cramped space. It was wonderful how a man so big could manœuvre himself through the jagged hole in the steel and crawl into the space beyond. She heard him tossing bricks about and enlarging the cavity at which he had been working all the day. She wondered where she was, for she had been a sick woman when she had been dragged into that terrible chamber, and had no recollection of how she had come in. Only she knew that people were searching for her, and that the awful forces which now held her prisoner were determined that she should not be found. She had been hidden in the depths of the earth, in hideous places alive with terrifying life, and this at least was better.

When he came back she said:

"Mr. Stuart would give you a lot of money if you took me to him."

He chuckled.

"Ye've told me that a hundred times, ye fool!" he said, and mimicked her: 'If you take me to Mr. Stuart he'll give ye a lot of money!' A lot of money he'll give me!"

"I nursed his children," she wailed, "and his poor wife. And when I got married he gave me a beautiful wedding ring."

"Aw, shut up!" snarled the man. "Haven't ye got anything more to talk about? A hundred million times ye've told me about nursing his babies and your blasted wedding ring!"

"When I told him about Clarissa, he said he'd give me a thousand pounds," whispered the woman. "I was that surprised to see him I nearly fell down!"

Blind Jake ignored her. He had heard this story before, and it had lost all its novelty.

"He never knew about the twins, and thought he had no children alive."

"If ye hadn't been a hook or a soak, y' could have told him where she was; but don't worry yer head: They've found her. A fine lady she is, with plenty of money! I heard 'em say that she was a fine lady with plenty of money," he added simply.

His faith in these mysterious employers of his knew no bounds.

"I was fond of my drop," confessed the half-witted woman, "and they sent me to prison for nothing at all. And the home was awful!"

Suddenly Blind Jake lurched forward and dropped his hands upon her shoulders. She opened her mouth to scream, but he put his face close to hers.

"If y' squeal ye're dead, my lady! Be quiet!"

His sensitive ears had caught the sound of footsteps on the floor above, though they were so completely deadened that none but a blind man would have heard them. He crept closer to her side, put one great arm around her shoulder, the other he held just in front of her face.

"If y' squeal, ye're dead," he said again, and then somebody knocked at the little door at the end of the chamber and the voice of Larry Holt demanded:

"Is there anybody here?"

Fred Lends His Keys

IT HAD been Diana Ward who had called Larry's attention to the great rusty boiler at one end of the house, the boiler which had supplied the steam and the power for the laundry. Larry tried the thick iron door which opened into the furnace, but it was fast. He tugged again and it did not move.

"Nobody could be here," he said, shaking his head. "What do you think, Harvey?"

"They would suffocate anyway in there, sir," replied Sergeant Harvey.

The girl was looking distressed.

"Is there nowhere else?" she asked. "I did hope——"

She did not finish her words.

"No, miss, we've searched the whole of the place now," said the sergeant. "Would you like that door forced open, sir?" he asked. "It will take some hours."

Larry shook his head.

"No, I don't think so," he said. "I am inclined to agree with you that if anybody was concealed in the boiler, supposing there were room enough, which is unlikely, they would die of suffocation."

"Do you think," asked the girl as they came away, "that Mr. Grogan was telling the truth? I know he was," she added quickly. "I don't know why I ask such stupid questions."

"Oh, he was telling the truth all right," said Larry. "Fred isn't a model of virtue, but in this case, I believe him. It's just the luck of the game," he said bitterly. "Sometimes I feel that I'm never going to fathom this mystery."

"It will be solved, and solved within a week," she said, and she spoke with such assurance that he could only stare at her.

"Then you're going to solve it," he said, "for I have reached the point, and it is the most dangerous point that a detective can arrive at, when I am suspicious of everybody. Suspicious of Dr. Judd, of the innocent Mr. Dearborn, of Flash Fred, the Chief Commissioner, and you," he added good-humouredly. But she did not smile.

"I wondered how long it would be before you suspected me," she said gravely.

She went off with Harvey and he returned to the hospital, for he had a few more questions to ask the injured crook.

Flash Fred listened attentively, and when Larry had finished:

"God knows I have never trusted a policeman in my life," he said piously, "but I think you're different, Mr. Holt. In one of my pockets you will find the key of my safe deposit. The hospital people have the clothes. It's the deposit in Chancery Lane, and I'm trusting you," he said whimsically. "There are things in that box that I shouldn't like anybody to see, but you will find what you are looking for without disturbing them. There's a bundle of war stock," he said uneasily, "which I bought by the sweat of my brow."

"Somebody sweated, I'll bet," said Larry cheerfully. "You needn't be afraid, Fred, I shan't pry into your secrets, nor shall I use anything I find there to jail you."

Fred was ill at ease.

"I knew I was taking a risk when I told you about this business," he said, "because you were certain to go farther in it, and I was just as certain to help you. If I'd been out and about, it would have been easy, because I could have given you the keys."

"What are the keys?" asked Larry.

"They're duplicates that I had made," said Fred without a blush. "Strauss got them from the doctor's key-ring when he was asleep and took the impressions. Strauss ain't a bad fellow, but he dopes; I never did hold with those evil practices," said the virtuous Fred. "You want a clean eye and a clear brain to get on in life, don't you, Mr. Holt?"

"And eight nimble fingers, plus two nippy thumbs," said Larry.

He secured the keys without difficulty, and half an hour later he walked into Room 47, humming a tune and jingling Flash Fred's nefarious possessions in his pocket.

Diana, after a great deal of persuasion, had been induced to take up her residence under Larry's eye. The motherly nurse had become a permanent institution at Regent's Gate Gardens, a circumstance which was not wholly to the liking of Mr. Patrick Sunny, who found himself forced to sleep on a camp bed in the kitchen.

"I am sorry to inconvenience you, Sunny," said Larry Holt that night, "and it is an inconvenience, I suppose?"

"Yes, sir," said Sunny. "It is an inconvenience."

"Not a painful one, I hope."

"No, sir," said Sunny. "It is not a painful one."

"The lady was in danger," said Larry, and this Sunny knew because the matter had been discussed very freely in his presence, "and it was impossible to leave her in her apartment."

"Yes, sir," agreed Sunny. "What collar will you be wearing to-day, sir?"

"Any old collar," said Larry with a smile. "Anyway, Sunny, the lady is safe sleeping in this flat."

"No, sir," said Sunny, and Larry was shocked, for it was the first time in his life that Sunny had ever disagreed with him.

"No?" he said incredulously. "Didn't you hear what I said? I said the lady is safe here."

"No, sir," said Sunny. "I'm very sorry, sir, and I beg your pardon."

"But no you mean, I suppose? Why isn't she safe?"

"Because you're not safe, sir," said Sunny calmly, "and if you're not safe, the lady's not safe, sir."

Larry laughed.

"All right, have your own way," he said; "and, Sunny——"

"Yes, sir."

"Will you close the kitchen door to-night? I could hear you turning around in your bed and it woke me up."

"Very good, sir, I will close the kitchen door," said Sunny, and in truth he did.

After Larry had gone to bed and the flat was in silence, Sunny carried his little camp-bedstead into the hall, placed it so that its foot was about fifteen inches from the door, balanced a broom, the head against the door, the end of the handle resting on the bed, and then he retired. But he shut the kitchen door.

At two o'clock in the morning a key was placed noiselessly in the lock and the door was pushed open a few inches, and the broom fell ruthlessly on Sunny's head. It might have brained him, but, by a fortunate accident, didn't.

Larry heard three shots fired in rapid succession and leapt out of bed and came into the passage, gun in hand. He saw an empty camp-bedstead, an open door, but Sunny was gone. He ran down the stairs and met that worthy man returning, leading by the collar a diminutive ruffian, upon whose evil face was stamped a twisted grin of pain, for he had a bullet in the fleshy part of his leg.

"Bring him in," said Larry, and closed the door.

Diana was standing in the passage when the man was marched through and hastily withdrew, to reappear again at the informal inquiry which Larry instituted.

It was an inquiry prefaced by a respectful apology on the part of Sunny.

"I beg your pardon, sir, for taking the loan of your pistol," he said, "and as to my bed being in the passage and disturbing you——"

"Say no more about that, Sunny my lad," said Larry with a grateful glance at his valet. "We'll talk about that afterwards. Now, my boy, what have you to say for yourself?" He addressed the unpleasant-looking prisoner.

"He ain't got no right to use firearms," said the man hoarsely.

Larry thought his hoarseness was due to his emotion, but it would seem that it was his natural voice.

"I'm shot, I am! I was coming down the stairs as quiet and as peaceful as possible when this fellow came out and shot me."

"Innocent child!" said Larry, unpleasantly. He felt over the man's pocket and took out a long-bladed knife, the edge of which he tested with his finger and thumb. It was razor-sharp.

Larry looked at the man again. He was about thirty-five, hollow-cheeked and sunken-eyed.

"Let me see your hands," said Larry, and the man with a scowl put them out. "Have you any convictions?"

"No, sir," said the man sullenly.

"Who sent you here?"

"Find out!"

"I am going to find out," said Larry softly, "and you will be a little damaged in the finding. Who sent you here?"

"I'm not going to tell," said the man.

"I think you will," said Larry, and led him into the kitchen and shut the door.

When the police arrived ten minutes later they took charge of a very shaky man.

"He has told all he knows," said Larry. "He was sent here to cover another man who escaped. He swears he does not know who the other man was, but it was evidently not Blind Jake."

"How did you induce him to tell?" asked the girl, a little fearfully.

"I threatened to wash him," said Larry, and he spoke no more than the truth. "It was not the threat of the washing, of course," he explained, "it was

144

the being in that room alone with me and the fact that I could strip off his coat without an effort, and the possibility that the washing was merely a preliminary to some form of horrible torture which I had invented which made him talk—his wound is nothing, by the way. It will probably be healed by the time he sees the divisional surgeon. And now I think we can all go to bed. I want to see you, Sunny, before you retire for the night."

What he said to Sunny set that stolid man strutting for the rest of the week.

A Breakfast Proposal

ATHIN white mist overhung the park and shrouded the deserted stretch of Rotten Row, and the one or two riders who had come out at this early hour for their constitutional merely served to emphasize the desolation of the place.

One of these horsemen was Sir John Hason, Chief Commissioner of Police, who made it a practice to ride before breakfast, and he neither expected nor invited company. He was, therefore, surprised and a little annoyed when a horseman came up from behind him and, checking his mount to a walk, fell in by Sir John's side.

"Hallo, Larry," said John Hason in surprise. "This is an unexpected apparition! I thought you were a ghost."

"I shall be that too, one of these fine mornings," said Larry, "unless I'm jolly careful. I knew you would be riding, so I hired a hack from the local livery stable and came out. Besides," he said, "I want a change of air and I want to talk, outside the stultifying atmosphere of your office."

"Anything new?" asked Sir John.

"There was an attempt at assassination last night, but that's so usual that I hate reporting it as a novelty," said Larry, and told the story of the two o'clock visitation.

"It's the queerest case I've ever heard about," said Sir John Hason thoughtfully. "Not a day passes but somebody new comes in. You still attach importance to the charwoman?"

Larry nodded.

The Dark Eyes of London

"You know London better than I, John," he said, for between him and his old school-mate there was no formality on such occasions as this. "Who is Judd?"

"Oh, Judd!" laughed the Commissioner. "I don't think you need worry your head about him. He is a man of some standing in the City, though I seem to have heard that his brother was rather a waster. The Judds practically own all the shares in the Greenwich Insurance Company. It is not a very big concern, but it has successfully resisted every attempt on the part of the insurance trusts and the big companies to absorb it. That shows character which I admire. They inherited the shares from their father and built up what looked to be a very shaky concern into a fairly prosperous business."

"I was looking at the board of directors last night," said Larry. "It is in the Stock Exchange year-book. I sat up after everybody had gone to bed and tried to puzzle things out. Do you know that John Dearborn is a director of that company?"

"Dearborn the dramatist?" asked Hason quickly. "No, I did not know. Of course, the directors in a company like that," he smiled, "are merely the nominees of Judd. Judd is a very good fellow, I am told, and spends a lots of money in charity. He practically supports the Home which Dearborn is running. He may have been given an ornamental directorship in order to bring in a little money to his institute."

"I thought of that too," nodded Larry. "Who is Walters?"

"Never heard of him," said John Hason.

"He's another director of the Company, and also an ornamental person, I should imagine. And Cremley? Ernest John Cremley, of Wimbledon."

"He is most certainly an ornamental person," said the Commissioner. "I know him slightly, a man with very little brains and an insatiable appetite for cards. Why do you ask?"

"Because these two men are also directors of the Macready Theatre Syndicate," said Larry quietly. "Judd's name does not appear, but there is another strange name, which is probably a nominee of his."

"Where are we getting to?" asked the Commissioner.

"We're getting here," said Larry, reining in his horse and bringing it round so that he stood side by side and facing his chief, "that Judd controls the theatre where Dearborn's plays are produced. So there is some association between Judd and the superintendent of the Blind Mission in Paddington."

Sir John digested this fact before he spoke.

"I don't see that there is anything particularly blameworthy about that," he said; "after all, Dearborn is only the victim of Blind Jake, and from what you told me in your report last night, Judd is the victim of nobody except our friend Flash Fred. I can well understand why the doctor wanted to save his brother's name," he went on. "Judd adored that younger brother of his, thought he was the finest fellow in the world. I have never seen a case where brothers entertained such affection one for the other. The week David Judd died the doctor shut himself up and would not see anybody. What the——!"

The Commissioner's note of startled surprise was justified, for Larry had suddenly brought round his horse and was riding furiously across the park, taking no small risk from the low railings he leapt.

He had seen a figure, unmistakably tall, muffled to the chin in a pea-jacket, slouching along the path that led to one of the gates of the park.

The man heard the gallop of hoofs and ran as straight and as swift as a deer, gained the gates and ran out into the street. The gate was too small for Larry to ride his horse through, and he flung himself off and, leaving his mount to his own devices, he ran out into the street. He saw no more than a car pull away from the kerb and move rapidly eastward.

He looked around for a cab, but there was none in sight, and with a shrug he came back, found his horse, mounted and trotted slowly back to where Sir John was sitting.

"Where the devil did you go?" asked Sir John.

"I saw a gentleman I am most anxious to meet," said Larry a little breathlessly. "One Blind Jake, who was taking his morning constitutional in the park, with his car waiting to pick him up like a perfect gentleman. If I had had a gun I would have given Tarling another Daffodil Mystery to solve. I should have been glad to have found flowers for Blind Jake!"

The Dark Eyes of London

Lew

WHEN he got back to the house Diana was dressed and sitting down to breakfast.

"I thought you weren't coming back," she said with a little sigh.

"Why the sigh?" asked Larry.

"Because—I thought you weren't coming back to breakfast," she said.

He told her of the chase in the park.

"That rather upsets my theory that Blind Jake is still at the Home or at the laundry," she said, "because the house is being watched, isn't it?"

"On both sides," said Larry, "but there are a dozen ways this fellow could get out, and the fact that he goes for an early morning constitutional, and the people who are behind him consider that his health is of sufficient importance to put a car at his disposal, rather proves that he is confined during the day."

They were alone, for the nurse chaperon had not finished dressing.

"I don't know how this case is going to end, Diana," said Larry after a little silence, "and this is a most prosaic moment to say what I want to say, but—but—but after this case is ended, I don't want you to remain at the Yard."

She went a little pale.

"You mean I am not satisfactory?" she said. "As a secretary?"

"You're very satisfactory, both as a secretary and an individual," said Larry, trying hard to maintain command of his voice. "I don't like your—I don't like your working."

There was another silence.

"I don't think I shall work after this case," she said quietly. "I thought of leaving, too."

This was an unexpected reply, and it filled him with a sense of panic.

"You're not going away?" he asked, and she laughed.

"You're really a most inconsistent person. You dismiss me in one breath and hope I'm not leaving you in another," she said, and she was treading on dangerous ground and was well aware of the fact. "After all," she went on,

148

solemnly mischievous, "there are so many jobs where competent girls are wanted."

"I know a job where a competent girl is wanted," said Larry, swallowing something, "and her job is to look after a flat and share the modest fortune of a detective-inspector who may be something better one of these fine days."

She was helping herself to a triangular piece of toast when he spoke, and she let the toast drop.

"I don't quite know what you mean," she faltered.

"I mean," said Larry. "I want to marry you—go to the devil!"

She looked up open-mouthed, in time to see the door shut upon the outraged Sunny.

"I'm awfully sorry," stammered Larry. "I didn't mean that last remark for you, dear. I really mean——"

"I know what you mean," she said, and laid her hand on his. "You mean you want me?"

"I want you so much," said Larry, "that I can't find words to make my want plain."

She did not speak. She suffered her hand to stay under his, and her eyes catching the distorted reflection of her face in the polished coffee-pot, she laughed. Larry drew his hand away quickly, for he was a sensitive man.

"I'm rather a fool, I'm afraid," he said quietly. She had not moved.

"Put your hand back." Her voice was no higher than a whisper, but he obeyed. "Now tell me what you were saying. I was laughing at myself in the coffee-pot. I don't look like a person that anybody could propose to at half-past eight in the morning."

"Then—then you know you are being proposed to?" he said huskily.

She nodded, and her shining eyes turned to meet his.

"And—will you?" he asked, finding it difficult to frame the words.

"Will I what—be proposed to?" she answered innocently. "I think I will, Larry dear: I rather like it."

And then she was in his arms, and he was holding her tightly, tightly.

And then Sunny came in, and they did not see him. He stole forth silently and made his way to the landing outside the door and rang the elevator bell. The girl who worked the elevator was a great friend of his and supplied him with much information which was of value.

"Louie," he said, and he was more than usually sober, "can you tell me where I can get lodgings near at hand? I think I shall soon be sleeping out."

"Sleeping out, Pat?" said the wondering Louie. (She called him Pat because it was his name, but more because he had graciously permitted her that liberty.) "Is your master getting a housekeeper?"

"I think so," said Sunny very gravely indeed. "I think so, Louie."

Larry may have walked to the office that morning, or he may have ridden, or floated. He had no distinct recollection of what happened, or how he got there, except that he knew that Diana Ward was by his side and that he was hopelessly, ridiculously, overwhelmingly happy in his love. It had been the most extraordinary courting, and the proposal had been as amazingly unconventional. He had pictured such a scene, but it had been set in a quiet drawing-room under shaded lights, or in some bosky dell, or in the shade of an old tree along some backwater of the ancient river.

"Not at breakfast," he said aloud, "oh dear, no."

"Not at breakfast?" repeated the girl. "Oh, you are thinking—yes, it was funny."

"It was wonderful!" said Larry. "I feel all puffed up."

"Then I'm going to take some of the puffed-up feeling out of you," she said calmly. "I want you to make me a promise."

"I'll promise you anything in the world, Diana," he said extravagantly. "Ask me for the top brick off the chimney-pots, or a slice of the moon——"

"Nothing so difficult as that. I merely want to——And yet perhaps it will be more difficult," she said seriously. "Will you promise me that under no circumstances you will ask to be released from your engagement?"

He turned round to her, and almost stopped in his walk.

"That's an easy one," he said. "Whatever makes you think I should want to break off this wonderful——"

"I know, I know," she interrupted. "It's very wonderful to me, and yet"—she shook her head—"will you promise that whatever happens, whatever be the outcome of the Stuart case, whether you fail or succeed, whatever revelations come, you will not break your engagement?"

"I promise you that," said Larry eagerly. "There's nothing in the world which would induce me to take back a word I've said. I am living in mortal terror lest you discover how you are throwing yourself away upon somebody who is not worthy of you. If you do, I swear I will sue you for breach of promise! My fine feelings are not to be trifled with."

When they reached Room 47 they found two men waiting in the corridor. One was a plain-clothes officer, the other was a wizened little man who sat pensively on a form, his hands on his knees, staring with unseeing eyes at the floor.

Larry stopped at the sight.

"What's this?" he asked.

"Oh, I'm sorry," said the girl penitently, "I should have told you—I sent for him."

"Why, it's Lew!" said Larry in surprise, and Diana nodded.

"You told me that I could call for any witness I wanted," she began, and he stopped her.

"My dear, of course you can," he said.

He looked at the old man curiously, and Lew, oblivious to all things, sat in his dark and silent world, consuming his own thoughts.

"Bring him in," said Larry. "How are you going to make him talk, or convey our wishes to him?" He shook his head pityingly. "I never realized before what a terrible affliction this combination of circumstances might be," he said. "Can you talk to him?"

"I think so," said the girl quietly, "but you must realize that he has no idea where he is. For all he knows, he may still be in that dreadful house of the blind, still under the care of the men who have treated him so cruelly."

Larry nodded.

"When you said he was dead I thought you were mad," he said, "but I understand now."

"I want a shot-gun," said the girl, "and I want a uniformed officer." She turned to Larry. "I am going to see whether I have forgotten all I learnt in the Blind Hospital," she said. She took the old man by the hand and he followed her obediently.

She caught his two wrists gently and raised them to her face.

"A woman," he said; then she took up the little vase of flowers on her desk and held them under his nose.

"Roses, ain't they?" he said. "This is a hospital."

She beckoned the uniformed policeman who stood at the door and again raised the old man's hands, letting them rest lightly on the collar of his tunic, and his buttons, then she raised them to his helmet.

"A copper!" said Lew, and shrank back.

She gave him the flowers again, and again raised his hand and brought the gnarled old hand to her cheek.

"I'm in a hospital and a policeman's looking after me. Am I wanted for anything?"

She took his head between her hands and gently shook it.

"I'm not, eh?" he said, relieved.

Larry was watching the play, fascinated.

"Am I safe from them swine?"

She took his head between her hands and forced him to nod.

"Do you want me to talk?"

She repeated the movement, and pushed a chair up to him, guiding him down to it.

The plain-clothes officer had brought the gun and she took it from him, and lifting Lew's hand passed it lightly over the barrel and the stock. He shivered.

"Yes, that's what they've done to me," he said. "You want them for that, don't you? It was cruel hard on a blind man. What are you pinching my left hand for?"

Again she made him nod, then she pinched the right hand, and without waiting for his question made him shake his head.

"I see, I see," he said eagerly. "The right hand is no and the left hand is yes. Is there somebody here—high?"

She signalled yes.

"Do they want me to tell?"

Again she signalled the affirmative, and he began his story.

He and Blind Jake had been companions in misfortune. He had been a slave to the big man, almost since his youth, and had lived a life of terror, dominated by this extraordinary villain.

"He done things that would make you curl up if you knew! Jake did," nodded Lew. "Things that I don't like thinking about, that haunt me at nights."

Then five or six years before Lew's own brother had joined this extraordinary band of criminals.

"A fine big fellow he was, too," said Lew proudly, "and he could see! He used to go round the fairs pretending he couldn't, but he had grand eyesight, could read newspapers and books. A big chap, sir, with long bushy whiskers down to here. A grand fellow was Jim, but a hook."

Then they had come under the influence of this extraordinary power, to which Blind Jake was used to refer in such reverent tones. They had been sent to carry bodies from a house, and Jake had assisted, and so had Jim and Lew. He didn't know that they were murdered, but he thought they were.

"A clever gang they are. Why, six years ago, do you know what they did?" He seemed almost proud of the genius of these terrible men. "We chucked a man in the river with a weight round his legs. You'd think they'd be suspicious, wouldn't you, when they found the body? Not they! What do you think the weight was attached to, guv'nor? A big block of salt, that fitted just round the cove's legs, and as soon as the salt dissolved, up he came."

"Was he alive when you put him in?" asked Larry, and the girl shivered.

The man could not hear, but he answered almost as though he could.

"He may have been dead, I forget," Lew went on. "He didn't holler or anything. God's truth, I didn't know they was going to put him in the water! How was I to know? But in the water he went. And then Jim disappeared. I don't know what happened to him. He just went away and we never saw him again. That was four years ago in May, as far as I can remember."

Lew had got frightened after a while and began to suspect the danger to himself, if he did not know it already, and was fearful of Jake and his threats, more fearful of the mysterious vanishing of his brother. He could not write Braille, but he had got a man in Todd's Home, a "straight 'un," to write the message that he intended putting in the pocket of the next victim. Possibly he had heard from Jake that there was a "job" at hand.

"I think I will go now," said the girl, suddenly white.

Larry took her out into the corridor and brought her a glass of water.

"I'm quite all right," she smiled bravely. "Go back and listen."

Lew was talking when Larry returned, and when he had finished, Larry knew almost all there was to be known about the murder of Gordon Stuart.

That evening there was a conference of all heads of departments, presided over by the Chief Commissioner.

"We may not be able to convict on the evidence of this man," said Sir John gravely; "we will get the warrants if you like, but I think with a little more rope, and the knowledge we have, we could catch them red-handed."

Larry came back to his office—the girl had gone home—in time to hear his telephone bell ringing.

"Is that Mr. Holt?" said a strange voice.

Now it is unusual to receive a call at Scotland Yard from anybody but police or public officials because the numbers of the various departments do not appear in the telephone book.

"I am Inspector Holt," replied Larry.

"Dr. Judd asks you whether you can come to his office at once. He has something important to communicate."

Larry thought a moment.

"Yes, I will come immediately," he said.

He picked up Harvey, and a cab deposited them at Bloomsbury Pavement.

At this hour Larry expected the building to be deserted, but there was a light showing in one of the upstairs windows. The long narrow vestibule was also illuminated.

Larry walked quickly through the vestibule; the porter's little recess was empty. At the far end were the doors of two automatic lifts, one of which was in position.

"Shall I come up with you?" asked the sergeant.

There was no reason why he shouldn't, and yet——

"No, no, stay here," said Larry.

He stepped into the lift and pushed the ivory button marked "Fourth Floor" and the elevator jerked upward. At the fourth floor it stopped and Larry, pushing open the grille, stepped out on to the landing. Immediately opposite him was a glass door, behind which a light shone. The words "Dr. Judd" were written legibly enough, and he turned the handle of the door and stepped into an empty room. He called, but nobody answered him, and, puzzled, he came back to the landing.

Every sense in Larry Holt's system was alert. Dr. Judd was not the kind of individual who would indulge in a silly practical joke, or attempt to hoax him.

Then he had a mild surprise. He had come by the left-hand elevator, which had now disappeared, and in its place was the right-hand lift, which must have been on a higher floor when he had reached the landing. What was more remarkable, the lift door was wide open. Who had come up?

He looked along the corridor, but there was nobody in sight.

"Is everything all right?"

It was the hollow voice of Harvey coming up the elevator shaft.

"I'm coming down," said Larry, and stepped through the open grille into the waiting elevator.

His foot was poised, he was in the very act of bringing it down upon the floor of the lift, when he realized in a flash that what he had thought was solid wood flooring was no more than paint and paper. There was no possibility of drawing back. His balance had shifted, and the full weight of his body was thrown forward.

He had the fraction of a second to think, and then, utilizing every ounce of strength, every atom of impetus he could get from his left foot, which still rested on the solid edge of the landing, he leapt forward and gripped the moulding of one of the panels at the back of the elevator. He had less than half an inch to hold on by, but by the extraordinary strength in his hands he maintained his hold, even as his feet crashed through the paper flooring and the whole weight of his body was flung upon his fingers-tips. He hung thus, suspended in space, a fifty-foot fall upon the stone flags beneath him.

"Quick, come up!" he shouted. "Fourth floor. I'm trapped!"

He heard the rattle of the other lift and the whine of the motor, and at the same time he heard another sound above him, and, glancing up, saw a face looking down from the opening on the fifth floor.

Then something whizzed past him and struck the panelling of the elevator with a crash. For a second he nearly released his hold. He felt the lift shaking unaccountably, and then, to his horror, the ascending lift passed him.

"Here, here!" he shouted.

The face above seemed to be growing dimmer; but again he saw the hand poised, something struck him on the shoulder, he released his hold and fell.

Larry Inspects a House

LARRY jerked open the gates on the ground-floor, and staggered from the lift-shaft to meet the dumbfounded Dr. Judd standing in an attitude of surprise, and incredulity expressed on every line of his countenance.

"Whatever has happened?" he demanded anxiously.

"A miracle!" said Larry, with a touch of grimness. "I seem to have fallen about four feet. You sent for me, Dr. Judd."

Dr. Judd shook his head.

"I'm afraid I don't understand what this is all about," he said. "Will you come up to my office?"

"I don't think that is necessary," said Larry. "You sent a telephone message asking me to come here at once because you had something important to communicate to me. I'm going up," he said viciously. "There's a gentleman on the top floor whose acquaintance I should like to make."

"I assure you, Mr. Holt," said the doctor earnestly, "that I have never sent for you or communicated with you in any way. I sent my porter out on a message and then remembered that I hadn't any cigarettes and foolishly left this great building unattended. You didn't step into the wrong lift, did you?"

A slow smile came to Larry's face.

"I rather fancy I did," said he.

"Good heavens!" gasped the doctor. "Why, you might have been killed!"

"I don't exactly know what happened as it is," said Larry.

"Only one lift is working," explained the doctor. "Something went wrong with the motors and we're working them on balance. That is to say, one elevator comes down while the other goes up. Taking advantage of the fact that to-morrow is Sunday, the workmen were repairing the floor of number two elevator, which has worn rather thin—"

"And spread some pieces of paper and canvas in its place, I presume?" said Larry, who was impolite and well aware of the fact. "Anyway, I'm going up now," he said, and they went together in the sound elevator.

Harvey was half-way down to his chief, and they met him.

"Thank God you're not hurt," he said.

Larry shook his head.

"I could have only been six feet from the ground when I dropped. I didn't realize that this infernal elevator was descending all the time the gentleman was shying things at me."

"Somebody throwing at you, sir? I thought I heard a bit of iron strike the bottom of the shaft."

The elevator only went as far as the fourth floor. The upper floor was reached by a stairway. Larry came up to the darkened landing to find, as he had expected, that his assailant had gone. Which way he had gone there was no need to ask, for in the ceiling at the end of the passage was a square patch of light where a trap-door had been raised, and beneath there was a pair of steps.

"I can't tell you how sorry I am," said Dr. Judd, when they rejoined him.

He looked unusually pale and his voice quavered.

"Some fool must have played a practical joke which might have had very serious consequences. How did you save yourself?"

But Larry was in no mood for narrative, and he left a perturbed Dr. Judd with a curt "Good night."

"And to-morrow, Harvey," said Larry, "I shall be at the office at half-past nine, and I want you to be there to meet me. The clearing-up process begins in earnest to-morrow and this day week, please God, there will be no Stuart mystery."

*

"My dear," said Larry Holt at breakfast the next morning, and his tone was at once paternal and apprehensive, "I said one large prayer last night, and it was one of thankfulness that your prophecy is coming true."

"About capturing the gang?" she asked.

"Something like that," said he, rising.

"Are you going without me?" she asked in surprise as he rose from the table.

"Yes," he hesitated, "I am going to pursue a little clue which may be a very big clue indeed."

She looked at him doubtfully.

"I couldn't come with you, I suppose?" she asked.

He shook his head.

"No, this is a job which I must do entirely on my own," he said. "Anyway it is necessary that I should break the law to make my investigations, and I cannot be responsible for leading you from the straight path."

"I don't think it would worry me very much," she smiled, "but you don't want to tell me, that's it, isn't it?"

"You've guessed it first time," said Larry. "The noble Sunny will look after you and escort you to Scotland Yard, and he will be bulging with weapons of a lethal character."

Sunny blushed, but recovered immediately.

"Yes, sir," said he, "I'm thinking of sending your overcoat to be cleaned for the winter."

"What on earth has that to do with escorting Miss Ward to Scotland Yard?" asked Larry in astonishment.

"Nothing, sir," said Sunny, "except it will be very cold round about November, and they take a long time to clean overcoats."

"In fact," said the girl with a smile, "Sunny is being nicely domestic and is taking a very optimistic view of the outcome of this case. Where will this clue lead you?" she asked. "I'd rather like to know, because—" She stopped. "Well, in case you are ever missing."

"It is leading me to Hampstead," said Larry.

She drew a deep sigh.

"I was dreadfully afraid it was somewhere else," she said.

He wondered why she was afraid, but it was not a subject that he wished to pursue because he had lied outrageously.

Half an hour after he reached the Yard, two slightly soiled men in the shabby uniform of the North Metropolitan Gas Company walked out the Whitehall end of Scotland Yard, one carrying a bag of tools, and boarded a bus. They were set down within a quarter of a mile of their destination and walked the remainder of the journey, stopping to survey the house wherein Larry had decided would be found the solution of Gordon Stuart's death.

It was an unusual-looking house, bare and grim, with few windows, and those heavily barred.

"The man who planned that must have thought he was designing a prison, sir," said Harvey.

"Maybe he was," replied Larry. "Harvey, if what Lew the blind man told us is true, then we have come to the end of the chase."

Harvey was shocked.

"But this is only a look-over, sir?" he said. "You don't really expect to finish the case on this one inspection?"

Larry nodded.

"When I enter that house I am pulling into material shape every dream I have dreamt, every theory I have evolved. I stand or fall by the result."

"Does Miss Ward know—?" began Harvey boldly.

The Dark Eyes of London

"This is the one thing that Miss Ward doesn't know," smiled Larry. Crossing the road, he mounted the steps and rang the bell.

The door was opened by a manservant, and to him Larry Holt spoke shortly and with authority, and they were ushered into the hall.

"Remember, you are to keep our visit a secret," said Larry.

"You can depend on me, Mr. Holt," said the man, who had turned a sickly green at the detective's appearance.

The hall was wide and lofty, panelled in oak from the tesselated marble floor to the ceiling. The only furniture was a table and a chair, Larry noted. There were no lights visible, and he gathered that illumination was furnished by lamps concealed in the cornices. Other illuminations were furnished by a long, narrow window of frosted glass, through which the shadow of the bars could be seen. There was no stairway leading from the hall, but there was a doorway immediately facing the street door, which Larry guessed concealed the staircase. On the other side of the hall was a second door, and these were the only apparent means of egress from the passage.

He opened the door on the right and found himself in a large and beautifully furnished salon. The walls were hung about with pictures and tapestries, and on the polished floor were a half a dozen Persian rugs, which Larry could see were worth a fortune.

There were six stained-glass windows in this room, and each was a masterpiece. By their side hung heavy velvet curtains which could be so drawn that the window excluded all light. One silver electrolier hung in the middle of the apartment, and there were no other lights, though here again Larry supposed that the main illumination came from concealed lamps.

He walked across to the big fireplace with its silver grate and fixtures, and examined two letters which lay open upon a table by the side of the big arm-chair. They were of no importance, and he continued his search.

From the main apartment another door opened on to a flight of stairs, which led to a suite of bedrooms, a little drawing-room and a large study, which was over the salon and covered practically the same area.

His search upstairs was more or less perfunctory, though his examination of the corridor from whence the bedrooms gave was of a more careful and exacting character. But he came down again to the salon, satisfied in his mind that what had to be discovered was to be looked for on the lower floor.

He found the servant in the room when he came down and dismissed him sharply.

"Go back to the hall," he said, and sulkily the man obeyed.

And now Larry gave every minute to an examination of the panelled walls of the room—particularly that wall which was opposite the door through which he and Harvey had entered. So cunningly had the panelling been arranged that it was a long time before he found the concealed door; and then it was not where he had been looking, but on a level with the stained-glass window. He remembered then having seen from the outside a small semicircular obtrusion from the main wall of the building.

"Here we are, Harvey!" he said exultantly, as he pulled up a carved wreath which seemed to be part of the wall's decorations and disclosed a tiny keyhole. He took the packet of keys from his pocket and tried first one and then the other. At the fourth trial a lock slipped back and the door opened inwards.

He was right! He knew it at that moment. The joy of accomplishment set his heart beating faster—the knowledge that he had at last a tangible something to show, not to the Commissioner, not to his superiors, but to the girl who was more to him than career or life, brought a new colour to his cheeks and a brighter light to his eyes.

He was in a small bell-shaped apartment, with a domed roof, a room so small that the door, when it was opened, touched the opposite wall. It was made of concrete, and a flight of steps leading down to the cellar were also of this material.

The first thing that caught his eye was an electric switch and this he snapped down, illuminating a lower landing. There was another door to the left, and a further flight of steps which disappeared in darkness. No effort had been made to conceal the keyhole of the door, and one of his keys opened it.

He found himself in a low-roofed concrete chamber, about five foot six in height and, as near as he could judge, about ten feet square. He searched for, and found, the electric switch and illuminated the apartment.

"What do you think of this, Harvey?"

"What are they running?" asked Harvey in surprise. "An electric light plant?"

Larry shook his head.

"No," he said, "this isn't a light plant. I know very little about machinery, but I have an idea that this gadget is a pump."

He examined the machinery more carefully.

"Yes, it is a pump," he said, "one of the type which is used in ships to trim the ballast tanks."

A thick cable was suspended on brackets along the wall, and he felt this gingerly.

"Electric," he said. "This is where he gets his power."

On the wall was a switchboard and what seemed an independent lever. He examined this closely and before he went on to yet another machine.

"And this is the ventilating plant," he said, pointing to a barrel-shaped instrument. "You notice the bad-air exhaust?"

"He's a thorough gentleman, this," said Sergeant Harvey.

"Very," agreed Larry, and they walked out of the room, locking the door behind them.

"A door over there leading to the yard," said Larry, pointing to the wall opposite the machine-room.

Harvey saw no door, but followed his leader down a further flight of stairs.

"Ten steps," Larry warned, and then he came against a door. A heavy door of ferro-concrete hung upon hinges of toughened bronze. This Larry confirmed before he went any farther. He expected to find bronze, and would have been surprised if the hinges had been made of any other material. He had two fears: one that the doors would be fitted with bolts and the other that they were impossible to open from the inside. This latter fear, he saw, was groundless, for the keyhole was covered from the outside by a screw cap. He twisted the cover off and opened the door. It swung back heavily, and he measured the edge.

"Four inches thick!" he said grimly. "He takes no chances."

Behind the first door was another of steel, and this too he unlocked. And now he paused and he felt his breath grow laboured.

"Take note of this room to which we are coming," said Larry Holt, "for it was here that Gordon Stuart died!"

The Death Room

HE CARRIED a flash-lamp in his hand, but it was some time before he discovered the switch, which was set high in the wall, near the sloping roof of the stairs on the farthermost side of the door. A click, and the void before them was illuminated. He could see nothing from where he stood save a brass bedstead, destitute of clothing. Down two steps and three paces along a narrow passage, and he was in the room. Floor, roof and walls were of cement-work, and he saw that what he had thought was one was really two rooms, the second being fitted up roughly as a bathroom. There were no windows of any kind, and he had not expected them. The air was heavy and stale, and evidently the two ventilators near the ceiling were not in working order.

But it was not the bathroom nor the bedstead to which his eyes strayed; it was to a great block of granite in the centre of the room. In the stone, which was a cube two feet in each direction, was a large steel bolt, and from this bolt ran a thin rusted chain, also of steel. Each yard of the chain ran through a block of lead, which Larry judged to be ten pounds in weight, and there were three of these. The chain terminated in a brass leg-ring.

"Yes," said Larry, "I think so."

He picked up the ring and examined it, and, trying first one and then the other of his keys upon the little lock, the opening of which was protected by a sliding cover, presently he saw the two catches snap back, and heaved a sigh.

"Thank God for that!" he said. "I was afraid I'd missed the key."

The Dark Eyes of London

He looked round at Harvey and Harvey's face was a study.

"What is this, Mr. Holt?" he asked, bewildered.

"The operating room of the 'Dark Eyes,'?" replied Larry briefly.

"Do you mean to say that these devils——"

Larry nodded. He was walking around the walls, looking for a place where he could conceal the waterproof bag he carried in his pocket. There was not so much as a crack into which it could be hidden, for the big holes set in the wall near the floor at regular intervals were, he knew, of no value for his purpose. Then his eye fell upon the granite block, and, exerting all his strength, he pulled at it. Slowly it canted away. There had been no necessity to cement to the floor a block of that weight.

"Give me a hand to ease this down, Harvey," he said, and the two men lowered the block on its side.

It had fitted truly, and its base was perhaps only an inch deeper than the floor. Where it had stood the workmen had not taken the trouble to make its foundations secure, and there was a depression in the cement, irregular and shallow, but large enough for Larry's purpose. He took the waterproof bag—it was no more than a sponge bag—from his pocket and began to drop various articles into the bottom. Key followed key and then:

"A handcuff key, if you've got one, Harvey," he said. "I left mine in my room."

Harvey found a handcuff key in his waistcoat pocket and passed it across to his superior.

"And this, I think," said Larry, and took something from his pocket and placed it in the bag.

He smoothed the bag and its contents as flat as possible, and it just fitted into the depression. Then the two men lifted the stone and put it back in its place.

"May I ask," said the bewildered Harvey, "what is the idea?"

Larry laughed, and his laugh sounded hollow in that dreadful room, which had never heard laughter.

"Is the servant in this?" asked Harvey.

"I'm perfectly sure he isn't. This gang wouldn't trust a servant," replied Larry. "No, he probably keeps to his own part of the house, and doesn't even enter the reception-room except when his boss is at home, unless he is sent for. If you notice this house, it has been built for a specific purpose. For example, the room has a vacuum bracket in the wainscot, there is an electric lift from the kitchen, and a private stairway to the bedrooms and study upstairs. My theory is, but I haven't time to confirm it, that the servant lives in practically a house of his own, which has no connection with this part of the building. Did you notice a door opposite what I would call the engine-room? It wasn't easy to spot because it looked like the rest of the wall. In reality, it is of iron, camouflaged as concrete. It is on the ground level and leads to the yard at the side of the house, and incidentally to the garage."

Harvey shouldered his tools.

"This is a horrible place, Mr. Holt," he said with a shudder. "In all my thirty-five years of police experience I have never been so—shocked. It sounds silly to you?"

"Not a bit," said Larry quietly. "I am shocked beyond words."

"You really think that that is the place where these people have been done to death?"

"I'm certain of it," said Larry. "In that room Gordon Stuart went over to the other side."

They went back in the hall now. By the side of the door there was a narrow slit of a window covered by a strip of silk casement cloth, and Harvey went to this and pulled it aside.

"There's a car at the door," he said. "Just come up."

Larry stepped to his side and looked. A man had descended from a taxicab and was paying the driver.

"The Reverend Mr. Dearborn," said Larry. "How interesting!"

Larry hesitated only for a second, then he opened the door, and the Rev. John Dearborn, who had turned from the cab, and whose hand was on the spikes of the gate, bent his head suddenly as though he had remembered something, and beckoned the cabman.

The Dark Eyes of London

"My friend," he said, "I cannot see you, but are you still there?"

"Yes, sir," replied the cabman.

"I have remembered that I wish to call at the post office. Will you take me there?"

His hand groped out and the cabman took it, and leaning back opened the door again.

Before Larry could get down the steps the cab was on the move. The detective turned back with a little smile.

"David Judd can wait," he said softly.

"David Judd?" said Harvey.

"David Judd!" repeated Larry Holt. "Who said this is not an age of miracles, when the blind can see as John Dearborn sees, and David Judd, dead and buried, is rollicking round London in a taxicab. Harvey, there's a great detective in this city."

"There is, sir," said Sergeant Harvey heartily. "And the name of the same is Holt."

"It isn't, but it will be," said Larry softly.

The Woman in the Garage

WAIT!" said Larry. He was on the point of leaving the House of Death. "We may not get another opportunity of making a leisurely examination of these premises. I am curious about the side door." He led the way to the secret door in the salon, closing it behind him, then down the steps he passed and paused opposite the engine-room.

"Here is the door to the yard, I think," he said, and switched his flash-lamp over the wall.

The keyhole was difficult to find, but he discovered it after a while near the floor in the bottom right-hand corner. As he had expected, it opened on to a covered passageway from the road.

"Clever work," he said in honest admiration.

He was in the yard looking at the wall through which he had come. Nothing like a door was visible. Instead he looked upon something which

166

had the appearance of a window made up of four opaque panes. It stood out from the wall in the most natural fashion, a trim window-box filled with flowers on its ledge.

"Not much like a door!" said Larry, and added, "Clever work!"

He walked back to the gate and examined it closely. Then he returned to Harvey.

"The mystery of the automatic gate is solved," he said. "As I suspected, it is possible to reach the house and enter the yard and garage without the servants knowing anything at all about it. The last time I was here, I noticed what looked to be two peep-holes placed at a distance of four feet apart and rather low. They couldn't have been intended for purposes of observation because they were backed with iron. Did you notice anything about that car we saw in the laundry garage?"

"Yes, sir," said Harvey, "there were two bars sticking out in front under the head-lamps," and Larry nodded.

"I thought at first," he said, "that it was some new kind of motor-car invention, but it is clear now just what they are intended for. A car is driven up to the gate, and those two bars fit in what I called the peep-holes; a lock is pressed back and the door opens, and presumably closes behind them, thus dispensing with the attendance of any servants and avoiding the inconvenience of their coming and going being noted by the people in the house. I think we will look at the garage, and then we will go," he said.

The door of the garage was at the far end of the drive and extended across its whole width. Larry searched amongst his keys, and presently he found what he was looking for.

"I wondered what door this tumbler lock was on," he said.

He slipped the key in the hole and turned it, and as he did so he heard a slight movement within the garage.

"Did you hear that?" he said in a whisper.

Harvey nodded, and drew his truncheon. Then suddenly Larry threw open the gates wide. He saw a car, but apparently the garage was empty of people. The wheels of the car were wet.

The Dark Eyes of London

"That came in this morning," said Larry.

There was no place where the smallest of men could conceal himself, he thought. And then he heard a scream, shrill and painful, the scream of some one in agony, and he sprang to the door of the big limousine and pulled it open. Then a tornado loosed itself at him—a great, gibbering shape leapt at the two men and by sheer weight flung them down, dropping his huge mass upon them.

Larry was stunned for a second, and then, as he struggled to his feet, he heard the door of the garage slammed and the click of the lock as the key was turned. The two men threw themselves at the door, but it did not give an inch.

"The woman!" cried Harvey suddenly, and pointed to the car.

There was an inert heap lying there, and Larry leapt on to the step and, lifting her out in his arms, carried her to where a ray of light penetrated from the small roof-window.

It was a woman of fifty, grey and bedraggled. Her face had not known soap or water for weeks; her hands were almost black. But now through the grime her white face showed in a deathly grin, and the claw-marks of Blind Jake stood out in purple relief upon her lean throat.

"Get some water, Harvey; there's a faucet there," said Larry, loosening the woman's blouse. "She's alive," he said. And then he realized. "My God!" he said in a low voice. "It is the charwoman!"

Whilst he attended to the poor wretched creature, Harvey had searched the garage and had discovered an axe. In five minutes the lock was smashed and the door was open.

"Take this gun," said Larry, slipping his revolver from his pocket. "It hasn't been much use to me, but if you see that swine, shoot him. Don't argue with him or think you can stop him with your truncheon, Harvey."

But Blind Jake had gone, as he knew. That blind man, with the most precious of his faculties destroyed, had again been a match for him.

The woman was showing some signs of a return to life. Larry had dragged her into the air and was sprinkling water on her neck and face. Her eyes fluttered and opened, and she looked up with a frown.

"Where is Miss Clarissa?" she asked thickly.

"That is what I am going to ask you," said Larry.

The cab came soon after, and they carried the woman through the side door, up the steps, and through the beautiful salon. They paused to set her down in the reception-room, and Larry looked round at the evidence of comfort and luxury, bought with the suffering and misery of God knows how many innocent souls who had died that this villainy should be gilded and scented and live in fragrance.

Then his eyes dropped upon the incongruous figure that lay on a thousand-pound Persian rug, who had done no harm but know and recognize Stuart, and must for that reason be condemned to hide in dark places under the care of a fiend like Blind Jake.

Strauss, the ex-convict butler, waited in the hall, nervously rubbing his hands.

"You're not in this, are you?" asked Larry.

"No, sir," said the man shakily. "I thought when you came that my gentleman had sent you, because I had—found a few things."

"Like a black enamelled link, eh?" said Larry. "How many pairs did he have of those?"

"Two pairs, sir. I had to tell him when he asked me what had become of them, because really I did not steal them—he had half given them to me because three of the brilliants were missing."

"Don't worry, Strauss," said Larry. "He has got them back now, though he had to burgle a pawnbroker's to get them."

A knot of idlers gathered on the pavement to watch the spectacle of two, apparently officials of a gas company, carry an unsavoury woman, who looked seventy, down the steps into the cab.

She had recovered consciousness before the cab had gone far, and was trembling violently, looking from one to the other of the men.

"You're all right now, Emma," said Larry kindly.

"Emma?" she repeated. "Do you know me, sir?"

"Yes, I know you," said Larry.

"Then I'm safe?" she said eagerly. "Oh, thank God for that! You don't know what I've been through. You don't know what I've been through!"

"I can guess," said Larry.

"Where are you taking her?" asked Harvey in a low voice. "I didn't hear what you told the cabman."

"I am taking her to my flat," said Larry, and Sergeant Harvey looked his surprise. "I can't afford to fill the hospitals with the witnesses for the crime," said Larry with a faint smile. "And, besides, this woman is not ill; she's just tired and hungry."

"That's right," said Emma eagerly. "I know I must look terrible, but they never gave me a chance of washing myself. They dragged me from one hole to another. I'm not a common woman, sir, although I've done charwoman's work. I was nursemaid and brought up a little girl, sir—the daughter of my missis. Brought her up like a lady, sir. Little Clarissa Stuart."

"Clarissa Stuart?"

"I called her Clarissa, sir," said Emma. "If I could only see her again!"

"You called her Clarissa," said Larry slowly. "Was not that her name?"

"Yes, sir," said the woman. "Clarissa Diana, but I used to call her Diana." Larry started back as though he had been shot.

"What is your name?" he asked in a husky voice.

"Emma Ward, sir. Diana Ward I called the young lady, but Diana Stuart is her real name, and her father is in London."

"Diana Stuart!" repeated Larry slowly. "Then Diana Stuart is the heiress to whom Stuart left his money. Diana Stuart!" he repeated in a tone of wonder. "My Diana!"

The Heiress

MRS. EMMA WARD had told him practically all there was to tell about herself before the cab had drawn up at the entrance of the flat.

It was she who had failed to register the birth of Diana and her twin sister, and this failure had, curiously enough, saved her life; for when the gang had discovered, as they did a few hours earlier than Larry, that Gordon Stuart had left an enormous fortune to the daughter whose existence he had discovered through an accidental meeting with the charwoman at Nottingham Place, they lost no time in securing the one witness who could prove the legality and the circumstances of Diana's birth.

Never had Larry so congratulated himself upon any event as he did upon the fact that he had engaged a chaperon for Diana. Once before had that nurse been useful; and now she took charge of the unhappy woman who, to the scandal of the neighbourhood, he brought to his flat; and it was a presentable and tidy lady of middle age who came into his sitting-room an hour after her arrival within reach of hot water and clean towels.

"I am going now to see Miss"—he baulked at the word—"Miss Stuart," he said.

The woman started.

"Do you know where she is?"

"Oh, yes," said Larry. "I know! She has been with me for——" He was on the point of saying "years" and honestly believing the word he framed; and then, with a queer sense of surprise, he realized that weeks, and very few weeks at that, would most accurately describe the length of his friendship with "Miss Diana Ward."

He had thought of telephoning the news to her, but somehow he wanted to tell her himself; and there were other things he had to say—things which were hard to think about. He thought it all over on the way to the Yard. Diana Ward, poor and dependent, was a different girl from Clarissa Stuart, an heiress to millions of dollars. He could ask Diana Ward to marry him and look forward with happiness to a union where each brought to the other only the treasure of love. Diana Stuart was a rich woman. He did not doubt that she would be sweet and generous and desirous that the marriage should go through; but after a time she would realize how enormous were the possibilities which great possessions offer. And then she would regret in a nice way, he told himself; for he defended her even as he accused her. And that was the end of the case, he thought. Kudos would come to him, though he could take no credit for that; and the long-deferred promotion—that also would come and he would sit in the office, an Assistant Commissioner, and exercise his function. But all the success he had secured was Diana's. Hers was the brain that had disentangled the knottiest of the problems and had made the tangle of clues into one straight case.

It was curious that he did not also credit her with having discovered even more. Perhaps it was the natural vanity which is latent in all men, which made him guard so jealously the claim to one achievement—the discovery of her identity.

The end of the case! And the end of all hope for him, as he knew. There was never another woman in the world like Diana Ward. She was the first in his heart and should be the last. He had renounced her in his mind and had drawn a grey veil over the future, by the time he stood outside Room 47 with his hand upon the door-knob, hardly daring to turn it because of the loss which would be his. And his first words expressed aloud the thought that followed that moment of hesitation.

"Diana," he said, "I am the most selfish brute in the world."

She showed all her white teeth in a silent laugh.

"I waited for you for over an hour," she said.

"Good Lord!" he gasped. "I was taking you to lunch."

"Yes," she nodded, "that was what you were talking about?"

He shook his head.

"I wish to Heaven it was," he said. "There I am again, thinking of myself and being sorry for myself, when I ought to be on my knees, thanking Heaven for the good fortune which has come to you."

She jumped up.

"You have found Emma!" she said.

"I have found Emma Ward," he replied slowly, "and I have found—Clarissa Stuart."

He walked towards her, both hands outstretched.

"Oh, my dear, my dear," he said, "I am so glad for you."

She took the hands in hers and lifted one to her cheek.

"Aren't you glad for yourself too?"

He was silent, and she looked at him quickly.

"Larry," she said, "I have known all about this for days and days—ever since the day I fainted at that boarding-house in Nottingham Place. Don't you remember?"

He frowned.

"Of course. But why——"

"Why, you silly," she said, "I knew it was Aunt Emma's ring. I always called her 'aunt,' though I knew she was not my aunt. And then I guessed who Gordon Stuart was. I knew nothing would make her leave her wedding-ring behind. Do you know where she went in such a hurry?"

He shook his head.

"To find me," she said simply. "I guessed that. I knew it instinctively before I had heard of that ring. My father gave it to her. She used to tell me how she was married when she was in my father's service, and how my father presented her with this strange wedding-ring for all she had done for my mother."

"You knew!" he said wonderingly. "But you never told me."

"You went on a chase to-day"—she lifted her finger reproachfully and shook it in his face—"and you never told me! You said you were going to Hampstead and you went to Chelsea."

"You knew that too?" he gasped. "Do I get any credit out of this infernal—this case?" he corrected quickly.

"You get me," she said demurely.

He pressed her hands together.

"Diana, I've got a serious talk coming with you, and it's about——"

"I know what it's all about," she said. "You can save yourself the trouble. You can't marry a rich woman because you're afraid she'll want to keep you. You would much rather marry a poor woman—and keep her, if she would submit to that indignity."

There was fun in the eyes that were raised to his.

"Larry!" She shook his hands with quiet impatience.

The Dark Eyes of London

"It makes a difference, doesn't it?" he asked.

"Not to me, Larry," she replied. "And anyway, it doesn't matter." She dropped his hands and walked back to her table. "Because you've promised."

"Promised? What have I promised?"

"Hear this man!" she scoffed. "You promised me that, whatever happened, whatever was the outcome of the Stuart case, it would make no difference to our marriage."

"Did you know?" he asked in astonishment. "Was that why you made me promise?"

"Of course I knew. I've been a rich woman for quite a long time, and I'm so used to the feeling that I can hardly restrain myself from taking a cab whenever I see one!"

He walked over to her and laid his arm about her shoulder.

"Diana—" he began, and then asked: "Or is it Clarissa?"

"Diana, always," she said.

He kissed her.

"And always."

The End of Jake

THE MAN who called himself the Rev. John Dearborn sat behind the locked door of his study, and methodically burnt papers in a little fireplace that was at the back of his chair. His blue glasses he had dispensed with, and under his eyes, keen and alert, the heap of manuscripts, old letters, receipts and other data, were sorted, and melted away until there was only a package left small enough to go into his pocket. He slipped a rubber band round these and put them on one side. Then he took up a heavy wad of manuscripts and dropped it into an open bag which was beside his desk; and as he sorted and read and destroyed, he whistled a little tune thoughtfully.

From one of the drawers in the desk he took out a thicker package of manuscript bound in a stiff cover. He turned the leaves of this idly, and sometimes the excellence of the writing induced him to read on and on.

"That's damned good," he said, not once but many times; for John

Dearborn was a great admirer of the genius of John Dearborn.

At last, with an air of reluctance, he closed the manuscript volume and put that more reverently in the bag.

The house was empty, for the hawkers had not begun to stray back; and except for the little man who acted as doorkeeper and kept the Home swept and garnished, and the old cook, who was dozing in her kitchen, the Home was deserted.

Presently he finished his packing and patted first one breast-pocket and then the other, until he found the letter he wanted. He took it out and studied it for a while. It was a brief, hand-written note which Larry Holt had written to him the day after his first visit to Todd's Home. He took up his pen and, with one eye on the copy, he fashioned a word taken from the letter, and compared the two efforts. Then from the open writing-case which lay on the desk he extracted a sheet of headed notepaper and began to write slowly and laboriously, and all the time he wrote he whistled his gay little tune. He finished at last and addressed an envelope, also taken from the writing-case; and when this was blotted, and the letter sealed and put into his pocket, he strapped the case and placed it on the floor by the side of his bag. Then he unlocked a wardrobe let into the wall and took out some clothing, which he laid on the back of a chair; and now he was singing with soft diminuendo, yet with evident enjoyment, one of the "Indian Love Lyrics."

He stripped his sombre clerical garb, tore away his white choker collar, and began to dress. He was a man about town now in smartly tailored tweeds; and he put the clerical costume into the wardrobe and shut the door. Then he sat down at the table, his face in his hands, thinking, thinking.

He had dressed almost mechanically, and he had a strange feeling of dissatisfaction. All the exits would be guarded; even the panel, the roof-path, the way through the boiler-room.

"I'm mad," he said, getting up.

He looked down at the bag and the writing-case, and there was regret in his expression. He peeled his coat and slowly undressed again. This time he did not go to the wardrobe, but to a long black box under the window, and he took out various articles of attire and viewed them with distaste.

"A wretched mountebank," he called himself, and was genuinely contemptuous.

But it had to be this or nothing. Blind Jake could find his way by the underground channel. He had the sharp instincts of the blind, could walk like a cat past the sentinels, and even creep through narrow passages where it seemed impossible that his big frame could go.

John Dearborn dressed and took up a canvas bag from the box, laying it on the table. He turned the contents of his leather grip into this bag, then went to the front room of the Home and looked out into the street. Two policemen, he knew, were guarding the end of the cul-de-sac. Nobody used this front room except himself, for storing odds and ends of furniture, old account-books and the like; but it had the advantage of possessing a door which was only a few feet from the front door.

He put down his sack and came out, closing the door carefully, before he went back to his study and locked himself in. He sat there for ten minutes waiting, and then came a gentle tap-tap on the panel. He crossed the room noiselessly, opened the door just wide enough for the caller to slip through.

It was Blind Jake, and his face was strained and puffed, and on his broad forehead the blue veins stood out.

"I only just got here, governor," he said breathlessly.

The other was eyeing him with a steely look.

"What are you doing here, Jake?" he asked softly. "I told you not to leave the woman under any circumstances until I came."

"Well, you didn't come, master," said the blind man. It was pathetic to hear the pleading, the humility, in his tone. His blind eyes were fixed on the cold man whom he loved so well and had served as men serve fate. A great rough cruel hound of a man, strong enough to crush and maim the master he worshipped, yet ready to cringe and whine at a sharp word. Blind Jake had given all for John Dearborn, had been the readiest minister of his vengeance and the slave of his cupidity. Blood was on his hands, and there were nights when strange faceless shapes came in and out of his room and were visible.

Cold hands touched him on these nights, cold stiff fingers felt for his throat, and he could feel the rough wipings of sodden sleeves and the drip-drip-drip of water.

But none of these things mattered. The sweat poured down his puckered face, his big lips were dropping, and perhaps the blind man felt some thrill in the atmosphere, for he asked with a little whine:

"Is there anything wrong, governor?"

"Where is the woman?" asked Mr. Dearborn, and his words dropped one by one like steel pellets.

Blind Jake shifted uneasily on his seat.

"I left her. I couldn't do——"

"You left her!" Another tremendous pause. "And they found her, eh?" John Dearborn's voice had grown very soft.

"Yes, they found her," said the man. "What could I do? Governor, I'd have done anything for you. Haven't I used my strength for you, master? There's no one as strong in the world as me, old Blind Jake. There's no one who can work as cunning as I can! Haven't I worked for ye; haven't I carried 'em out for ye? Haven't I croaked 'em for ye, with these hands, master?"

He held them out: great cruel hands, knotted and roughened, their backs speckled brown, their palms yellow with callosities.

"You lost Holt," said Dearborn calmly, dispassionately, as a judge might speak. "You lost that woman You lost the girl. And you come and talk to me of what you have done."

"I've done my best," said the man humbly.

"And they'll catch you, too. And you can talk."

"I'll have my tongue torn out before I talk against you," said Blind Jake violently, and smashed his fist down on the table so that it cracked and quivered. "You know that I'd die for you, master?"

"Yes," said Dearborn.

He slipped his hand, the left hand that had no little finger, under his coat, and pulled out a short, ugly automatic pistol of heavy calibre.

"You'll talk," he said. "You're bound to talk, Jake."

The man leant forward, his big face working convulsively.

"If I die——" he began. And then John Dearborn, taking deliberate aim, fired three shots, and that great mountain of muscle swayed and slipped by the table into a heap on the ground. Blind Jake's day had come.

The Get-Away

DEARBORN slipped the revolver in his pocket, unlocked the door and stepped out. The little man who acted as porter was standing, his mouth agape.

"What's wrong?" he said quickly. "Who's shooting?"

"Go out and fetch the police," said John Dearborn calmly. "Somebody has been killed."

"Oh, my heaven!" whispered the little man.

"There are two policemen at the end of the road. Hurry," said John Dearborn sharply, and listened to the flip-flap of the messenger's slippers as he shuffled up the street.

Dearborn waited a while, then entered the front room and closed the door, standing against it listening. He heard the rush of feet, distinguished the policemen, heard them clump through the passage and the chatter of an idle bystander or two behind them; then he opened the door. A policeman was bending over Blind Jake.

"That's him all right," he said. "Jim, clear these people out and stand on duty at the door until the inspector comes. You'd better blow your whistle."

A police whistle shrilled through Lissom Lane, and the little knot of curiosity-mongers who had been turned unceremoniously from the scene of the tragedy grouped about the door.

"What's happened?" asked Mr. Dearborn, and the policeman smiled good-naturedly.

"Now, postman," he said, "you go along and deliver your letters." And John Dearborn flung his bag over his shoulder.

For he had chosen the uniform of a letter-carrier, and it had proved a most effective cloak. He got away within a few minutes of Larry's arrival. The detective was on his way to interview Mr. John Dearborn, and the handcuffs he had in his pocket were expressly intended for that gentleman.

Larry saw the little crowd about the door and knew that something unusual had happened. He came to the study and looked silently upon the massive body of his enemy. Blind Jake had died immediately. He had never known what had struck him, or guessed the vile treachery of the employer he had served so well.

"The man must be in the house somewhere, sir," said the policeman. "This little fellow heard the shots, and the superintendent sent him out to get a policeman. We both came down together, me and my mate."

"Was the front door left unguarded at all?" asked Larry.

"Only for a second, sir," said the policeman. "We both came in together."

"That was the second our friend got away," said Larry. "I don't think it's any use searching the house."

He was accompanied by the officers who had been charged to effect the arrest of Dearborn, and their inspection and examination of the room produced nothing of importance.

Larry drove back to the Yard and interviewed the Chief Commissioner. Then he went to the girl.

"I've heard the news," she said quietly. "Sergeant Harvey has just been in. Do you think Dearborn's killed him?"

"Dearborn is David Judd," said Larry.

"Dr. Judd's brother?" she said in surprise, "But he's dead."

He shook his head.

"That elaborate funeral was well staged, and I am perfectly certain that David even went to the length of providing the body. He is a very thorough gentleman. You remember Lew telling us of his brother who disappeared, a fine-looking fellow with a beard?" She nodded. "That is the man we shall find in David Judd's grave," he said.

"Is Dr Judd——" she began, and there was no need to finish the sentence.

"Dr. Judd is in it up to the neck," said Larry. "The story of Dearborn is explained very easily. Dearborn was a partner of Judd's, and something that happened at the office—either some crime or some murder, perhaps, which David had manœuvred in order to draw insurance—had come to the knowledge of one of the clerks. This man stole a large sum of money and went to Montpellier, and from there began to blackmail David. David went after him and shot him. Probably the murder was unpremeditated, because David is not the sort of man who would shoot in the open square. But at any rate he did shoot, and he was seen by Flash Fred, who reached the body in time to learn from the dying man the name of his murderer. To a man of Fred's calibre, that meant that he had an income for life, and he hastened back to London, saw Dr. Judd, and probably stated the terms on which he would keep his mouth shut. Judd decided that David should conveniently die; and David, you remember, was a fine-looking man with a beard. Of their hirelings or acquaintances they chose Lew's brother as being the nearest in physical appearance to David, and he was unceremoniously destroyed and buried as David. Incidentally, a very large sum of money was drawn from the underwriters on the heavy insurance policy which had been issued to David.

"They must have had this scheme in mind for some time, for a month before David's death Dr. Judd had completed the purchase of Todd's Home. It was not so much a charitable institution as a business proposition, for Todd's Home had deteriorated into a kind of superior doss-house, frequented by the lowest of the low amongst the blind mendicants of London. It was there that the famous Dark Eyes had their head-quarters, and it was from them that David must have learnt of Todd's.

"The Home was bought, and the day after David's 'death' the Rev. John Dearborn appeared as the new superintendent. It is perfectly true that he cleared out all the bad characters and had certain structural alterations made; but he only did this because he wanted to clear the taint from Todd's Home, to give it a good character, and to employ the house as his head-quarters without fear of police visitations. When the laundry company went broke, it was Judd who bought the premises, and the alterations were carried out by David himself with the assistance of his gang. David, I might remark, is an architect and built the house in which his brother lives. We know they employed foreign workmen, and that that house was built for one specific purpose," he said gravely.

"With the laundry premises in their possession the Dark Eyes came back to Lissom Lane, and came and went amongst the blind, who could not see them and who were ignorant of their presence."

"What about Dr. Judd?" she asked.

"I am arresting him," said Larry. "And I am arresting him in the very place from whence your father disappeared—in that famous Box A at the Macready Theatre."

"Will he be there?" she asked in surprise.

He nodded.

"He is there almost every evening," he said quietly.

"But why not take him now?" she asked, puzzled.

"Because Box A and its mystery has yet to be cleared up," said Larry; "and I have an idea that I shall clear it."

At eight o'clock that night he walked into the vestibule of the Macready Theatre.

"Dr. Judd, sir?" said the attendant. "Yes, he's in Box A. Is he expecting you?"

Larry nodded. Harvey was for accompanying him, but the other shook his head.

"I'll go alone," said Larry.

He went swiftly down the passage and, stopping only for a second outside Box A, he turned the knob of the door and stepped in.

Dr. Judd's eyes were fixed on the stage, and the detective had stopped to speak to him when something dropped on his head, something fleecy and warm. It felt like a bag lined with wool. It had been saturated with a chemical which took his breath away and momentarily paralysed him. Then he felt a string pulled tightly round his neck, and whipped out his pistol. Before he could use it, it was gripped. Something sharp hit the hand that held it, and he let go with a cry of pain, muffled in the bag. Every breath he took choked him. He struck out, but his arms were seized from behind, and he was flung forward on the floor. Dimly he heard the voice of Dearborn.

"The atomizer, Peter!"

A nozzle was pressed under his chin into the bag, and something pungent was sprayed under his nostrils. He tried to fight his way out of their grip, but a knee was in the middle of his back, and then he lost consciousness.

"You're really a genius, David," said Dr. Judd almost ecstatically. "So perfectly timed, so beautifully done! Wonderful, dear fellow, wonderful!"

"Open the door and look out, Peter," said David, and the doctor obeyed.

The passage was empty. Immediately opposite the door of Box A a curtain was draped on the wall, and through this he disappeared, and there came a rush of cold air as he opened the fire-exit door which led to the side street, where a car was waiting.

A minute later David Judd had picked up the detective as easily as though he were a child, had lifted him into the interior of the limousine and had taken the place at the wheel.

He came to the house in Chelsea, and brought the car with a sweep straight to the closed gates of the covered driveway. In that solid gate were the two big circles, and before David Judd's car were two steel bars that projected beyond the line of the lamps and just beneath. Slowly and skillfully he brought the car up the inclined slope from the roadway, so that the ends of the two bars rested in the "peep-holes." Then he drove the machine forward. There was a click and the gates swung open. The car rolled in, and as the wheels passed over a narrow transverse platform that gave slightly under its weight, the doors closed again.

David Judd stopped opposite the door that looked like a window, opened it and, lifting Larry in his arms, passed inside. The lights were burning on the stairs leading to the cell, the doors of which were wide open.

He threw the detective on the bed, picked up the bronze anklet and snapped it about one of Larry's ankles; and then, and only then, did he pull off the heavy leather bag which covered Larry Holt's head. It stank of formaldehyde, and he threw it into the bathroom.

Larry's face was purple; he had all the symptoms of one who had been strangled, but as the night air reached him he gasped. David leant over and felt his pulse, opened his eyelids and smiled.

He went out softly, locking the two doors, and paused at the first landing, to enter what Sergeant Harvey had called the "machinery room." He turned over a switch and the electric ventilating apparatus hummed drowsily.

David went again into the yard, stopping only to lock the doors behind him. He had no time to lose; the engines of his car were still running, and he jumped into his seat and began to go slowly backward. As the wheels reached the narrow weighbridge, the gates opened again. They would remain open twenty seconds and would then close of themselves; and the car had hardly backed on to the road before they came together noiselessly.

Swiftly the car sped back. This time it turned northward and jolted to a standstill opposite Larry Holt's flat.

A Letter from Larry

DIANA had gone home—it was queer how in a few days she had come to regard Larry's flat as her home—before dinner. Her work was done, and there remained only the stern, grim processes of arrest to be accomplished. At any moment she expected the telephone bell to ring and to hear Larry's voice telling her that the brothers were under lock and key.

She had a book on her lap, but she was not reading. Her nurse and chaperon was sewing in her room. Sunny was standing outside the door of the flat, which was ajar, discussing certain matters with Louie, the lift girl, in a low voice. Probably Sunny had secrets of his own, but it was certain that the discovery of a person who agreed with him in most of the things he said, and most of the statements he made, had fascinated this agreeable man.

Diana sat, her head bent, her hand softly caressing her throat, and her mind was on the future rather than upon the tragic past. She rose once and went into Sunny's little room, where the woman she had called "aunt" was sleeping peacefully; and she smiled as she walked back along the passage at the thought of this female invasion of Larry's bachelor quarters.

She had taken up the book when Sunny knocked and came in.

The Dark Eyes of London

"There's a note for you, miss," he said, and handed a letter to the girl. It was in Larry's writing, and she tore open the envelope and read:

"Dear Diana,—The most extraordinary mistake has occurred. Dr. Judd has given an amazing version of the death of your father. Will you get into the car which I have sent and come down to his house at once—38 Endman Gardens, Chelsea.—Larry."

She glanced at the embossed note-heading. Larry had written from Endman Gardens.

"Is there any answer, miss?"

"Yes," said the girl. "Tell the chauffeur I will come down at once."

"Are you going out, miss?" said Sunny dubiously.

"Yes, I am going to Mr. Holt," she said with a smile.

"Would you like me to come with you, miss?" said Sunny. "The master doesn't wish you to go about alone."

"I think I'm all right this evening, Sunny," said the girl kindly. "Thank you very much for your offer."

She dressed quickly and went downstairs. The limousine was waiting at the door, and the chauffeur touched his cap.

"Miss Ward?" he asked. "I'm from the doctor's." He spoke in a gruff voice as if he had a cold.

"I am Miss Ward," she replied, and sprang into the limousine.

The car stopped before a dark and silent house.

"Is this the place?" she asked.

"Yes, miss," said the man. "If you go up those steps and ring the bell, the servant will take you to the gentlemen."

It was Dr. Judd himself, jovial and smiling, who opened the door to her and ushered her into a magnificent room.

"You don't mind waiting here a little while, Miss Stuart?" he said.

The name sounded oddly to her, and he laughed.

"I suppose you're not used to being called that name, eh?" he said with excellent humour. "Now I'm going upstairs to see our mutual friend, and I will bring him down to you. Perhaps you could amuse yourself for ten minutes. Our little conference is not quite ended."

She nodded, and settled herself in the chair. The ten minutes passed, and twenty minutes, and the twenty minutes became forty minutes, and nobody came to her. The silver-toned clock on the mantelpiece chimed sweetly.

"Ten o'clock!" she said in surprise. "I wonder what is keeping him?"

Yet she had no fear, and did not doubt for one moment that Larry was in the house.

The room was luxurious, beautiful, more beautiful than any Diana had ever seen. She sat by the side of a great open fireplace where a small fire was burning, for the night was chilly, and she looked round approvingly upon the pictures, the tapestries, the rich hangings, and the soft panelling which was the background for all. There was not an article of furniture in that room, she thought, that had not been chosen with care and judgment. The rugs upon the floor were antique Persian; the carved table might have been looted from an Eastern emperor's palace.

She lay luxuriously in the depths of a great chair, an illustrated newspaper on her knees, and brought her gaze back to the fire and her thoughts to Larry. She wondered what important matters he was discussing and what was the explanation which the doctor had offered. After a while she looked up at the clock again. Half-past ten! She put down her paper and walked restlessly about the gorgeous apartment, and then she heard the click of a door and Dr. Judd came in from the hall.

"I hope you haven't been lonely," he said. "He will be in very shortly."

She took it for granted that the "he" to whom the doctor referred was Larry Holt.

"I was getting worried," she smiled. "What a beautiful room this is!"

"Yes," he said carelessly, "it is beautiful, but one day we will have a more wonderful saloon to show you."

"Here he is," said the doctor; but it was not Larry who came in. She sprang to her feet with an exclamation of alarm. The man who had entered was John Dearborn. He made no pretence now. His glasses were gone, and his fine eyes were surveying her with amusement.

"Where is Mr. Holt?" she asked.

Dearborn laughed softly.

"You would like some supper," he said, and slipped back one of the panels by the side of the fireplace, revealing a silver tray on which a meal for one had been laid.

"We do not eat at night." He carried the tray to the table and spread a lace cloth.

The girl's colour had gone. She was in mortal peril, but her voice did not quiver.

"Where is Mr. Holt?" she asked again.

"Mr. Holt is quite happy." It was the doctor who spoke. "We will let you see him later."

The strange words and the stranger tone frightened her, and she got up from her chair and picked up her wrap.

"I don't think I will stay any longer, if Mr. Holt is not here, Dr. Judd," she said, addressing that jovial man. "Can you take me home?"

The doctor did not reply. He had pulled open a drawer of a lacquer bureau and had taken out a thick pad of papers and handed them to Dearborn with a broad smile.

"You're going to have a delightful time, Miss Stuart," he said. "Really, David, it is most good of you. I thought you would be too tired to-night."

The girl looked from one to the other, not daring to credit her own senses. Dr. Judd, who had hitherto been polite to a point of obsequiousness, was ignoring her.

"I don't think you heard me, Dr. Judd," she said steadily. "I want you to take me back to my—to Mr. Holt's flat."

"She is thinking of her clothes," murmured the doctor, addressing his brother. "You will see that they are sent for, won't you, David?"

"Sent for?" gasped the girl. "What do you mean?"

David Judd—already she had ceased to think of him as "Dearborn"—had settled himself in the chair which she had lately occupied, and was turning the leaves of his manuscript book.

"I think you had better eat first. You must be very hungry."

"I will eat nothing in this house until I know what you mean by saying that my clothes will be brought here," she said hotly. "I am going back alone."

"Dear young lady,"—it was the doctor who laid his big hand on her arm—"please do not distract David. He is going to read one of his beautiful plays to you. Do you know that David is the greatest dramatist in the world—the supreme force in modern drama, rivalling, and indeed excelling, the so-called genius of Shakespeare."

David looked at his brother and their eyes met.

He was so earnest, so self-convinced, that she had no words for a moment. Then:

"I am not in a mood to hear plays read, however beautiful they are," she said. She had to keep a tight hold on herself, for instinct warned her that her plight was desperate.

"I don't think she will go back to-night," said the doctor, almost regretfully. "Perhaps to-morrow, when you are married to her?"

He spoke timidly, pleadingly, and there was a question in his statement.

"I shall not marry her," said the man called Dearborn sharply. "I thought we had arranged that, brother? Jake is dead, but there are others. Does it matter who marries her?"

Diana was dumb with indignation and horror. They were discussing her marriage with one of them, each trying to induce the other to wed her with a calmness and an assurance which left her speechless. At last she found her voice.

"I do not intend marrying either of you," she said. "I am engaged to—Larry Holt."

Both men were looking at her, and in the doctor's rubicund face there was an expression of distress.

"It is a pity," he said. "The whole thing could be arranged if Mr. Holt were with us. Unfortunately, though he is with us in the body, we are spiritually as far as the poles apart."

"With us in the body?" she repeated, and was seized with a violent fit of trembling. She had realized that the letter which lured her to this terrible house was a forgery, and her hope of rescue was centred on the certainty that Larry would discover her absence and come after her.

And then the two men exchanged glances, and Dearborn rose and put down his book with an air of resignation. He beckoned her and passed to the other end of the apartment, and there found a door which Larry had overlooked; for the edge of the panels which covered it so overlapped that no crevice was visible.

"I designed this house myself," he explained simply, "and built it myself with only twenty workmen from Tuscany."

Later she was to find much of that was true. The chamber in which she found herself, led by the fascination of a growing horror, was unfurnished and unadorned. She heard a strange humming sound and a curious vibration beneath her feet. Then David stopped, fumbled with something on the floor, and opened a little trap-door less than a foot square. It revealed a pane of glass, and when her eyes had become accustomed to the unexpected perspective, she saw beneath her a small room, evidently lighted from the ceiling.

She had no time to take in the details of the room; her eyes were focused upon the figure that sat on the edge of the bed. With his handkerchief he was binding a wound in his hand, and at first she did not recognize him. Then he looked up, for, though he could not see the occupants of the room above, he had heard the sound of the trap opening.

She stared and screamed, for it was Larry Holt who sat there, and he was chained by the ankle.

Diana Pulls a Lever

DEARBORN put his arm about her waist and dragged her from the room into the saloon. When he released her, her knees gave way under her and she dropped to the floor.

"Everything must be seemly," said Dr. Judd gravely. "We cannot countenance a vulgar scene. Do I speak your mind, brother?"

"Exactly, my dear," answered David Judd.

Diana stared up at him from the floor, resting her shaking body upon her arms.

"What are you going to do with him?" she asked wildly.

Again the brothers looked at one another.

"You tell her, Doctor," said David gently.

Dr. Judd shook his head.

"I think you should tell her, my dear David," he answered. "You are so very delicate in these matters, bless you—and remember," he added, "that she is your wife."

David had seated himself and was leaning over the arm of the chair, his immobile face fixed upon Diana's.

"When I have finished with him," he said, "I shall drown him."

She started up, her hand to her mouth.

"My God!" she breathed.

The dreadful truth came upon the girl with a rush. These men were madmen! Madmen who preserved all the outward appearance of sanity, who day by day and for years had conducted a business with sane men and never once betrayed the kink in their unwholesome minds. She shrank back from them, farther and farther back until she was against the panelling of the opposite wall. They were her father's murderers! She thought she was going to faint, but dug her nails into her palms in a tremendous effort to keep her senses. Mad, and the world rubbed shoulders with them and never suspected!

"Shall I read?" asked David quietly.

"Yes, yes, read," she said eagerly.

They were to kill Larry when he had finished reading!

That was the thought which obsessed her as she turned her drawn face to the man. The vanity of this monomaniac was flattered, and he betrayed his agitation in his stumbling speech as he read the first two pages of his manuscript.

Then his voice grew calmer, and the girl understood in a wondering way that he was imparting into these dead and lifeless words a beauty which only his mind could see, but which, in some extraordinary way, he was conveying also to her.

Dr. Judd had slipped from his chair to the big bearskin rug before the fire and sat with his legs crossed, his hands clasped before him, his large, eager face turned to his brother. And here was another curious circumstance which the girl noted numbly. Those lines which seemed brilliant to David were brilliant also to the other, and when he paused self-consciously, as if for applause, it was always the doctor who anticipated his desire.

"Wonderful, wonderful! Is he not a genius, Miss Stuart?" asked Stephen.

She glanced quickly at the other, expecting to find him embarrassed, but he sat bolt upright, a complacent smile upon his heavy face, a benevolence in his eyes. And they were planning murder! They had murdered many men in this terrible house, she thought, and wondered. Had they sat here whilst their victims fought their last fight in that horrible dungeon, the one reading and the other listening to these trite sentences, these age-worn situations which both believed were the work of a supreme genius?

"This is not my best work," said David, as though reading her thoughts. "You like it, of course?"

"Yes," said the girl in a low voice. "Go on, please."

She hoped to keep them occupied throughout the whole of the night. She knew that the police would be searching for Larry, and perhaps one of them knew this house in Chelsea. But those hopes were to be shattered, and her heart gave a wild leap as she saw David close the manuscript book and put it tenderly on the table beside him.

"Brother," he said, "I think——?"

The doctor nodded.

"And it would be a gracious thing, and a picturesque beginning for all the happiness which lies ahead of us, if this fair hand——" He took the unresisting hand of Diana in his, and again he did not complete his sentence.

He took his keys from his pocket, the keys that Flash Fred had so carefully duplicated, and Larry had duplicated again, and walked to the door through which the girl had entered the room. He smiled to himself as he inserted the key and the door swung open.

"Will you come this way, dear girl?" he asked. She hesitated, then, summoning her courage, followed him down a flight of steps.

Again there was a door at the end. A little room filled with machinery she saw, when he put on the light. He walked to a switch.

"You shall have the honour of releasing our friend—we bear him no malice—Mr. Holt."

"Release him?" she asked huskily. "Do you mean that?"

She hesitated, her hand upon the black lever in the wall.

"Why do you not open the door and let him out?" she asked suspiciously.

"That will open the door and release him. Believe me, my dear, I would not in this hour deceive you."

It was the doctor who spoke in his softest tone, and she hesitated no longer. Her brain was in a whirl. She could not analyse either their motives or their sincerity, nor could she appreciate the fact that to these men deception was a habit of thought. She swung the lever back and it came more easily than she had expected. Then she looked at the door.

"Let us go and meet him," said the doctor, and put his arm round her shoulders.

She shivered, but did not attempt to escape, and so he led her up the stairs and back into the salon, closing and locking the door behind him.

Then, before she could guess or anticipate his intentions, the arm about her shoulders had become a grip as firm as a vice, and she found herself pressed closely to the big man.

"My wife, I think, brother," he said.

"Undoubtedly your wife," said the doctor; "for the world is yours to pick and take from, my dear."

"My wife," repeated Dearborn without emotion, and brought his lips to hers.

She was frozen with terror, incapable of movement. Why did not Larry come? Then, as suddenly as he had seized her, the doctor released his hold and took her cold hand in his.

The Dark Eyes of London

"Come back to the fire, wife," he said. "I will finish the third act of this great work of mine, and by that time Mr. Holt will be dead."

In the Trap

LARRY sat on the iron bedstead of the cell, his aching head between his hands. He had anticipated many ends to that night's adventure, but never did he imagine that he would be trapped like a rat, and that the mystery of Box A would be solved in so startling a fashion. So that was the explanation of Gordon Stuart's death. He had accepted the invitation of Dr. Judd to go with him in his box, and there had met the sinister figure of Dearborn. He had either been drugged or clubbed to insensibility and had been carried in John Dearborn's strong arms through the emergency door in the passage and whisked away to the House of Death.

If he had not anticipated such an end to the evening, he thought, he had at least made some preparations. Instinctively he had known that of all places on the face of the earth where his quarry would be run down and "Finis" might be written to the Stuart case, no other spot was so likely as in this terrible mansion which the Judds had built for themselves, and the object of his visit that morning had been twofold. He desired to know and to see with his own eyes the evidence of the men's wickedness; but he had also a wish to understand the ultimate danger to himself and to the girl.

He smiled as he thought of Diana, sitting snugly at home, and wondered what she would feel if she knew his position.

His captor had taken from him every weapon he carried, but that did not worry Larry overmuch. He got up from the bed and walked about the room, but the weight of chain at his ankle made it necessary that he should gather a yard of it slack in his hand. He gave one glance at the black holes in the wall near the floor, for it was from these that danger would come. Well and truly had these men planned their execution-room. No cry for help, no sound he might make, would penetrate through these concrete walls. The light in the ceiling was protected by a thick and heavy globe of glass. It reminded him of a bulkhead light.

He wanted to test the length of the chain, for he had ample time, he thought. Dearborn would be in the house by now. He heard the click of the trap-door above and looked up, but saw nothing. He waited for another half-hour, then pushed over the big block of stone to which the chain was fastened. Before his eyes could fall upon the bag he had left there in his earlier visit, the light went out.

Curiously enough, he had not provided for that contingency, and he drew a sharp breath. The bag was there: his fingers touched and pulled it out, and he groped inside for the keys. Had there been light, there would have been no difficulty in selecting that which unlocked the anklet; but now he tested three, and none of them fitted the bronze clamp about his ankle.

He heard a sound, a low, gurgling sound, such as water makes when it is poured from a bottle; and then about his feet came an eddy of cold air. He tried another key, and that too failed him. Worse still, it remained fixed in the lock, and he could not pull it out.

He heard the rush of the water coming through the small holes in the wall, and the dull throb of a pump. He tugged at the key, great beads of sweat running down his cheeks, and then, with a sigh of relief, it came out. The water was over his boots now and rising rapidly.

There was only one more key to try; the rest were too big for the purpose. He drew that out, but the ward caught in the string of the bag in which he had put them, and the key fell into the water. He groped down; it had gone! Again and again he flung his hand through the swirling water, and his fingers groped along the rough concrete floor. Presently with a cry he felt it and, lifting his ankle with an effort, he inserted the key. It turned. The anklet opened, and he was free.

There were still the two doors, and he knew that, with the pressure of water, it would require his utmost efforts to open them.

The water was up to his waist now, and he waded along the passage and up the two steps, holding the waterproof bag between his teeth. The key turned easily enough, but there was no handle to pull, and every second increased the pressure of the water. He set his teeth and, gripping the key in both hands, he pulled steadily, steadily . . .

The Passing of David

DIANA had heard the dread words without understanding them at first. "By that time Mr. Holt will be dead!"

She opened her mouth to scream, but no sound came. She had killed Larry! Her hand had pulled the lever which drowned him! That was the word Judd had used. Drowned him—but how? As the thought took more definite shape she swayed toward the doctor and gripped his shoulder for support. She would not faint, she told herself; she would not faint! There must be a way of saving Larry. She looked around for some weapon, but there was none; and then she grew calmer. They were madmen and must be humoured. But the time was short.

Again she assumed an attitude of attention, but her mind and eyes were busy, and as David Judd leaned forward she saw something that brought a thrill of hope to her heart. His jacket was open and showed just a glimpse of white shirt where his arm passed through the waistcoat, and against that strip of white was a sharp black line. She looked again and saw it was an automatic pistol, worn in a holster under the armpit. She remembered reading of desperadoes who carried their guns that way, so that they might be ready to hand; and possibly David had read too.

He was in the midst of an impassioned love scene when her hand darted forward and closed over the butt. With a jerk she pulled it free and stepped back, overturning the little table on which her supper tray had been laid.

"If you move I'll kill you," she said breathlessly. "Open that door, and release him!"

The two men were on their feet, staring at her.

"You—you interrupted my reading," cried David, in the tremulous voice of a hurt child. He did not seem to be conscious of any danger.

"Open the door," she breathed, "and release Larry Holt, or I'll kill you!"

David frowned and put his hand on the mantelpiece. She saw his fingers touch a button, and as the lights went out she fired.

The explosion deafened her. A second later his strong arms were around her and he had flung her into the chair and stood glaring down at her.

"You interrupted my reading," he almost sobbed, and Dr. Judd, a frowning figure, looked anxiously from her to his brother. "And now," said David petulantly, "I will not marry you."

His big hand gripped the edge of her bodice and dragged her to her feet. His eyes were wet with tears, the tears of pride, of humiliation. Then, with the sudden caprice of a madman, he released her.

"He is dead now, I should think, brother," he said, turning to the doctor, and Dr. Judd drew a sigh of relief and nodded.

"Yes, he is dead now," he said. "The water rises at the rate of one foot in two minutes, I think."

"One foot in a minute and fifty seconds," said David.

"Spare him for God's sake!" cried the girl hoarsely. "I will give you anything—anything in the world you want! If it is money, you shall have it!"

"I think she ought to see him," said David, ignoring her frenzied appeal.

"There is no light," said the doctor and shook his head.

"Of course not. How stupid of me! We always put the light out," said David, whose fit of anger seemed to have passed. "Then the water comes up through the little holes at the bottom of the cell very, very quickly. It is pumped from the roof of the house. We have a large tank there, you know," he went on, "and the person we drown cannot rise because of the weight of his feet. Once a man got on the bed—do you remember?"

"I remember," said the doctor in a conversational tone. "We had to put nine feet of water into the cell before he died."

She listened numbly. It was a nightmare, she told herself, and presently she would wake.

"And that takes a long time to pump out. It was very thoughtless of him. So much had to be done," David continued, and his brother was looking at him for the first time anxiously.

"We had to dry the bed," David went on, "and did you notice the chain was rusty, brother? That isn't right. It is an eyesore to me."

The Dark Eyes of London

He turned and looked at Diana thoughtfully.

"My wife," he said in a low voice, and there was a sudden fire in his eyes which terrified her. "My wife," he said again, and caught her to him with a horrible animal cry that set her shrinking.

"I want you, Judd!"

He spun round. Some one had come into the room and was standing now with a pistol aimed straight at the man's heart.

It was Larry Holt.

The End of the Chase

DON'T MOVE," said Larry. "Resistance is useless. Listen to that."

There was the faint sound of a crash in the hall.

"Those are police officers, and they are inside the house," said Larry laconically.

Slowly David pushed the girl away from him and faced the intruder, looking at him from under his heavy brows. Larry did not see the man's hand move, so quick was the motion. A wind fanned his cheek, a panel splintered, and the two shots sounded like one to the half-fainting girl.

David Judd stood for a moment erect, then staggered a little.

"My beautiful plays!" he said, and choked.

Then, without another word, he crashed to the floor, dead.

"David, David!" Dr. Judd threw himself upon the body. "David, don't act! I will get you beautiful actors for your work. I don't like to see you doing it, David! It frightens me. Tell him not to!"

The big man, his florid face gone white, looked up appealingly at Larry Holt, who stood with his smoking pistol in his hand, his eyes fixed upon the two.

"Mr. Holt, you have influence with him," whined the doctor, his face streaming with tears. "Tell him, please, not to do this! It frightens me when he acts. Sometimes he acts for hours in this room—little pieces from his own wonderful plays. You must ask him to read you some, Mr. Holt. David—!"

He shook the body, but David was beyond the voice of his brother.

Then the doctor stood up. He came across to Larry, laying his large hand on the other's like a frightened child. Larry was so overwhelmed by the tragedy of it all that he could not speak. This grown man, whose brilliant brain had conceived and dared so much, was for a moment like a little child.

Suddenly the doctor's head came up.

"I am sorry," he said huskily. "Poor boy!"

He looked at Larry Holt long and steadily.

"Mr. Holt," he said, "I have been behaving childishly, but I am perfectly sane. I accept full responsibility for all my acts—and all the acts of my brother. I know quite well what I have done."

Harvey had burst into the room and stopped dead at the scene, until Larry beckoned him forward.

"Take him," he said.

"I wish we had finished you," said Dr. Judd as they led him away.

The girl was in Larry's arms now, her face hidden against his shoulder.

"This is the end of the bad road," he whispered, and she nodded. As they came into the vestibule, one of the police officers who filled the hall saluted him.

"We've taken the servant, sir. He was locked up in another part of the house."

"He knows nothing about it," said Larry. "You can safely release him. And, anyway, I haven't taken the trouble to get a warrant for him."

A tall man came out of the broken doorway which Larry discovered led to the servants' quarters, and took the girl's hand in his.

"You've had a terrible experience, Miss Stuart," he said, and she recognized the Police Commissioner, and tried to smile. "I have my car here. You had better come along, Larry. Harvey can charge Dr. Judd."

They drove back to Scotland Yard, and Larry said very little on the journey. He sat by the girl's side, her hand in his, and answered the questions the Commissioner put to him briefly and without elaboration. It was when they were back in the Commissioner's office that Larry spoke.

"John," he said, "I hope you are not going to report this matter to the

Government as an achievement on my part."

Sir John looked at him with an inquiring frown.

"Of course I shall," he said. "Who else takes credit?"

Larry put his hand on the girl's shoulder.

"Here is the best detective we have had in Scotland Yard for many years," he said simply.

Diana laughed.

"You silly man," she scoffed, "of course I am not. Who was the best detective you could have had to deal with this case?"

"You," he said.

She shook her head.

"The best detective was Dr. Judd, if you could have secured his services. And he was best because he knew most of this matter, knew all the secrets which we were trying to discover. I was in very much the same position; I was inside the game. Once I knew, as I did, that Clarissa Stuart was myself, I was able to mystify you. For when it was clear that poor Emma—I nearly called her aunt—poor Emma Ward was the charwoman who had seen my—my father, and had left in such a state of great agitation, there was no doubt whatever in my mind that it was my father. And when that was clear, the rest was rather easy. I knew then that I was the objective of the gang. No, Larry, you are and you have been wonderful."

Larry shook his head, with a smile.

"Anyway," said the Commissioner dryly, "does it matter who gets the credit?"

"Why?" asked Larry in surprise.

"I mean, so long as it goes into the family," said Sir John, and the colour came to the girl's face.

"There's a great deal in that, Sir John," she said, "and now I am going to take him home."

That night, after she had gone to bed, and Larry sat before his little fire, his bright brier between his teeth and his mind at peace, Sunny came in to him, bearing an armful of laundry.

198

"Two of your collars are missing, sir."

"And the man who wears the collars was nearly missing, Sunny," chuckled Larry. "Do you know, one of the first things I thought about in that infernal place was whether you'd get the news in time to stop the papers."

"I could have always sent them back, sir," said Sunny gravely.

"You're a cheerful soul," said Larry. "Well were you named Sunny! And Sunny," he said, "I want to tell you that I'm going to be married."

"Yes, sir," said Sunny, and his brows knit in thought.

"Well?" said Larry.

"Well, sir," said Sunny slowly, "I think you'll want some new socks. They dress very smartly at Monte Carlo."

"By Jove!" said Larry, and then his face fell. "We can't go to Monte Carlo in the summer, you silly ass. It would be too hot. No, I'm going to Scotland for—for—after I'm married."

Sunny was interested.

"Then you'll be wanting a kilt, sir," he said.

Three Cigarettes

TWO MONTHS later, Dr. Judd sat on the edge of a very small bed and smoked three cigarettes, one after the other. It was a rainy morning, and the square of glass which gave light to the cell seemed to collect all the greyness and drabness of the day and transmute the faded light of heaven into a lead.

The doctor smoked luxuriously, for he had not tasted a cigarette for the greater part of two months. Presently the door of the cell opened, and Larry came in. Judd jumped up to his feet and greeted the visitor with a smile.

"It's awfully good of you to come, Holt," he said. "I intended saying nothing, but in the circumstances it seems to me only fair to a man of your position, who has put in such a large amount of earnest and excellent work, that you should know the truth."

He was altogether sincere: Larry knew that.

"My brother David and I—and this you will understand—were on the most affectionate terms from our early childhood. David was my care and my responsibility, and he was also my joy. We had both been left by our mother at a very early age, and our father was an eccentric gentleman who had very little use for children. So we grew up and went to the same public school and to the University together, and I think I am right in saying that we were wholly sufficient for one another. I had an admiration and a love for David beyond anything that is human," said the doctor, lowering his voice and looking down.

Larry nodded. He had recognized this quality in the two men.

"I hope you will not think that I owe you a grudge because you killed David," he said. "Far from it. I recognize the inevitability, and in my heart I know that nothing could have saved David. He died as he would have wished; and in some respects I am very glad for all that has happened. At the trial I made every effort to prove to the judge and the jury that I was perfectly sane, and your evidence helped to secure the conviction which I knew was inevitable. I thank you for it. As I say——" he went back to the story of his early life, and told stories of the childhood of he and his brother.

"When my father died," he went on, "he left us the Greenwich Insurance Company, a small impoverished concern which was then on the verge of bankruptcy. I can safely and honestly say that I have never respected the sanctity of human life. To me a human being is like any other animal—a kind of dumb Lew," he explained easily, and Larry could hardly restrain a shudder at the light-hearted way he referred to this human wreck.

"I tell you that before I go any further, lest you expect anything in the shape of an apologetic attitude on my part. If you do, you will be disappointed. The business to which my brother and I succeeded was bankrupt, and I think we got our first idea for the subsequent operations when we had to pay out a risk which had been taken by my eccentric father, and a risk which he should never have undertaken.

"The idea of the scheme was partly mine and partly David's. We began our experiments three months later, when we drowned a man, whose name I need not tell you, since it would serve no useful purpose and no person is under suspicion for his death. We had insured him in our own office—a very simple process—without his being any the wiser. I myself had signed the medical report, and David, who was a clever draughtsman, in addition to being a brilliant engineer—the career for which he was trained—signed all the necessary forms in his name. We chose the man carefully. He was one who had no friends and was regarded as being something of a recluse. The policy was made payable in favour of a fictitious name which my brother had taken in Scotland, where he had furnished a small house and where he lived for the purposes of collection.

"We made a large sum of money by this death, for we had reinsured the life and there was little to do but to collect from the underwriters. My brother was always something of a poet, and when he was at Oxford he wrote two or three plays, which the managers of the London theatres rejected. I need hardly tell you," he said with the utmost gravity, "that they were wonderful plays, though not, of course, as good as those I produced later at the Macready Theatre."

"The Macready was your property, was it not?" said Larry, and the doctor inclined his head.

"I bought it some time ago for the purpose of producing dear David's dramas," he said. "It was the one thing for which I lived: to establish David's name. He had very early on taken the name of Dearborn, and it is curious that you had not compared the name that appeared on the playbills six years ago with the Rev. John Dearborn."

"They were compared," said Larry, "and our conclusions were drawn, but not until a late stage in the investigations."

"Our next experiment was on a man named—well, I need not give this name, either," he said. "We had to wait a reasonable time before we bled the underwriters. And here occurred an unfortunate thing. One of our clerks discovered that the person to whom the money was paid was my brother. He found it out by the veriest accident, and began to blackmail David, and finally, fearing the consequence of this line of action, he stole a considerable sum of money from the office and went to France. David followed him and shot him in Montpellier. You know that part of the story very well, Mr.

The Dark Eyes of London

Holt," he said with a good-humoured smile. "Flash Fred saw the act committed, and lived on me for years, but only because he never accepted an invitation to dinner in my house," he added with a little smile.

"And now I come to the Stuart case. David, who did a great deal of investigation of his own, had, as you know, disappeared as the result of Flash Fred's recognition. We gave him a very handsome funeral, and——" He hesitated.

"And the body was the brother of Lew," said Larry quietly.

"Quite right," agreed the doctor. "He was an awkward man, and he—had to go! The whole thing had been simplified by now," he explained. "My brother had built our beautiful house, and the death chamber with its water, its pump and its ventilator, had been created by his genius. It was my idea that we should buy up Todd's Home, and curiously enough, I had completed the sale before it became necessary for dear David to disappear. Mr. Grogan has not told you, in all probability, that we sought by every means in our power to induce him to come to the Macready Theatre to see a representation of one of my brother's dramas. He saved himself, not by any superhuman cleverness, but because he had the low cunning of the rat which walks around the cage of a trap, knowing that the trap is there, yet unable to realize just how it works.

"I will return to Stuart," he said. "We had laid our plans when Stuart came into the box, and our plans did not include any injury to him whilst he was in the theatre, because we thought it would be a simple matter to persuade him to pass through the fire door into the car which was waiting in the private road which is the property and stands upon the grounds of the theatre.

"Stuart came. My brother, of course, was not there, though he was near enough at hand if I wanted him. Boxes A, B and C were never let to the public, by the way. To our surprise he came in the most exalted mood, and told us that he had discovered a daughter. And then, for the first time, we knew that he was not an obscure stranger, but a very rich man. We took him back to the house and he went willingly, and there we had a discussion, dear

202

David and I, as to what should be done. We came to the conclusion that there was nothing definite to be secured from this man if we let him live, and it was very necessary, indeed vitally necessary, that money should come in at once. I had spent a great deal of money, some hundred thousand pounds," he said airily as he lit his second cigarette, "on art treasures, and another hundred thousand upon the theatre, and we were being pressed very hard. We decided that Stuart should go."

He puffed at his cigarette and blew a ring to the ceiling.

"He showed fight," he said briefly. "By the way, I have reason to believe that one of the cuff-links which were torn off my shirt in that struggle was retrieved by you, Mr. Holt. Where did you find it?"

"In the dead man's hand," said Larry, and Dr. Judd nodded.

"I was afraid I had not been very thorough," he said, "but I am relieved, because I thought that David was to blame—David was careless in some matters.

"He had told us, had Stuart, all about his charwoman, had given us her address; and there and then we decided to find this Clarissa and marry her to some one." He shrugged his shoulders. "It did not matter whom, so long as we could first of all prove her birth and then control her money. The next day my brother went to confirm the man's story, but he found difficulty. The woman in charge of the nursing home—it was a converted farm, if you remember, where Mrs. Stuart died—had disappeared. And even the offer of a reward did not produce any results. We had no difficulty in finding and capturing the charwoman. Blind Jake, who was a faithful servant of ours—and nobody regrets his death more than myself, but I also realize that it was necessary, or had the appearance of necessity—Blind Jake, I say, hurried her away, and from the information she was able to supply us with, I could trace Clarissa Stuart as Diana Ward. I might add, for your information," he said, addressing Holt, "that the inquiries did not take more than half a day."

"There is one question I should like to ask you, doctor," said Larry quietly. "The lift accident was arranged by whom?"

"By David," said the doctor with a little smile as though he were amused at something. "David was on the floor above, and it was David who dropped things on your head. They didn't reach your head, of course, which was unfortunate. Then he had an easy exit along the roof to the next building, and I never admired you so much as when you refrained from going up those steps left so invitingly under the open trap-door. You would have come down very quickly," he added significantly. "And that, gentlemen, really concludes my story." And he took up the third cigarette, for the second had been smoked very vigorously.

"Why did you spare Lew?" asked Larry. "He was one of your helpers and knew your secrets."

"I was prepared to spare almost anybody unless my life was endangered," said Dr. Judd. "Certainly I did not want to find all my good plans tumbling to the ground through the death of some wretched beggar who was quite harmless. I only killed when it was necessary or profitable," he said. "Blind Jake had his own vendettas, and his attempt upon Fanny Weldon was a purely private affair in which we were not interested."

A man came in through the door of the cell, a short, stocky man who was bareheaded, and Dr. Judd took one long whiff of his cigarette, dropped it on the floor of the cell and put his foot upon it.

"The executioner, I presume?" he said pleasantly, and turned round, putting his hands behind him.

The stocky man strapped him tight, and the white-robed clergyman, whose ministrations he had refused and who was waiting outside the cell door, came in and walked slowly by the doctor's side.

And so he went out of sight of Larry, who waited behind. He saw the broad shoulders for the last time as they passed through the narrow door leading from the prison hall to the exercise yard, and he waited, feeling inexpressibly and unaccountably sad.

A minute passed, and then there was a crash that came like thunder to his ears and made him start. It was the crash of the falling death-trap. Dr. Judd had met his brother.

www.ingramcontent.com/pod-product-compliance
Lightning Source LLC
Chambersburg PA
CBHW031336170626
46807CB00002B/727